Henry Ki

Some Time in Ireland

Henry King

Some Time in Ireland

Reprint of the original, first published in 1874.

1st Edition 2024 | ISBN: 978-3-36884-750-0

Verlag (Publisher): Outlook Verlag GmbH, Zeilweg 44, 60439 Frankfurt, Deutschland
Vertretungsberechtigt (Authorized to represent): E. Roepke, Zeilweg 44, 60439 Frankfurt, Deutschland
Druck (Print): Books on Demand GmbH, In de Tarpen 42, 22848 Norderstedt, Deutschland

SOME TIME IN IRELAND.

A RECOLLECTION.

*Quæque ipsa . . . vidi,
Et quorum pars [haud] magna fui.*
VIRGIL, ÆN. ii. 5.

HENRY S. KING & CO.,
65 CORNHILL AND 12 PATERNOSTER ROW, LONDON.
1874.

PREFACE.

WRITERS professing to describe social and family life in Ireland have mostly selected their types from roistering squires or ruined country gentlemen.

My aim is to depict, from the vivid recollections of my earlier years and from my later experience, views, feelings, habits, and principles, more really and truly characteristic of the gentry of Ireland.

I lived in those stirring and eventful times when Daniel O'Connell agitated and strove for, and eventually succeeded in obtaining, the religious and civil enfranchisement of his Roman Catholic countrymen, but signally failed in his efforts for the Repeal of the Union—that same measure which under the name of Home Rule is as persistently clamoured for as in the days of the arch-agitator.

I have also attempted to represent the very strong opinion which has prevailed, that—ever since the Union—Ireland has socially declined, and that she can never regain her rightful level as long as England compels her legislators to assemble in St Stephen's, Westminster,—as long as she permits Absenteeism,—and as long as she absorbs the rank, wealth, and intelligence of the country. As long as this lasts, Ireland will have a real grievance.

M. L. C.

May 1874.

CONTENTS.

Book the First.

CHAP.		PAGE
I.	SCENES FROM MEMORY,	1
II.	SUNDAY OBSERVANCES—WEEK-DAY FARE,	11
III.	HOMŒOPATHY AND ALLOPATHY,	17
IV.	WE SMART FOR IT,	21
V.	TRAINING AND DRESS,	29
VI.	PRIOR TO COMPETITIVE EXAMINATIONS,	37
VII.	OUR AMUSEMENTS,	46

Book the Second.

I.	IRELAND'S NEEDS,	54
II.	DUNLESS,	62
III.	LIFE AT THE SEA-SIDE,	81

Book the Third.

I.	PRIESTLY DENUNCIATIONS,	91
II.	AN ESTATE AGENT,	97

CONTENTS.

CHAP.		PAGE
III.	THE REBELLION OF '98,	105
IV.	DANIEL O'CONNELL,	119
V.	BEHIND THE SCENES,	129
VI.	TERENMORE CASTLE,	135
VII.	IMPOLITIC CONFIDENCES,	142
VIII.	PARTY-SPIRIT RUNS HIGH,	149
IX.	WE ESCAPE WITH OUR LIVES,	160

Book the Fourth.

I.	ONLY A LETTER,	174
II.	A BRUTAL MURDER,	185
III.	EXTENUATING CIRCUMSTANCES,	189
IV.	AUNT EVIE,	195
V.	MY MOTHER,	202
VI.	TO WATERFORD,	205

Book the Fifth.

I.	AN EVENTFUL SUNDAY,	211
II.	THE EVANGELICAL WAVE,	222
III.	THE WIDOW MOLLOY,	228
IV.	TITHE MASSACRE,	237
V.	THE YELLOW POSTCHAISE,	248
VI.	THE CURRAGHMORE BALL,	256

Book the Sixth.

CHAP.   PAGE
I. MADAME BONAPARTE WYSE, ... 276
II. ANECDOTES—EPISCOPAL AND CLERICAL, . . 288

Book the Seventh.

A REAL IRISH GRIEVANCE, ... 302

SOME TIME IN IRELAND.

Book the First.

CHAPTER THE FIRST.

SCENES FROM MEMORY.

> The first effort of Reason
> Sought some explanation
> Of Nature's great problem,
> Mysterious Creation ;
> Babes come at all seasons—by night and by day,
> They come at the dawn and they come at the dusk,
> Whence come they—these babes ? Your answer, I pray ;
> None ventured to answer—evolved from Mollusk.

I WAS born some time in the present century.

The sage advice was once given to me,—Never state your age without producing the voucher— namely, the duly signed and authenticated copy of the baptismal register, because your accuracy will be suspected—at least by your own sex, and you may think yourself well off if you be not weighted with not more than five years over and above what you really carry.

Most people ask—few take—advice : I am of the few—at any rate in regard to the advice above given.

A

My readers, therefore, will know no more of the day of the week, the month, the year of my birth, than I did myself when I drew my first breath in a large, rambling, and (what an Englishman would call) semi-dilapidated old country house, within two miles of the Cathedral city of Landford, in the south-west of Ireland.

The connection of our family with Ireland was not of ancient date. We came over with other Cromwell settlers, and for services—real or supposed—were endowed with the mansion and lands of Kilkreen in the county of Innisfellah. We never affected, nor desired to be considered native Irish; nor would such a pretension—if made—have been admitted by the genuine natives, who regarded us as heretical supplanters of the rightful owners of the soil.

The youngest child—if a girl—is generally the pet or the pest of the family—its plaything or its plague; I, the youngest, was certainly not made the one—nor did I make myself the other. I was quiet and silent, and observant of all that passed; I treasured up what was said, and reasoned—after my own little fashion—on what I heard.

One of the earliest occasions which I can recall of my reasoning faculty being brought into play was when I was one day sitting—still as a mouse—on a footstool at my father's feet, during a conversation he was holding with a friend and neighbour—one Jack Summerville.

My father patted me on the head, and made some reference to the day on which I was born. I was all attention, for I expected to hear how I came into the world at all, and what were the incidents of my early life previous to the date of my recollection.

I was not destined to be enlightened on these points—on which I had often speculated. The door was half opened, and our butler thrust in his curly head and round face, and in a whisper—as if he were afraid of disturbing some sick person in the room—said, " Misther Summerville, the Misthress has come to say that she has got a fine boy, and—glory to the Saints—she's getting on as well as she can."

" Why, Jack," exclaimed my father, in a tone of deep commiseration, " this is your sixteenth ; and what on earth can you possibly do with them all ? "

" My dear fellow," said Jack, " don't distress yourself on my account. When I found myself the father of eight children, I was preciously down in the mouth —I don't deny it. It was a question that I oftener put to myself than I could answer—How are they to be provided for ? It was a dead weight upon my spirits, and often made me very irritable. But as child after child continued coming, I got used to it ; my spirits and good temper returned ; and now that I have sixteen—just twice your number, Mr Rochford, I have a blessed feeling of irresponsibility stealing over me; I just shift the responsibility from myself to Providence. It is so utterly out of the power of me, Jack Summerville—an Irish squireen, with his lands heavily mortgaged—to house, clothe, feed, and educate sixteen children, that there is manifestly nothing else for them to do but to take to the trade of mendicants; and when they set out on their professional tramp, the first on whom they must try their vagrant whine will be good, generous Mr Rochford, who can't have the heart to refuse the poor beggars a few coppers—with some praties and broken victuals."

"Jack, I am ashamed of you; how can you jest upon so serious a matter?"

"My dear Mr Rochford, I have come to you in the most serious mood—not to consult you, but to inform you of the decision at which I have arrived. I have resolved to emigrate; and, by the time my wife is well again, I—with all mine and a couple of my labourers—will be ready to start for Australia."

In those days, the emigration of an Irish country gentleman—though his estate might be mortgaged up to the hilt—was a thing undreamt of; but the reasonableness of the step at once struck my father, who both expressed his approbation, and offered all the assistance in his power.

Jack Summerville's bold venture proved entirely successful. Instead of professional mendicancy, Colonial eminence has been the lot of the boys, and marriage with wealthy Colonists that of the girls. If other heavily mortgaged landlords and squireens had followed in the wake of Jack Summerville, it would have been the better for themselves, their families, and their country.

My father so often related his interview with Jack Summerville, that I have no doubt of the above narrative being due quite as much to my recollection of his description, as of the scene itself.

One childish incident was vividly impressed on my memory, through the same instrumentality as the first sight of a lake was upon Montesquieu's—by his having his ears soundly boxed by his father.

My third sister Mildred, was removed from the nursery to share with my second sister Eveleen a double-bedded room. Nothing was ever purchased in our house which, by any shift, could be dispensed with—where it was a matter only of domestic comfort. So that, when the question was raised of providing additional bedding, a visit of inspection was made of all the bedrooms — ending with the nursery. Nurse Reilly—the autocrat of the nursery, with whom I slept—was found to be the fortunate possessor of palliasse, mattress, and feather-bed.

Soon an order came from my mother that nurse was to give up her feather-bed. To kill two birds with one stone, the governess—Miss Lacey—who was always complaining that her bed was so hard it made her bones ache, was to have nurse's soft bed transferred to her, while her mattress was to serve for my sister's use. Our housemaid Bridget, who in concert with the other servants, bore Nurse Reilly no good will, carried out my mother's order with spirit.

Nurse Reilly's temper rose to fury-pitch. She "dared swear"—and she did not refrain from cursing. "Bridget was a vile sneak, and a slieveen, and came of a bad stock. The misthress was hard to her own flesh and blood,—wasn't she taking the bed from under her own child? And was not she as good as the governess any day? What call had she to *her* bed —let alone Miss Katy" (my name was Kathleen)!! "She supposed they would next be left nothing but bare boards to lie on—bare boards, my jewel!" said the nurse to me, while she shook her clenched hands in Bridget's face.

I clung to nurse's gown, and filled up the pauses during which nurse took breath—by screaming in my tiny passion, "I won't sleep on the bare boards"—my selfish instincts being thoroughly roused at the prospect of the loss of my soft bed.

"Never you mind what *she* tells you, Miss Katy," said the housemaid; and, carrying off the feather-bed which had been indignantly pitched into the middle of the nursery by the infuriated nurse, she fired a parting shot—" Nurse Reilly, be sure you confess the big lie you've told that Innocent, the next time you go to confession to Father O'Flaherty; and by the blessed St Peter and St Paul, and all the rest on'em, if you can't get him to give you absolution, you'll have to roast for it."

Nurse Reilly's high-pitched threat, " The next time you, Bridget, set your foot in my nursery, I'll do for you entirely, entirely," and my sympathetic screams, brought the governess on the stage; who, evidently convinced by the expression on Nurse Reilly's face, that she would prove an ugly customer, made a scape-goat of poor me, boxing my ears, shaking my small person, and peremptorily ordering me to "stop that horrid noise." Of course I only screamed the louder, as if that would relieve the smarting pain of head, ears, and face.

Nurse rushed to the rescue; and, taking me up in her arms—though, as I afterwards thought to myself, she did not use such naughty words to the governess as she did to Bridget—she nevertheless, in no gentle terms, dared Miss Lacey to lay her hands upon me again. " What call had she to meddle and make with her child? Let her keep her hands for them she was paid for bating and taching. Wouldn't she take it out on Miss Mildred's ears the next time she came to play with Miss Katy."

"Impertinent, insolent woman, your mistress shall hear of your conduct," screamed Miss Lacey.

"*Our* Mistress"—with a forcible stress on the "*Our*"—"will, I'm thinking, larn you your proper place is in the schoolroom, and not in my nursery; so be off with you, and as I told you afore, keep your fists and your cuffs for them you've to look after, and leave my child to me."

"*Our* Mistress!" was all that Miss Lacey could utter, so choked with rage was she at being thus placed by Nurse on the same social level with herself.

"Well," persisted Nurse, "I see no difference betwixt the two on us; the Misthress pays you a few more pounds wages than———"

Miss Lacey would hear no more—she rushed away.

The boxing of my ears was the first lesson I had in vicarious punishment.

Long after my ears had ceased to tingle, the recollection of the scene was kept alive. Nurse's account of it was constantly repeated in my hearing, not only to the fellow-servants and village cronies, but to all the nursery-maids whom we encountered in our walks.

Although strictly forbidden by my mother to take me beyond our own grounds, Nurse invariably took me into the town, or to the bridge which divided us from Landford. Indeed, Miss Lacey did the same with my sisters; she liked some variety after the monotony of teaching—it was pleasant to see faces and shops.

My sisters not unnaturally agreed with Miss Lacy on this point; and many were the altercations between my mother and the governess on the subject of country-walks and town-walks.

"Miss Lacey, I do not like it at all," complained my mother; "I cannot see the necessity of these daily walks into Landford; my daughters' faces will become too common; besides, their every-day dresses are not smart enough to wear in the town, and if they take to their best suits they will become shabby long before the change of season comes round."

"But, Mrs Rochford, the walks in the grounds are so very damp."

"Miss Lacey, I do not object to *country* walks."

"O!" groaned the governess, "such roads! no pathways! mud, and ruts, and puddles in winter, and dust enough to smother one in summer!" And then as a climax—"Really, madam, after the monotonous labour of teaching four young ladies English, French, and music, my spirits require more change and variety than what is afforded by the grounds of Kilkreen."

My mother felt there was no help for it, and so she

compromised the matter with—" Then, twice a week, Miss Lacey."

In the end, however, the Irish climate being on her side (as it generally rained four days out of the seven), and Sunday being a free day, Miss Lacey and my sisters got their way.

CHAPTER THE SECOND.

SUNDAY OBSERVANCES—WEEK-DAY FARE.

"Here's a dish I love not."
Much Ado About Nothing, Act I.

"Like a sickness did I loathe this food."
Midsummer's Night Dream, Act IV.

OUR family always attended the Sunday morning service at the Cathedral Church of Landford. We occupied a large square pew in a gallery on one side the nave, and a similar pew on the other side—directly opposite to ours—was set apart for the officers of the regiments quartered in the city.

I am afraid that the eyes of Miss Lacey and of her two elder pupils were not confined to their Prayer-books so much as they ought to have been. There was at least some ground for suspicion of glances having been directed to and returned by their opposite neighbours in scarlet and gold uniforms, as, on descending the staircase common to the two galleries, one or two officers always contrived to be exactly on the same level with Miss Lacey and her pupils, and then Miss Lacey would say, in an unwonted sweetly-modulated tone, "Nora, where shall we walk this afternoon?" Nora, looking cautiously behind, in order to be sure of her mother being beyond hearing distance, would answer in the softest of voices, "The Mall, dear Miss Lacey; I am reckoning on hearing that exquisite band." The bait being thus thrown and taken, the three quickened their steps so as to be in time to see the regiment fall into line and march back to barracks.

In those days Sunday was observed much in the same way as it is on the Continent, except that all the shops were closed. There was always a line regiment quartered in the town, which was reinforced by cavalry whenever the turbulent population had to be kept in order. The military element was greatly appreciated in the town and in the neighbourhood. The gentry cordially fraternised with their gallant defenders, and exercised lavish hospitality. The officers, on their part, gave handsome mess dinners for the gentlemen, and balls for the ladies. Landford was considered the pick of Irish quarters, and interest was made for crack regiments to be sent there.

The soldiers were marched to and from the morning service at the Cathedral with due military pomp. Crowds of artisans and workmen, who had turned out of the Romish chapels (the word church being strictly

SUNDAY OBSERVANCES. 13

confined to the Protestant places of worship), kept the step alongside the military, or followed in their rear, excited by the brilliant march music, delighting in the sight of the red coats, and forgetting for the moment that it was by the British army that Ireland was held in subjection to the detested English Government.

It was the usual thing for our parents to remain for luncheon with some friend or other who possessed a house on the Mall—the fashionable promenade of Landford—where, on fine Sundays, the regimental band performed from three to five o'clock. The carriage took all the rest of us back to Kilkreen directly after the service; but later in the afternoon Miss Lacey and my two elder sisters, Nora and Eveleen, having wrung permission from my mother, returned to the town by the ferry-boat, which crossed the river Dour, a distance not exceeding ten minutes, whereas the route by the road occupied nearly an hour. It was their especial delight to walk up and down the Mall for two hours, listening to the band, and exchanging nods and smiles and greetings with the friends of their own age and class. We ranked among the aristocracy of the County of Innisfellah, of which my uncle had been one of the representatives; and as trade, commerce, and some professions were not recognized as gentlemanly callings, I fear that we were in the habit of assuming silly pretentious airs, which were of course resented by those who thought themselves as good as ourselves. What cared we for what was said or thought of us by those whom we never met in society? We were ready enough, however, to receive the advances of the smart junior officers whose acquaintance had been made in the drawing-room, of whom a certain number were always invited to accompany their Colonel to our parties.

The children of our family were eight in number. First came two daughters, Nora and Eveleen, followed by three sons, Horatio, Patrick, and Rowland; the tail of the family—the unwelcome additions, as they were called—consisted of Mildred, Aileen, and me Kathleen the youngest.

Children were children actually—not metaphorically —in those days. Whether or no, I at least thought as a child, I was treated as a child. I was brought up to regard myself as a Nobody, and was expected to be contented with such an amount of domestic comfort as most English servants would turn up their noses at. I question, moreover, whether any medical officer would consider our dietary sufficient for the children inmates of a Union.

I beg my readers to observe that in the following description I am not drawing upon my imagination— it is a simple statement of facts.

For breakfast we had " rounds " of very stale bread,

to be washed down with skimmed milk—butter was a luxury reserved for those who had attained the honourable rank of being "introduced." At noon we were supplied with more dry bread—water this time taking the place of skimmed milk. The governess had butter—and O, how we envied her! We three younger girls dined in the nursery, the same room being common to eating and sleeping—night and day nurseries were then unknown. Meat was allowed us only four days in the week; on the other days our fare was gruel or vegetables. How many scrag ends and cold slices of mutton it fell to our lot to consume on meat days!

The cook did not waste much time or care upon our meals. She *might* have thought with Wordsworth that "plain living" and "high thinking" went together, and wished to have *her* share in our spiritual training. She might, on the other hand, have considered that anything was good enough for "them children in the nursery."

One day we had an animal set before us, at the sight of which Mildred, Aileen, and I were so terrified that with screams of horror we ran down the staircase into the dread presence of our mother. I well remember standing at the open door of the drawing-room when my mother demanded of the other two an explanation of so turbulent a proceeding,

"O, mamma, mamma, please do come up to the nursery; cook has sent us a dead cat for our dinner!" cried Aileen.

"And I am so hungry," whined Mildred.

"Dead cat, indeed!" said my mother, evidently amused, instead of being angry and sympathetic as we expected. However, she followed us up to the nursery, and, to our surprise, burst into a fit of laughter,—"You silly children, it's a cold hare."

We, having never seen such an animal before, being, too, on most affectionate terms with a number of cats, to which the cold cooked hare bore a startling resemblance, could not be induced to feed on a probable favourite. We rejected our mother's explanation as unsatisfactory. The hare was a hare and nothing else to her; it was a cat and nothing but a cat to us; and, hungry as we were, and much in awe, too, of our mother, we would have starved rather than eaten a morsel of a creature we had nursed and fondled.

My mother cut the matter very short. "If you children are not satisfied with the remains of what we feasted on yesterday, you must dine on bread and vegetables,"—and we did. To this very day I never see a hare brought to table but that nursery scene comes back fresh to my recollection.

CHAPTER THE THIRD.

HOMŒOPATHY AND ALLOPATHY.

Si tibi deficiunt Medici, Medici tibi fiant
Haec tria—Mens hilaris, Requies, Moderata Diæta.

To keep the doctors from your door, three things are quite enough—
Be merry, do not fag your brain, and chiefly do not *stuff*.
Translation.

WHEN we left the schoolroom and were introduced into society, we were allowed the privilege of a free breakfast and dinner table. The reaction from a spare diet to the unrestrained indulgence of appetites so long controlled, resulted at first in alternations of repletion and depletion. The family apothecary was good for two days a week, and pills and potions swelled his Christmas bill for medical attendance.

But even when womanhood had been attained, and we graced the table of our elders, meals had neither the number nor the variety now considered indispensable. We knew nothing of hot luncheons or afternoon teas. Entrées and sweets were strangers —

except on very special occasions. We thought ourselves well off with fish, flesh, and fowl, which were provided in wasteful abundance. Nora and Eveleen had been promoted at an earlier age—together with the governess—to dine with their parents, but as *growing*, in contradistinction to *grown up*, girls, they were restricted to one dish, and they did not fail to air their grievances in the schoolroom during the evening studies :—" Only drumsticks of turkeys and chickens ! No early potatoes, asparagus, or peas !" Perhaps it *was* tantalising for them to sit merely as spectators of delicacies which others were enjoying.

In spite of — perhaps in consequence of — the simple dietary of the nursery, as described in the last chapter, we children throve excellently well. We passed without loss or damage through the usual disorders of measles and whooping-cough ; I in particular emerged, unmarked, from a terrible attack of confluent small-pox when I was twelve years old. The case was one of such extraordinary severity as to be the object of curiosity and interest to all the medical men in the neighbourhood. I had a vision, though nearly blinded, of a group of elderly and middle aged men standing round my bed—gazing on my disfigured countenance with an interest truly professional. My mother never left my bedside, constantly fomenting my face and restraining my hands from touching it. Being pitted with the small-pox would be the annihilation of all my chances of being married. Had I been left to myself, I should certainly have arisen a hideous object for life: thanks to my mother's unwearied care, there remained not a blemish on my beauty. Just at the same time a motherless cousin of ours was attacked with the same disorder; fancying his strength would be as great out of, as in, bed, he got out and fell flat on the floor; his face was a crushed mass, of which he ever after bore the mark—" all owing," as he said, " to a fellow not having a mother."

Bad as our illnesses were—whenever we had any (though I cannot say they were very bad)—the remedies were decidedly worse. O the nauseous compounds we had to swallow! I ought not to say *swallow*, for they were literally *crammed down* our protesting and resisting throats. Pills at night, black doses in the morning, must have aggravated or prolonged the complaints. My mother went through long courses of coaxing, bribing, and threatening, in order to make us take the prescribed medicines: she rarely succeeded in getting more than half the quantity down our throats—the rest was spluttered over the bedclothes.

Homœopathy, and (thanks to homœopathy) a

vastly mitigated allopathy, are blessings for which children of the present day cannot be too grateful.

I always yielded to bribery, which was administered in the most seductive form—either of as many oranges as it was safe for me to eat, or of as many pennies as a bag suspended from the top of my bedstead could hold.

When I reached the convalescent stage, and all danger was over, my complete restoration to full health was left to the agencies of nature and time to accomplish : as to change of air, such treatment was not then included in the pharmacopœia. Indeed, for fully nine months in the year there was no possible place for us to have migrated to, which would not have been much inferior in point of situation and necessary comfort to our own home.

CHAPTER THE FOURTH.

WE SMART FOR IT.

" Crackling, blazing, spittings, hissings,—
Splutter, flutter, grillings, frizzings;
Round and round the spits turn over;
Bubblings, boilings, 'neath each cover;
Tossings, turnings, raspings, toastings;
Stewings, fryings, bastings, roastings;
Caldrons reeking, coppers steaming,
Scullions melting, faces streaming.
Great the care and calculation
For the birthday's grand collation."
Opera Buffa.

TAME and monotonous as was our home life, we had nevertheless our field days. Our delights were stolen delights—perhaps all the sweeter on that account.

During the winter a certain number of dinner parties were given. On these occasions an early dinner was provided for Miss Lacey and my two elder sisters in the schoolroom. To have an undefined position strictly defined, is about as agreeable to an individual as to have an uncertain boundary line rigidly marked out is to the weaker of two adjoining nations. The wound inflicted on the self-love of the governess through her not being admitted to a place among the guests at the dinner table, was borne in a manner which could hardly be regarded as an example to her pupils of Christian meekness. Her vexation was not confined to her own bosom, nor smothered in our presence. She keenly felt the humiliation of her position, more especially in the eyes of the servants—*that* was where the shoe pinched the tightest; and she knew well enough that Nurse Reilly would not be slow to take advantage of the opportunity of showing her that, after all, she was no better than herself.

Nurse once put her head in at the schoolroom door and asked in a malicious tone, "As Cook wanted her help in the kitchen, had not Miss Kathleen better have her dinner with her sisters?"

"Leave your brat in the nursery, she shall not come here," was the tart reply.

I felt the slur cast upon my social position by being called a "brat," but Nurse soothed my offended dignity by taking me with her to the kitchen upon my promising not to move from her side, "or the cook would hit me with the rolling-pin," and above all, "not to tell the Misthress, or there would be *something* to pay."

The kitchen—in preparation for a dinner party— was a sight indeed! What with the entire female staff, and the running in and out of the men-servants and the "followers"—what with the huge joints, the pride alike of the kitchen and dining-room—what with the roaring fires, the heat, the confusion of tongues, the cook's temper vented in expressions not the most refined—it *was* a scene. It is a wonder that I escaped both moral and physical contagion; I suppose I did, because I never remember having been reproved afterwards for any of the phrases in vogue in low life below stairs.

My mother's orders were most peremptory, that Miss Kathleen was never to go near the kitchen, nor to be taken to any of the cottages; Nurse Reilly persistently disobeyed in both respects *when the Misthress's back was turned.*

My youthful acquaintance was of a very motley description. All my reflections on what I heard and saw I confided to Nurse's ear, and I turned to her as to an oracle for an explanation of such terms as "the quality," and "heretics" as applied to us, and of such words as "cotter," "squatter," "conacre."

In kitchen and cabin I was a great favourite. Cook gave me jam-tartlets and plum-cake. Often a gilded gingerbread man was presented to me as an offering of respectful homage by some admiring gossoon who had expended all his worldly wealth in its purchase at the neighbouring fair.

While I had a lively time of it in the kitchen, it

was quite the reverse with my sisters in the schoolroom. They were Miss Lacey's *souffre-douleurs*, and had to undergo outbreaks of ill-temper which were carefully controlled in my mother's presence. "A nasty spiteful vixen," Nora would call her when she purposely set her a difficult sum. And Eveleen was not behind-hand in abuse when ordered to write out some passages of Telemaque in correct English; "would not she pay her off by holding up to her the slight mamma had put on her by not admitting her to the dinner-table?" So she began, "Nora, don't you long to be eighteen? I know I do."

"Of course I do, Eveleen, and I have only two years to wait. But why do you long so to be eighteen?" "Why, because I shall then always appear at table when there is a dinner party."

These personal remarks were sure to be followed by a smart rap from that ready instrument, the round rule, on the bare shoulders of Nora and Eveleen for being "impertinent." Frocks, low-bodied and short-sleeved, were then worn by young ladies in nursery and schoolroom. Frequently my own as well as my sister's ears, neck, and arms, have been red and swollen from the outpourings of temper of a revengeful woman entrusted with the sole charge, without appeal (for double woe if complaint was made), of four helpless girls. If the brothers are born to adversity in public schools, the sisters are no less the victims of a vicious system of tyranny in Home Education. The saying of the wisest of men, that "it is good to bear the yoke in our youth," meets with the ready assent and approbation of all—*who are not subjected to it.*

My mother, knowing pretty well what Miss Lacey's feelings would be on learning that she was to dine with the girls in the schoolroom, and was only to appear with them in the drawing-room in the evening, directed that some of the delicacies should be taken to her in order to console her for being excluded from the dinner table. My sisters catered for themselves. Bridget was talked over and prevailed on—nothing loth, as she was the footman's sweetheart—to stand in the hall and take from him the dainty dishes on their way back to the kitchen. My sisters had taken up a position in the study where the guests had deposited their wraps, and to them Bridget handed in the delicacies, on which (as the time was short) they ravened like very beasts of prey. Bridget kept imploring them in vain to put some restraint on their appetites, "as cook would be cute enough to find out that more had been taken from the dishes than had been eaten by the company and the governess; and, bless us, what will the Misthress say when she goes next morning into the larder!"

A very meagre, bone-displaying appearance the

joints, ham, and turkey did put in the next morning; and as to the game, a gastronomic anatomist alone could determine, from the small remains, their original proportions. In addition to Miss Lacey's permitted portion and the young ladies' surreptitious appropriations, there were the hangers-on, who had to be paid in kind for their services. The butler had a man to do the work he was too lazy to do himself; the footman (not to be behind-hand) had also his help; and what with the cook's assistants, in addition to the home staff, and the friends who came to see the fun and to have a frolic after "the quality" had left, it was no wonder that on the day after the feast the contents of the larder formed but a sorry show. The number of bottles of wine accounted for by the butler as having been drunk by the guests would have given a bottle and a half to each lady, in addition to three bottles to each gentleman.

Of course it was well known who the real depredators were, namely, the *hangers-on*—that especial curse of almost every Irish house of any pretensions. It provoked my mother to see the joints hacked and hewn. She was a beautiful carver—a most necessary accomplishment in those days—and prided herself upon supplying from the breast and choicest parts of poultry and game a larger number of slices than any lady of her dinner-giving friends.

On ordinary occasions the servants were "allowanced," and every article of consumption except meat was kept under lock and key, else swift and sure ruin would have been the result. The supplies for daily use were given out every morning to the cook, who, with an eye to the house-followers, generally contrived to get one-third more than was actually required; and it not unfrequently took my mother a good hour to cool down after vainly striving to reduce these extortionate demands.

The Irish ladies of the first quarter of the present century had—apart from their national beauty and vivacity—very few opportunities of distinguishing themselves in any rôle save the daily routine of domestic life, varied by heavy dinners and balls, few and far between, public or private. An authoress would have been voted a decided bore if not socially ostracised.

Locomotion, before steamers and railways had revolutionised the age, was difficult, tedious, and expensive. I suspect that my parents' knowledge of foreign parts was derived only from Cook's Voyages and Bruce's Travels. The cities of Europe, with their matchless treasures of architecture, painting, and sculpture, were known by name only. School books supplied but scanty information respecting the great capitals and their contents, and the boundary lines between nation and nation. There were no travellers to report to us what they had themselves actually seen —snow-capped Alps, the smiling valleys of Switzerland with their deep-blue lakes, and Italy's glowing skies and rich sunny landscapes, and thus to make us dissatisfied and discontented with the objects, natural and artificial, of our own country, by a contrast with those of more favoured lands.

CHAPTER THE FIFTH.

TRAINING AND DRESS.

" O Liberty! what crimes are committed in thy name!
O Fashion! what miseries follow in thy train!"

THE sunshine went out of my life when nurse and nursery were exchanged for governess and schoolroom. The warm blood was chilled, and the light free spirit was fettered, except when the exuberance of youth would burst through the shackles with which we were harnessed to an educational scheme rigidly drawn up and enforced.

Our school-room was appropriately furnished with wooden desks and hard high-backed chairs. Daily family prayer had not come into use, but our school work began by reading aloud, verse by verse, the psalms and lessons for the day. Very little of the meaning we understood or cared to understand, our thoughts being chiefly directed to the way of escape from reprimand, or rap from the ever ready rule, as the punishment of mispronouncing some hard Scriptural name; and O, how hard we found many of them! I hope the recording angel took note of our sufferings and of the tears which we shed.

It was in much discomfort both of body and mind that I received the first seeds of knowledge. My seat was a straight-backed chair. My feet were inserted in an apparatus which enforced the position of "Heels together—toes out,"—a veritable young ladies' stocks. In order to keep my head erect and guard against an ungraceful stooping posture, a metal collar was fastened round my neck, padded with wash leather for preventing abrasion of the skin; while, to bring my shoulders down, I wore "monitors" as they were called, consisting of leather straps brought round the shoulders and crossed behind the back, from which hung a flat leaden weight. Under such bodily conditions were my early studies pursued. We were told that the result of this treatment would be a graceful carriage when we developed into womanhood.

I admit that the same hard lines had been already measured out to my elder sisters, and—as they were assuming elegant forms—the physical training which had been successful with them was not likely to be either discontinued or relaxed in our case. But, whatever might be the gain to our personal charms, it was obtained at the cost of much trial of temper and of much bodily torture, to escape from which so many artifices were resorted to as seriously to impair the nice sense of right and wrong. We tried every conceivable position which might give us ease; we fidgetted about in our seats, and were never still for two minutes together; we contrived to push the collar from our chins, which were intended to rest upon it; we put an unoccupied hand behind and raised the leaden weight; we wrangled for half-an-hour at a time upon the necessity of being released from collars and monitors some minutes at least before beginning our writing lessons, and if the relief was refused, we had our revenge on the hard-hearted governess, as my mother always inspected our copy-books, and blamed Miss Lacey if our writing fell short of her expectations. The irritation of our tempers had not subsided when the music succeeded to the writing lesson, and we were released from our bonds not by grace or favour but by sheer necessity—the wrong keys which we persistently struck setting both governess and music-master half wild.

The ultimate object of this home education, with all its bodily inflictions, trials of temper, temptations to deceit, was after all only this—the making a sensation in our social world when we should be introduced! We could not help suspecting that all our accomplishments and graces were not meant for home adornment and for the formation of useful and agreeable members of society, but for securing for us a successful *debût*, on which a good worldly marriage was to follow as the natural consequence. The future partner for life must be well connected—if nearly allied to nobility so much the better. The cousin or younger brother of a nobleman with a very moderate income would carry off the prize in the matrimonial market—not only with the consent of the girl herself, but also of her more prudent parents—against a suitor of five times his income, who in tracing his pedigree had to travel a long way back before he came to the bifurcation of nobility and commonalty.

What immense strides have been made in the education, dress, and amusements of the children of the present day! An American once remarked—" We never see now-a-days either young folks or old folks." I suppose it must be owing to all ages dressing much alike—one cut and material does for all who *dress* in contradistinction to *being clothed*. How difficult it is, judging from mere outward costume, to decide who is the lady and who the lady's-maid! I have been told that the most accurate discriminators are the female pew-openers of fashionable West-end churches, whose trained eyes enable them to pronounce at a glance who's who.

Now, when babies emerge from long clothes, the form and fashion of their garments are pretty much the same as those of their elder sisters, mothers, and grandmothers. Do not all wear hats, post-boy jackets, chignons, plaits, long curls, and coronets,—flowers pendant, flowers rampant, flowers in wreaths, flowers single, flowers coquettishly peeping from between or from beneath,—bands, braids, tresses? I forget, there is one other style, but this is at present confined to a portion of the very youthful, the very simple, and the very poetical, namely, the hair falling naturally down the shoulders and back—as Eve is represented in the garden of Eden by Italian painters. *As yet*, our sexagenarians and septuagenarians have not ventured upon any artificial means of producing this graceful and innocent effect; who will venture to predict how long it will be before they do?

As the winter season drew on, there were great expectations on Nora's part—some hopes on Eveleen's: we three younger girls knew only too well what was in store for *us*. Five light-blue braided cloth pelisses, with as many beaver hats, which had undergone a seven months' imprisonment in a dark closet, again saw the light of day. The law of primogeniture was observed in Nora having the privilege of a new pelisse, hat, and feather; while—according to the law of descent—her last year's suit passed to Eveleen, her's to the next, and so on in regular succession.

Eveleen—who was by no means satisfied with the arrangement—gave her mother plainly to understand that it was monstrous that she, having attained the ripe age of fifteen, should have to put up with her elder sister's cast-offs. She was quite aware of her growing charms, and craved for suitable raiment to set them off to advantage. She was no modest flower content to blush unseen, nor to appear in public in Nora's discarded dresses.

"My dear Eveleen," said my mother soothingly (for nothing would have pleased her better than to gratify the girl), "with so many of you entailing so many calls upon your father's purse, I cannot ask him for seven pounds for a pelisse and hat for you, when the tailor and hatter can make Nora's look quite as good as new. Next year you shall have everything made expressly for yourself."

We three younger girls had to receive without a murmur the descending suits of our elder sisters. Eveleen might, unrebuked, burst into a passionate flood of tears over her disappointed hopes, but no such license of feeling was allowed to us.

We knew well enough there was not a single one of our acquaintances who would not be quite aware, when we entered the family pew on the Sunday of our first sporting our winter dresses, that Nora Rochford alone would be considered worth a critical inspection, and that—if any of the critics were the fortunate possessors of new instead of transferred dresses—they would be sure to mark their sense of superiority by significant glances during church time—only to be repeated on the Mall.

The Cathedral morning service, and the military band on the Mall from three to five o'clock, were the "Longchamps"—the parade-grounds for the display of the beauty, elegance, and fashion of the Landford ladies.

At those two particular epochs of the year which were known as "between seasons," when on the one hand our winter, and on the other hand our summer, dresses, became faded and worn, the governess was desired to attend the Parish church with her three younger pupils. Kilkreen Church was a dreary, white-washed building; the congregation was scanty, consisting of not above a dozen worshippers; and the service was cold and heartless, performed by the Rector in a slovenly, undevotional manner. We always called our "between season" Sundays "punishment Sundays."

Miss Lacey, debarred through the increasing shabbiness of our attire from Cathedral alike and Mall, was consequently in the worst of tempers. There was nothing for her but the monotonous society of her pupils, unrelieved even by a fashionable novel; for whatever amount of out-of-doors amusement and frivolity was regarded as legitimate, yet within doors (it seemed like straining off the gnat and swallowing the camel) anything approaching to light literature was strictly excluded. Nora and Eveleen, having spring dresses which did duty for autumn wear, were spared the humiliation of banishment to the Parish church. The parochial system had little hold even then upon the residents in the parish, who felt no obligation to be faithful to their appointed minister, if services more suited to their taste and temperament were to be found elsewhere.

CHAPTER THE SIXTH.

PRIOR TO COMPETITIVE EXAMINATIONS.

"I'll play the cook."
Titus Andronicus, Act V.

IT may perhaps astonish some of my English readers to be told that there were old families holding good positions in their neighbourhoods whose children were never visible except when detected in the act of swinging upon the entrance-gate, or surprised in some out-of-the-way nook in the shrubbery,—the boys with naked knees peeping through their corduroy suits, the girls with battered bonnets and with socks either hanging in wrinkles about their ankles or half-absorbed under the heels of well-worn shoes. When thus caught, the little savages incontinently took to flight.

There were large Country houses within a few miles of us where I never saw any children at all, though I knew there were plenty. In many families the younger branches were invisible, indisputably for economical reasons, but not for this reason alone. The daughters who had been introduced must be considered. To publish the number of those still remaining to be provided for would be the height of imprudence, as the more the children the less the marriage portion, and consequently the smaller the chance of marriage. Such arrangements were much too common for any unfavourable comment to be made.

A fair amount of liberty was accorded to the elder daughters. They might be seen taking daily drives on the jaunting car, or riding on horseback with fathers or brothers. Such privileges were enjoyed by Nora and Eveleen; we younger ones never took turns with them. Many a starting tear we furtively wiped away when the butler threw open the door of the schoolroom, and announced that Miss Nora and Miss Eveleen were to get ready for a drive with the Misthress or a ride with the Masther.

It was not the custom in my day for young married women to enter the lists and compete with the unmarried for the most eligible partners at balls; neither was it safe to attempt to carry on flirtations with them, as very little provocation—and sometimes hardly any at all—was sufficient ground for a duel. The young married women had had their day, and they unselfishly retired upon their matrimonial laurels, leaving a fair open field for others to try their chances of similar conquests. The most youthful bride, when she put off the bridal veil, assumed a modest lace cap, not the travesty of a cap, but of a size and shape to cover the head. Many a time I have seen a young bridegroom lay violent hands on his young wife's cap and fling it to the end of the room, and let loose her imprisoned tresses, declaring he would never have married her had he known that one of her principal charms was to be half concealed by day—and wholly by night under that hideous invention a nightcap.

When the family finances were inadequate to the supply of suitable dresses for both mother and daughter, the daughter's interest was first considered, while the mothers—with true motherly unselfishness —denied themselves what was due to their position. I have seen troops of well-dressed girls in a ball-room accompanied by chaperones in dresses furbished up for the occasion, a matron's black velvet being generally held good for the term of her natural life— unchanged in form as in material.

There resided, within four miles of Kilkreen, a Mr and Mrs Cullum, who had ten children, not a single one of whom I had ever seen. Mr Cullum was an easy-going, indolent Irish squire; he married a very handsome woman. The husband loved a quiet and retired life; the wife loved excitement and gaiety— neglecting home duties and family cares. Few days elapsed without seeing her drive past our gates, or meeting her on the road leading to Landford where she shopped and visited, and walked on the Mall with one or other of the officers whom she encountered by chance or appointment. Usually she was attended by one of the handsomest young men I had ever then seen. Mr St George was a distant connection of Mr Cullum; he used to stretch himself at full length on the opposite side of the car to Mrs Cullum, who was so placed as, with a slight inclination of their heads across the rail which separated them, their faces almost touched.

I was then of an age of blissful ignorance; but as Mrs Cullum and Mr St George drove past, Nora and Eveleen were wont to exchange glances and subdued remarks. Miss Lacey, who dearly loved a little bit of scandal, did not check either words or looks—it was her special delight to hear all that was talked about in our circle; and as my two elder sisters heard a great deal they were not supposed to hear, they would graphically retail (when their relations with their governess were of a friendly sort) many a piquant anecdote, redounding neither to the credit nor morality of the actors.

While Mr Cullum sat moping indoors, or was listlessly strolling about his ill-kept grounds, and Mrs Cullum was taking her pleasure in pursuits apart from husband and family, what wonder that the children of such parents should grow up uncouth in manner and uneducated in mind !

Time went on, and the eldest boy shot up into a fine grown man of nineteen, waiting for a commission in a Line Regiment. What young Irish gentleman ever condescends to enter into any profession but the naval or military ? In due course of time—his name having been placed on the Commander-in-Chief's list —the commission was obtained, and he was gazetted as ensign in His Majesty's —th Regiment. It was, however, at the cost of one more mortgage being added to the already heavily mortgaged estate. Taking our usual walk into the town, we were met on the bridge over the river Dour by Miss Anstey Costello—a middle-aged spinster, racy in speech and original in ideas, one of those characters indigenous to Ireland. As we came within hailing distance, Miss Anstey Costello—always bursting with her subject whatever it might be, and regardless of time, place, person, matter—halted, threw up her arms, and with a tone half comical, half satirical, and with an exclamation more forcible than reverent, shouted,—

" Girls, Jem Cullum has got his commission ; aint he a proud and happy boy ? And faith, my dears, he may well be, for Jem can neither read, nor write, nor spell, and before the next Gazette is out, no commission will be given except to those who can read a military order and sign their names legibly. I have read it myself in an order signed by Lord Fitzroy Somerset, the Duke's secretary."

Though we had never set eyes upon Jem Cullam, we could quite understand that he had got his commission in the nick of time.

I once overheard my sister Nora telling a story similarly illustrative of the state of education at that period. She was rather deep in a flirtation with a certain captain in one of the Light Infantry Regiments—otherwise the gallant captain might not have been so ready to tell tales out of school. The second son of a noble marquis had received an invitation to dinner in the neighbourhood; how to reply properly puzzled him; sprawling across the mess table he got as far as, " Lord William presents his comp—" and there he stuck: " I say, how do you spell compliments ? is it pla, ple, or pli—or what the devil is it ? for it staggers me, I can tell you." The captain helped him out of this difficulty. " Ah yes, I see, compliments to be sure ; any school boy knows that. But, ahem! how am I to go on now? There, old fellow, do you finish it for me ; and when you have done, come along to my room and have a pull at the claret; I broached a fresh hogshead this morning." Lord William had always a hogshead of claret on tap in his barrack-room. He died at an early age from an attack of fever, aggravated by the constant use of stimulants.

As a pendant to the two preceding examples of the low standard of intellectual culture prior to the era of the present competitive examinations and of the high-pressure education to which girls are now submitted, I give the following instance :—

Arabella Barton was a lovely girl of sweet seventeen. She had lived all the days of her girlhood in a remote country village. Her father could not afford the funds for boarding-school or governess; and though he was a clergyman and a fair classical scholar, and though her mother was educated up to the times in which she lived, yet neither parent thought it a duty devolving upon them to supply—themselves—what they had not the means of procuring from paid teachers. It was no uncommon practice for Irish parents to be totally neglectful of their duty in regard to the education of their children : if they could afford to pay for school or governess, they were ready enough to do so; but if not, then the children were left to pick up what smattering of learning they could receive from the village schoolmaster in his spare hours, who generally officiated also as the Parish clerk.

There had been a brutal murder of two process-servers. The neighbourhood was a seething mass of disaffection. No one knew what the end would be. The police force stationed in the parish of Greymount, of which Mr Barton was rector, was strengthened by a detachment of cavalry, commanded by Captain Sutherland. The Barton family were charmed with this interruption of the monotony of their village life; and an invitation to dinner was speedily sent to the Captain, though poor Mrs Barton was at her wits' end how to procure the necessary supplies. Fortunately, a clever Irish cousin who had resided many years in France was staying with them, and she came to the rescue. Even *her* inventive genius was severely tested, as few days passed without Captain Sutherland being a guest at the Rectory dinner-table. I asked the cousin how, with such a limited larder, she contrived to place a dinner fit to be eaten before a Cavalry officer who had been accustomed to a luxurious mess?

"In the first place," she replied, "I knew—and he knew too—that 'the Peelers' could not give him anything so good. In the second place, he was in love. In the third, there was a good vegetable garden, well stocked; a joint of meat was generally, though not always, to be had in the village; and there were plenty of long-legged, lean chickens at hand in the coop."

"Why, what could you make out of such scanty materials?" I asked in surprise, remembering our own kitchen scenes.

"You don't suppose," she said, "that I have spent so many years in the land of cookery without profiting by it. Give me a kitchen garden, a bone with a little meat on it, a few eggs, a pat of butter, and a few preserves, and I would engage to send up a dinner at which the Lord Lieutenant would not turn up his nose."

"Much less a man in love, who is no Lord Lieutenant," I said, laughing.

"He had reached that ecstatic state of love when common objects appear under angelic forms. I often used to say to myself, 'Poor man, when the fit is over and you get back to your right mind, you will think very differently, and it will be the old cry—That wretched, backward, uncivilized country! thank God I am not an Irish proprietor, with a rascally priest-ridden tenantry.'"

"And the denouement?" I asked.

"Just what all wished. Captain Sutherland proposed for Arabella, and was accepted; and, two days after, he was on his way to England to obtain his father's consent, which was readily given, as he was an only child, and his father was only too glad of his settling down as a married man, and giving up soldiering."

"But how did Arabella manage to carry on a correspondence with her lover during his absence?" I asked.

"She dictated, and I wrote—moulding the sentences into grammatical shape. It was not easy to transfer to paper the gushing expressions which came so glibly from her lips; I often found French the best vehicle, and therefore used French. Captain Sutherland was all surprise and admiration: how could she, in that retired village, have made herself mistress, not only of the bare language, but of the idiom? It was so modest of her to conceal her accomplishments from him; she must have been conversant with the best authors. Arabella's fortune was a thousand pounds; it was all expended upon the trousseau, and a visit to dear, dirty, delightful Dublin (as it is called) to purchase it, and upon the wedding-breakfast. Captain Sutherland and his wife have never set foot again in Ireland. Her deficiencies were soon discovered, and no sooner discovered than repaired; the best masters were engaged; and, stimulated by affection, and aided by much natural quickness and ability, she soon ripened into an accomplished woman."

CHAPTER THE SEVENTH.

OUR AMUSEMENTS.

" To rear a child is easy, but to teach
Morals and manners, is beyond our reach ;
To make the foolish wise, the wicked good,
That science never yet was understood."
Theognis. Translation by J. Hookham Frere.

VERY scanty were the amusements provided in the intervals of our lessons. A doll's house descended to me in due course, like my wearing apparel; it was in a ricketty condition, and the furniture was only broken rubbish. The doll herself had lost her right eye and her left arm, and—whatever it might have been in happier days—her nose was no longer after the Grecian type. I soon began to treat my doll as an Indian does his god when his prayers are not granted. A doll was, however, a necessity to me, and I invented one. I abstracted a pillow from my bed, tied a string tight round the middle to give it somewhat of a shape, dressed it up in my own clothes, and constituted myself its nurse. When tired of carrying my bantling about, I turned a chair upside down, placed another pillow on it, and, lo! by the force of imagination, there was a carriage ready to carry off my lady to make a morning call.

Another of my devices, for which I was soundly scolded by Bridget, was the travestying her duties by pouring the contents of the water-jug on the floor, and scrubbing the boards on my knees with a towel.

On wet afternoons a retail shop was established in partnership with my sisters in the schoolroom; the table represented the counter, the lesson-books the goods for sale, Nora and Eveleen were the proprietors, Aileen and Mildred the customers, and I was the errand-boy who had to take round the parcels.

I much doubt whether more real enjoyment is felt by the children of the present day in the possession of fashionable and scientific toys.

I have often been struck with surprise at finding how children catch up and dramatise in their own way the thrilling occurrences and crimes of the day. I well remember taking a niece of mine upon a visit to an old friend, the wife of an English vicar. We happened to go into the nursery, where, strewed upon the floor, lay several expensive toys which were neglected for another and a grim amusement. Etta, the Vicar's daughter, had dressed her biggest doll in a black satin dress, a linen cap was drawn over the head and face, a cord was fastened round the neck at one end, and attached to the bed-post at the other.

"What can Etta be doing?" asked my niece, evidently undecided whether to laugh or scream.

"I am going to hang Mrs Manning, the murderess," was the answer, and she at once carried her intention into execution; she gave a professional jerk to the string, and up flew the effigy. The next act was to jump up on the bed and pull the legs. The cutting-down process was then gone through. Then the black satin dress was removed and a white night-gown was substituted, and the executed criminal was placed in a box representing a coffin, which was solemnly borne down-stairs into the garden, where a grave had been already dug by a small but considerate brother, and consigned to the ground. The trial of the Mannings and its result had no doubt been read and discussed by the parents in the children's presence, who had thus got up a mimic representation as more exciting pastime than that to be got out of their artistic and scientific toys legitimately used.

My next visit, as it happened, was to my sister Mildred, who had some years before been married to an English rector. The parish was an unhealthy one, low, damp, and marshy; the death-rate was consequently high; and as the Rectory grounds adjoined the church-yard, the sound of the passing and the funeral bell could be distinctly heard by the family. One day my sister and I had been watching with much sadness and sympathy, on account of the particular circumstances of the case, a funeral procession winding its way to the church-yard. A young farmer's wife had been suddenly carried off by diphtheria, leaving five small children. My sister's two little girls, with their brother, had witnessed the scene from the nursery windows; shortly after the children rushed into the room where we were sitting, and gleefully exclaimed, " O we have had such a jolly time of it !" This jolly time proved to be an imitation of the solemn scene by the children—a doll representing the deceased, the little boy in his night-gown—" just like papa "—being the officiating minister.

I certainly cannot recal any special amusement being provided for me. Once, and only once, I was at a children's party; we never had them at Kilkreen. My only theatre for display was the dancing academy. I was incomparably the best dancer among a large number of pupils, but I never attained to the position of show-girl; my elder sister's cast-off frocks always kept me in the back-ground. On one occasion the wife of a Colonel asked Nora who " that ill-dressed girl " was who " danced so beautifully." Nora coolly answered that she did not know. As we were not an amiable family, I was soon told that Nora was ashamed of me. I keenly felt the slight that had been put upon me. What had I done that Nora should deny the relationship between us? Bursting with anger, I flew to my mother for redress. Alas! I got none. My mother sided with Nora, and even approved of her tact in preventing that "stiff English woman, with her national sense of family justice, commenting upon one sister being dressed better than another, which she would be sure to pronounce as so thoroughly Irish."

"My dear Kathleen," she argued with me, "you ought to see how impossible it is for me to dress all of you for public exhibition. It does not matter what opinion is passed on you *now*. Make the most of your present opportunities, and by-and-by when you have grown into a handsome, graceful girl (as I am sure you will do), you shall be suitably dressed, and we shall all be proud of you."

It was a far-off consolation; it was one of those happy prospects in the distance which were frequently held out to us, and with which we had to be, or appear to be, satisfied. I must do my mother the justice to add, that when the time came she faithfully fulfilled her promise.

I had but a small allowance of pocket money—an occasional shilling and an extraordinary half-crown constituted my privy purse. Reading was a passionate delight, and I expended all my cash in the purchase of such books as "Sandford and Merton," "Paul and Virginia," "Robinson Crusoe," and the successive volumes of Mrs Hofland's Tales. So well read was I in the contents of my juvenile library, that I could have stood a competitive examination in them with much credit. I invariably identified myself with the suffering heroine or hero of the tale ; — it took away the feeling of isolation — this hearty entering into their humiliations and trials.

As our birthdays were never kept—Irish ladies, above all others, being touchy about their ages being known—we neither looked forward to nor expected birthday presents. Christmas was the only day on which we had a special treat. On that festival the whole family breakfasted and dined together. Aunts and cousins, waifs and strays of society, were our guests on this occasion : besides these, it was open house to all acquaintances far and near, for whom a magnificent luncheon was provided—spiced rounds of beef of fabulous weight, raised game-pies of wonderful proportions, and various dishes proper to the season. We children particularly delighted in that particular currant cake called Barmbrack. The party which assembled at dinner—a magnified edition of that at luncheon—was so large, that we were pretty much left to ourselves and to the unrestrained indulgence in plum puddings and minced pies, for which we underwent the penance of a week's dosing of pills, powders, and black doses.

Book the Second.

CHAPTER THE FIRST.

IRELAND'S NEEDS.

" My poor opinion is that the closest connection between Great Britain and Ireland is essential to the well-being, I had almost said to the very being, of the two kingdoms. . . . I think, indeed, that Great Britain would be ruined by the separation of Ireland; but as there are degrees even in ruin, it would fall the most heavily on Ireland. *By such a separation Ireland would be the most completely undone country in the world—the most wretched, the most distracted, and, in the end, the most desolate part of the habitable globe.*"—BURKE, *Letter on the Affairs of Ireland.* Works, vol. ii., p. 62.

ABSENTEEISM has long been regarded as the great, if not sole, cause of Ireland's social depression; and few would deny, that if the money spent out of the Country by the Absentees were spent in it, a great change would be effected, placing Ireland on as high a level as Scotland has attained.

But is it not a great mistake to maintain that material prosperity and social elevation are indissolubly united?

It may suit the political party in power to hold up, in proof of their views of Irish prosperity, the sums invested by thrifty farmers in Savings' banks, the rise in the wages of agricultural labourers, the increase of exports, as evidences of Ireland emerging fast from the slough she had fallen into—that she is about to take her rank with countries of similar natural advantages, and to become a country "sought out, not forsaken."

But Ireland requires other elements to raise her to the position she is entitled to hold, and—deprived of which—she must ever occupy a low standard socially in the rank of nations.

Ireland needs not only resident landlords, but a wealthy, independent gentry, enterprising merchants, large and commodious dockyards, her excellent natural harbours made available for ships engaged in *import* as well as export trade, and, above all, she needs men of high reputation for Literature, Science, and Art, animated with a spirit of patriotism and of pride in the land which gave them birth.

In the year 1850 I was staying in the house of an old Irish proprietor, when the subject of Absenteeism was discussed.

"To England's party government or rather misgovernment, to her selfish policy, and to her wilful ignorance or disregard of Ireland's legitimate claims, Ireland owes her present unfortunate position," said my host, Mr Jenkinson. "It was by the grossest corruption, the most shameless bribery, and the most lavish promises of peerages, pensions, and government offices, that the Union was carried. While, from financial as well as other motives, moral high-minded England was boasting of keeping strict faith with powerful foreign nations, she had no scruple in employing any means, however dishonourable or demoralising, when *a Conquered Province* had to be dealt with. No sooner was the measure thus unrighteously carried than the social ruin of Ireland commenced.

" When I was a boy," Mr Jenkinson went on to say, " I always accompanied my parents to the County town, where we passed the six winter months. We had a house of our own, as had most of our principal county neighbours. There was excellent society—the Bishop and Cathedral staff, some rich Rectors, Officers of superior rank, and Governmental or Municipal officials whose offices (many of them sinecures) had been obtained through interest rather than by merit.

" Now, mark how all this was changed by the Union. When St Stephen's-green Dublin Parliament was absorbed by that of St Stephen's Westminster, our representative Peers and our Members of the House of Commons had to curtail their home expenditure in order to meet the expenses of a six months' residence in London ; they had also to put the screw on their tenantry in order to raise their rents. Gradually, both nobility and commonalty became dissatisfied with Ireland as a residence, when they came to experience the superior advantages which England possesses. Instead of making merely a Parliamentary stay in England, they began to make England altogether their home—taking only flying trips to their native Country; some never again crossed the Irish Channel, leaving the management of their estates altogether to agents.

"Less fortunate than England with her Bath, Brighton, Leamington, and other watering-places, Ireland had no such attractions, either for winning back those who had thus deserted her, or for retaining a hold upon others who had not the excuse of Parliamentary duties for following their example."

"Yes," interrupted Mrs Jenkinson, "it is really unendurable the dull lives we Irish ladies are doomed to lead. I am weary of my life—so monotonous—with only one unvaried topic of conversation—English misgovernment and Irish grievances. *My* grievance is the having to go on vegetating in this dreary country of ours."

"The English Government," Mr Jenkinson went on without deigning to notice his wife's interruption, "will find our country's wrongs a hydra-headed monster; strike off one head and another is sure to start up. An unhappy fatality seems to attend all her measures whether palliative or coercive, always trying some expedient or other." . . .

"Like Longfellow's blacksmith, always *something attempted*, but (the continuation has to be reversed) *nothing done*," I said.

"Exactly so," he continued; "and just see what comes of it all."

"Comes of it all, indeed!" cried Mrs Jenkinson. "Just like those roads they have been making to employ the people during the terrible famine, starting from nowhere and leading to nowhere. I wish to goodness they had made a road to take me out of the country."

"God knows," said Mr Jenkinson, "I would not keep you another day in the country if I could help it: only wait till our boys' education is finished, and they are started in life."

"I agree with you," answered Mrs Jenkinson, "as to the necessity of denying ourselves for our boys' advantage; but there are times when I cannot prevent the demon of discontent from obtaining a supremacy, and then I catch myself saying, 'Oh! that I were the wife of an English squire, that I might, when moped in the country, make flying visits to Brighton or mild Torquay.' Here in Ireland we have no winter resort; and when from sheer necessity we cross the channel for a change, we are taunted with being Absentees."

"Another evil result of the Union," said Mr Jenkinson, "has been our being compelled to send our sons to England for their education. In my day Irish schools and Trinity College were thought quite sufficient for boys and young men. Now nothing goes down but English public schools, and Cambridge or Oxford, else the national brogue would as effectually stamp them as the misplaced h's do the English cockneys."

"And I have to put up with the airs of a second-rate English governess," said Mrs Jenkinson, "who, when she feels dull in this isolated place, does not scruple to tell me that she must always think Ireland the most backward country in Europe, destitute alike of comfort and civilisation. No doubt she is right; still it is no more pleasant to have Home Truths forced upon us than Home Troubles. However, we are travelling along the high road which is to conduct us to England in time; and then farewell—a long farewell—farewell for ever I hope—to Ireland and the endless repetitions of its grievances social and political."

"What! and abandon all your duties as proprietors?" I could not help asking in amazement.

"Ah, I see," said Mr Jenkinson, "you have caught up the Saxon cry—' property has its duties as well as its rights.' For my part, when I see the English proprietors setting us the example, I shall be proud to follow it. Don't I know lots of owners of large estates who never think of visiting them, much less of spending a portion of the year on them, but either leave them shut up altogether, or else place their agent in occupation."

"But," I interrupted, "I am assured in England by those acquainted with the facts, that many owners are at this very time spending more upon the improvement of the land than the rent covers—that they actually are losers in point of income."

"Whew!" whistled Mr Jenkinson, "I know better than that. A property may have been rack-rented, or else may have been so let down that a large outlay of capital and the lowering of rents were necessary for bringing the property round. But has any one of these owners you speak of the conscience to tell me that, as shrewd, calculating Englishmen, they would keep possession of land which would be a never-ending drain upon their purses? Trust them! They are looking forward to the time when there will be a lull in agrarian crimes, and when that comes there will be three classes competing for estates and farms: —First, thrifty farmers will be bringing out their hoarded gains; secondly, there will be rich North-Irish manufacturers, who will be eager purchasers of estates, which they expect will entitle them to take rank as Country gentlemen ; and, thirdly, there will be speculators, who will make large investments, with the view of selling again when land rises in value. When that time comes—and it is not very far off— English owners will throw their Irish estates, on which they are now spending so much, into the market, and so recoup themselves."

Mr Jenkinson's prophecy seems to be undergoing its fulfilment. From the furious demand of Ireland for the Irish, and from the failure of every successive concession to satisfy the craving of that horse-leech— the Ultramontane Kelt—it is easy enough to see what must follow. Even already, large estates which have been for centuries in the possession of non-resident English noblemen have been sold at some forty years' purchase, and more are advertised for sale. Some few sales may have originated in conscientious motives, but the great majority has been caused by a dread of *total* confiscation, towards which Ulster Custom and Tenant Right (as interpreted by the Tenant and legalised by the late Land Act) have made a great advance.

Nothing now remains for this unhappy country but for Home Rule and an Irish Parliament to inaugurate a war of extermination between the descendants of the old Kelt proprietors and the Saxon Colonists.

CHAPTER THE SECOND.

DUNLESS.

"Arma virumque *cano.*"
Virgil, *Æn. I.*

"Such love might never long endure,
However gay and goodly be the style,
That doth ill cause, or evil end enure;
For Virtue is the band that bindeth hearts most sure."

It was with a thrill of delight that, one morning towards the close of May, we heard that John Mahoney was closeted with my mother.

It was an annual visit, was this of John Mahoney's; we well knew the object of it, and the probable result, namely, a four months' stay at the sea-side, which (as far as we three younger girls were concerned) meant partial freedom from schoolroom restraints, fewer formal walks, and our brothers' company during their six weeks' holidays. Nora and Eveleen had their visions of boating, picnicking, and unlimited flirting. My mother, too, delighted in the prospect; it was something to her to exchange the monotony of her home, which was always a dull one during the spring, as dinner parties and balls were then over, and there was nothing to replace them; so she entered with all a mother's sympathy into the lively anticipations of her two daughters. As for us three juniors, we were nobodies, and were not taken into account when the summer plans were under consideration.

On one occasion I overheard my mother saying,— " I do wish, Nora, that something to your advantage will come of our visit to Dunless this season. We shall be sure to have some of the young men from the upper end of the County. I must confess I am getting rather tired of the military; they are pleasant and agreeable, their uniform sets off a dinner-table and a ball-room, and many of them are first-rate dancers, but matrimonially regarded they are nowhere. They come and dine, and dance, and are good company, but then the route comes and sets them free from entanglements from which in a short time they would have found it difficult to escape."

My sister Nora had been made much of as the eldest daughter. Her natural disposition was not altogether amiable. She was disposed to be tyrannising over her younger brothers and sisters, and—when out of temper—to be antagonistic and impertinent to her parents. Indeed, she rarely was in good humour, unless she had a flirtation on hand (usually with some officer), which of course came to grief with the "Order of march." All this would vex and worry my mother, but my father would only remark, "If Nora chooses to act like a fool, she must take the consequences of her folly." Unfortunately *others* had to take the consequences also. She would resent—even scornfully—her mother's warnings that these flirtations would only end in disappointment; she would affront and wound the governess in some weak point; she would carry tales of some breach of rules, and get us punishment tasks. On the occasion just referred to, she answered her mother with flaming eyes and in a sneering tone—"If the bait you held out to papa for our going to Dunless is the chance of my getting a husband there, I hope you will be disappointed."

When eventually she did get a husband, we shed no tears at her departure. If any were shed at all, they were tears of joy.

This John Mahoney was the owner of most of the houses at Dunless—the principal summer resort of the upper ranks of our own and the adjoining Counties. As my father had been in the habit of engaging John's best house for several seasons, John paid him the compliment of giving him the first choice; and in this, as in previous years, my father's name was entered in John's greasy memorandum book as the tenant for four months, namely from July to October, of "Rathmahoney

House," which was the title given to the principal house in "The Row." The rent was then considered a high one—forty pounds for the whole term. The bargain, however, was never concluded without some altercation between the contracting parties—namely, my mother and John, as my father was much too easy-going to take any trouble in such arrangements. John was by no means indifferent to his own interests; he pleaded the situation and the size of the house and the excellence of the furniture,—" there could be no doubt of Rathmahoney House being snapped up the very moment it was known that it was to be let." Of course my mother depreciated,—" To my knowledge, Mr Mahoney, you have not spent five pounds on repairs for the last five seasons, and as for the furniture, it is perfectly disgraceful. You know what a quantity of things I have to send from this house before we can possibly occupy Rathmahoney."

"By my faith, my lady, an' you are the very first that I ever heard find fault with my house or its furniture."

John named the rent he wanted. My mother scouted the demand as extortionate, and offered about two-thirds.

John called St Patrick to witness that he "should be ruined entirely, entirely; and sure, my lady would not have it on her conscience to ruin a poor man."

E

My mother retaliated by telling John that he had better look to his own conscience, and he would find he was trying to make himself rich at her expense.

And so they went on, the one descending step by step and the other ascending the rent scale, until the middle point was reached, and the bargain was struck. A *vivâ voce* agreement was quite sufficient for both landlord and tenant in those days. One thing, however, John stipulated for—that my mother should be "close" as to the amount of the rent. "If it once got wind that my lady had beaten him down, there would be the black gintleman to pay; and sure if one would not give him what he asked, there was no reason why he should not square up by squeezing as much as he could out of another."

John's philosophical view of trading, it may be assumed, is extensively adopted, namely, making the unwary and the unsuspecting compensate for the screws, the bad-payers, and the non-payers.

During the last week of June the preparatory steps were taken for the transport of the family to Dunless. Bridget commenced by despoiling almost every bedroom of some of its furniture. Nora and Eveleen kept continually reminding her not to forget the toilet glasses, as those in Rathmahoney made a fright of every one. "They did not know their own faces in them."

"Now, Miss Nora, Miss Eveleen, don't keep on

worreting the wits out of me. If you lave me in pace you'll not be without a glass to see your pretty faces just exactly as God Almighty made them. If you stop me from getting the things ready in time, shure the Misthress will be down upon me."

While these annual flittings were in progress, Nora was seldom in the best of tempers. She liked her ease by night as well as by day, and could not bear the thought of having a hard bed to sleep on for the week that her feather bed would be on its way to Dunless; so she kept manœuvring for the delay of its removal, much to the vexation of Bridget, who confided her own notions to us. "It will be aisy times for us all when Miss Nora is off our hands, and I hope she'll meet her match this summer at the Sayside." I cannot say that we disagreed with Bridget upon this point.

The cook took stock of the kitchen utensils required; the butler of the plate, glass, and crockery; and great was the difference in their respective inventories at the commencement and at the close of the occupation of Rathmahoney House.

The household goods and effects having been stored in the waggon, and all being held tightly together by ropes, the kitchen-maid was gallantly elevated to the summit of this medley pyramid by some of the men-servants.

Molly the kitchen-maid liked a soft seat as well as her betters whenever she could get it, so she had contrived to crown the edifice with a feather-bed, on which she seated herself, and she was driven off amid the laughter of her fellow-servants at the comicality of her position. We rushed to the schoolroom window to hail Molly with waving handkerchiefs.

Molly was allowed two entire days for the unpacking and distribution of the effects over which she had *bodily* presided during the journey. In due course the rest of the establishment followed.

My father cordially detested these annual outings. A house in a Row was, he maintained, as bad as camping out; the eyes of "The Row" being always directed to their neighbours' proceedings as far as their field of vision extended—right, left, and in front.

The houses in "The Row" had no back entrances, the front doors were consequently never shut all day long. What with the visits of friends, the calls of various tradespeople, and the constant running in and out of the family, privacy and quiet were out of the question. In vain my father protested. It was the custom of the place, so he had to put up with the annoyance, though he never got reconciled to it.

The provisioning of "The Row" was carried on, necessarily, at the front doors. The scale of prices was very low; chickens were to be had for two shillings a couple, a fine turkey for three shillings. Fish was in unlimited abundance, and eggs and fresh-churned butter were charged at prices which would appear fabulously low to housekeepers of the present day. But then it must be remembered that there were in those days no railways to convey agricultural and other produce to the coast, nor steamers to take it across the Channel; and, also, that, though the population was numerically greater than at the present time, yet that portion of it which lived on a better diet than potatoes and butter-milk was considerably less.

It was customary to bargain for each separate article of food, except meat which had a fixed price; and as there was only one butcher, there was no opening for competition. The fishermen would shoot down from their shoulders the baskets of fish, fresh from the boats which, but a few minutes before, we had seen unlading their "take" on the primitive landing-jetty of rough wooden planks. A slim girl, half-clad, with bare feet and ankles, would carry a round basket, well poised on her head, full of the liveliest of live chickens; she would be accompanied by a fine specimen of her class, the wife of an Irish farmer (hear it, ye pretentious wives of English farmers), carrying on each arm a basket—the one filled with new-laid eggs, the other with rolls of fresh-churned butter. No matter what the weather might be, even if the thermometer were eighty degrees in the shade, she would be enveloped in a dark-blue cloak, which was not worn to conceal the baskets—quite the contrary, it was so disposed as to display them, being drawn up in folds under the arms, and kept in position by pressure.

A well-to-do Irish farmer's wife always possessed two blue cloth cloaks—one for commercial purposes, and one for going to Mass, as well as other special occasions, such as fairs, and funerals, and wakes, and weddings. My father strictly forbade all bargaining on his door-steps; consequently my mother always maintained that the housekeeping expenses at Dunless were one-third more than at Kilkreen, on account of her husband's absurd idea that ladies were out of their place in haggling with rough fishermen and sellers of country produce. Most of our neighbours pocketed their pride, distrusted the agency of their servants, and themselves bargained with the vendors of supplies, afflicting my father's sensitive nerves with the noisy tones in which the cheapening operations were carried on. It was great amusement to us, and after a short time we could accurately tell the dinners of most of the families of "The Row."

We children enjoyed the life at Dunless immensely. Our hours of study were reduced—the pains and penalties of collars, monitors, and dumb-bells were mitigated. Now-a-days children would soon make their grievances heard, if, on visiting the sea-side, spades and buckets, and implements for the construction of miniature aquariums, were not provided for them, with a reserve of story-books and toys for wet days. We had none of these advantages of an advanced civilisation. We hunted for and selected stones which had been flattened and polished by the action of the waves, or else we manufactured celts of which the proverbial pre-historic man might have been proud, with which we carried on our operations of erecting sand palaces, and of constructing dykes for arresting the encroachment of the incoming tide. We gathered jelly-fish, crabs, and star-fish, and consigned them to the skirts of our frocks, which we held together by one hand, while with the other we drew along trailing masses of sea-weed. Woe of woes if we met our mother on our way home laden with our marine treasures!

But where was our governess, that we were able to make such figures of ourselves? Our governess—and we knew it—was all the time engaged in a little amusement of her own on the sea-shore; if a little pool was to be leaped over, or a slippery rock to be crossed, there was a ready arm ready to help her. Major Burton was the protector of the unprotected governess; and it was owing to this diversion made in our favour by the Major, that we were thus left free to follow our own devices. Now and then, on returning home, we would be detected by our mother seated in the bay window, and saluted with—" Why, children, what plagues you are, making such a mess of your frocks and ruining your boots! If this sort of thing goes on much longer, you will be regular savages, with brown skins, coarse hands, and splay feet. Get upstairs directly, undress, and go to bed." But as our mother never thought of seeing her order carried out, we enjoyed unmolested the delight of sorting our shell-fish and hanging out our sea-weed to dry. Alas! our cherished possessions were doomed to be soon ruthlessly swept away. When the time came for the usual evening setting-to-rights of our room, the remorseless Bridget flung those "nasty, slimy, stickly creatures" as she irreverently called them, out of the window. Many a time I sobbed myself to sleep at the unexpected loss of my treasured spoils of the ocean.

The sea-air had a wonderful effect upon both our animal spirits and our imaginative faculties. As soon as a gale arose, out we would rush, heedless of prohibitions, reckless of consequences. Our great enjoyment was to take our stand upon one particular rock, against which the sea dashed with especial violence.

We positively danced to the rough music of the winds, and screamed in concert with the sea-gulls which swooped round us and then sailed away into the far distance, while the spray of the waves dashed over us drenching us to the very skin. Sometimes we fancied ourselves mermaids waiting for the call of our Queen to float away with her to her coral palace; sometimes we were shipwrecked maidens cast upon a rocky island. Occasionally we were rudely awakened from our romantic day-dreams by loud shoutings; they were not melodious enough for our mermaid Queen—could they be the yells of the savage islanders? No, the servants—who had been sent in pursuit of the adventurous truants—had tracked and discovered them. And pretty unromantic objects we were when brought back as culprits! clothes all wet and clinging to our figures, muslin bonnets shapeless and limp—they, as well as our cheeks, dyed with varying shades of green from the colour discharged from our veils.

My father was not at all more reconciled to Dunless when his three sons came home for the holidays. Like most Irish fathers, he considered the mere fact of placing them at the best public school which Ireland afforded as releasing him from all further responsibility. Dr Graham was then the master of the Waterford Grammar School. He was a sound classical scholar and a strict disciplinarian. He flogged the boys as severely for a false quantity as for a moral offence; the result was that he turned out some of the most distinguished members of the bench, the bar, and the other learned professions, Ireland at this present time can boast of.

On the evening of their arrival, the eldest, Horatio, surprised us by ensconcing himself in the easiest armchair he could find, instead of plaguing the governess or romping with us. "You are as white as a ghost, Horatio; what is the matter with you?" we exclaimed. As if to stop further questioning, he stripped off coat and waistcoat, and bared his neck and shoulders. It was a sight which almost sickened me—a mass of bruised flesh, black and blue. The explanation was given—a false quantity—and then came, "Hold out your hand, sir, and if it were not break-up day I would flog you." He refused to hold out his hand for the regulation cuts, because it was break-up day; he ran round the schoolroom, he dodged round the desks, he ducked under the forms, the Doctor pursuing and showering down blows with his cane whenever he got a chance.

My mother urged my father, in strong language, to write to the Doctor, and to threaten him not only with exposure which would be followed by loss of pupils, but also with legal proceedings which would entail heavy damages. My father took a more sensible view of the matter: "I have been flogged many a time for making false quantities, and my son must bear what his father has borne before him; if he chooses to resist, he must take the consequences. I do not see how the Doctor could have done otherwise, with due regard to the maintenance of his authority."

My mother, if she could not have her *way*, would at least have *the last word*. "Thank God, I don't belong to the male sex, to be beaten like a hound and flogged like a Newgate felon."

Horatio and his brothers, like manly boys as they were, sided with their father. But castigation from other than pedagogic hands seemed likely to be in store for them. They soon acquired a knowledge of the several peculiarities and oddities of the denizens of "the Row," whom they quizzed unmercifully, and on whom they played off some practical jokes. A hard task often devolved on my mother, of smoothing down matters when formal complaints were made to her: "Surely there must be some mistake somewhere; we are all of us sensitive, and apt to take things to ourselves which were never intended for us; her boys could not possibly have been intentionally rude or ungentlemanly—and who should know *that* so well as their own mother?"

Had not our family held the position which they did at Dunless, it would have gone hard with my brothers; as it was, they more than once narrowly escaped horsewhipping within an inch of their lives from the brothers and cousins of the mimicked and ridiculed ladies; "it would not do to offend the Rochfords, who kept open house and had the best people at their parties."

Interference on the part of the parental authorities became at last absolutely necessary, when the boys began to endanger their lives by taking, unattended, long boating excursions. Remonstrances were first tried; these proving useless, their caps and hats were removed. What did they care for that? it was all the more fun to go bareheaded. Next, they were locked up in their rooms, but they managed to effect their escape through the windows. As a last resort, their shoes and stockings were taken away; then they confessed themselves checkmated. To go bareheaded was nothing, but to be shoeless and stockingless was quite another thing; they would, in their turn, be the laughing-stock of "the Row." A compromise was made, of which the terms were—that they should never boat except under the care of a couple of sailors, never take "headers" from the jetty, nor remain in the sea above half-an-hour at a time.

The boys have occupied the stage long enough—they must now give place to their sisters.

Our governess, Miss Madden, announced to us one

morning that she wanted materials for a swan's-down trimming to her winter pelisse. All the farm-yards in the neighbourhood were forthwith put under request. Whenever a goose was to be killed timely notice was given, and off we started in high glee, knowing that during the operation of plucking we should be regaled in the farm kitchen with oatcakes and buttermilk.

We sometimes suspected that Major Burton must have received information of these expeditions, so unfailingly did he encounter us; and yet he did not want any goose-down, and he never joined us in the oatcake and the butter-milk; besides, his greeting always was—" What an exceedingly lucky chance it is that I should meet you, young ladies! Pray how are your estimable papa and mamma?"

We never had any time to answer the tender enquiry, as Miss Madden told us to be off to the farm and to say that she was coming; so off we bounded like antelopes, while she leisurely followed—the Major at her side.

Miss Madden had undeniably great personal attractions, of which she was quite aware, and which she did her best to set off to advantage. On this account she was no favourite of my elder sisters, who began to regard her as a rival. They even made spiteful insinuations to my mother about her and her admirers.

It was not long, however, before my mother received such enlightenment from those proverbial personages called " the friends of the family," about the *accidental* meetings of Miss Madden and the Major, as to impose on her the disagreeable necessity of speaking at once, and plainly, on the subject.

We were hard at work in the school-room one morning when we were startled by the footman throwing the door wide open, and with a conscious leer on his red round Irish face, announcing, " Plase, Miss Madden, the Misthress wants ye in the drawing-room."

Miss Madden, blushing and confused, obeyed the summons.

My mother began, " I hear from good authority, Miss Madden, that you are carrying on an affair with Major Burton."

" An affair, madam ! What can you possibly mean ? " asked Miss Madden, taking the injured-innocence tone.

" I mean what I have already said, that there are meetings between you and Major Burton."

" Madam, that is not my fault ; he has accidentally encountered us in our country walks."

" Nonsense, Miss Madden ; do you mean me to believe that meetings so frequent could be accidental ? And even if they were so, you should have had more regard for your own character and the example you were setting to your pupils, than allow him to accompany you."

"Surely, madam, you would not have had me act in such an unlady-like manner as to treat a visitor at your house like an importunate tradesman, and send him about his business."

"How could you dream for one moment, Miss Madden, of Major Burton's intentions being honourable, considering the great disparity of position between him and you?"

"Disparity of position, madam! Am I not a lady?"

"Undoubtedly, Miss Madden, as the companion and instructor of my daughters, but surely not in the conventional sense of the term."

Miss Madden burst into tears; she declared that there had been much exaggeration, and she promised that for the future she would forbid the Major joining her in her walks with her pupils.

My mother was fain to be satisfied with her promise, knowing that her dismissal would entail on herself the care of us three girls at a most inconvenient time, that of our brothers' holidays.

The next time my mother saw Major Burton, she appealed to his feelings as an officer and a gentleman, and she entreated him not to raise false hopes in Miss Madden's mind, nor distract her attention from her duties to her pupils. The Major only laughingly replied, "Mrs Rochford, if you throw such tempting creatures in my way, how can you expect me to be an icicle ?"

Whether it was from Miss Madden's faithfulness to her promise, or from the effect of my mother's appeal to the Major's sense of honour, certain it was that we never again encountered Major Burton in our walks.

It was not long after our return to Kilkreen from Dunless, that Miss Madden asked for a week's holiday in order to pay visits to the parents of former pupils. Major Burton, as it soon came out, applied for leave of absence at the same time. My father's suspicions were excited, and he made enquiries which satisfied him that Miss Madden was no fit companion for his daughters.

At the end of the week Miss Madden returned. She was ordered to confine herself to her own room, and to hold no communication with her pupils. On the following morning she was put into the Dublin mail-coach which passed our gates, and we saw her no more.

CHAPTER THE THIRD.

LIFE AT THE SEA-SIDE.

Fermôssi al fin il cor che balzò tanto.
Hippolito Pindemonte.
O shall man die once,
Die once and for ever? Impious thought!
He dies to live for ever. He expires
To rise an Angel in the realms of bliss,
And with new faculties and purer soul,
A purer world to inhabit.

THERE was much pleasant, unconventional society at Dunless. The community that went on of household goods, such as glass, crockery, and kitchen utensils, among the visitors, contributed not a little to promote sociability and friendliness. Families, who in their own country houses would have been exclusive enough, were glad to descend from their stilts, and entered with great zest into the unceremonious habits and amusements of the place. Besides, objectionable people were very rarely to be met with. No excursion trains brought crowds of holiday-seekers to vulgarize the place; neither were there purse-proud business-men, with over-dressed wives and daughters, to occupy the principal houses and to raise the prices of house-rent and provisions. The class frequenting Dunless were gentry : though some might not be rich, yet they were connected with the best families.

Dunless could boast of great charms of scenery. There were bold promontories stretching far out into the sea,—romantic caves, approachable only at low water,—a broad expanse of fine bright sand, studded with pools left by the retiring tide, glittering in the sunshine like so many mirrors; there were winding walks through bushes and low shrubs to secluded bathing-coves,—and narrow pathways along precipitous cliffs curtained halfway up from the base with sea-weed of exquisite tints of green, and brown, and red, and commanding a grand view of the Atlantic.

On account of its fine air, its fresh sea-breezes, and its romantic scenery, to say nothing of the absence of grasping, cheating lodginghouse-keepers and shopkeepers, I unhesitatingly give the palm to Dunless over all the English seaside resorts with which I have become acquainted. Bathing, boating, and pic-nic-ing occupied the day. The dinner hour was five o'clock, after which every body turned out for a walk to the new pier, to watch the arrival of the Mail-Packet from Milford. If any distinguished family was among the passengers, we carefully scanned the ladies of the party, in order to get an idea of the latest London fashions. Even a travel-stained dress, which had done its duty in the Park and other fashionable resorts during the season, was quite a study to many an observant mother and daughter living in such a behind-hand country as Ireland. The evenings were spent at different houses in turn. Card-tables were set out; the elders played whist, the youngers commerce. The elders would sometimes lose their tempers not only with each other, but also with " those young people who were making such a row ;" while the youngers were too much taken up with their own fun and laughter, to pay any attention to the remonstrances directly or indirectly levelled at them. Cheating-made-easy was shamelessly carried on among " those young people." Nora and Eveleen were the most innocently-guilty. Their next-door neighbours were—no doubt quite *accidentally*—the favourite companions of the boating or walking excursions ; and they—with more of gallantry than of obedience to the rules of the game—would discharge from their own hands, or refrain from taking up from the board, the aces or faced-cards which, from side-long glances, they saw would be advantageous to their fair neighbour's hands.

My father, being no card-player, found these meetings not at all to his taste ; accordingly, he never attended those which were held at other houses, and expressed his desire of absenting himself from those at our own.

"But, my dear Mr Rochford," argued my mother, "surely common politeness demands that you should receive your guests at your own house; you can vanish in half an hour if you like."

"Agreed; I consent, then, for half an hour only to being victimed at the shrine of politeness."

One evening a laughable mistake occurred. Among our guests was a middle-aged spinster—remarkably prim and stiff—named Lambert. My father, impatient to be off, and yet not quite sure whether the stipulated half hour had expired, stole up softly to the table where the whist-players were intent on their game, and taking it for granted that he was addressing his wife, stooped down and whispered in Miss Lambert's ear, "My dear, may I go to bed now?" Down fell the offended spinster's cards — up she started from her chair—"What have I to do with your going to bed, sir? What do you take me for? How dare you insult me thus—and in your own house?"

My father bolted. The whole company was convulsed with laughter. My mother immediately comprehended the situation, and as soon as she could recover her composure explained the mistake. It was long before Miss Lambert could be pacified, or brought to believe that it was not either a bad joke or a deliberate affront. She had not learned the lesson, that if, through malice or mistake, one of a company is made ridiculous, the wisest course is to fall in with the humour of the moment, and thus rob the ridicule of its point.

Most of the eligible young men who came for the season, lived *en garçon*. When a boating party or pic-nic was coming off, hampers filled with good things were sent from Rathmahoney House. There was neither wine merchant nor depôt at Dunless. Visitors had to import the stores required for the season from Landford. My father would waggishly remark, when these pleasurable parties were projected, " Girls, the young men will of course supply the wine: I always did when I was a bachelor."

" Goodness, papa," Nora exclaimed, " where are they to get it ? "

" The officers can have it over from their mess at Landford, and the other young men can get it from their fathers' cellars."

" Yes," broke in Eveleen, " and I should like to know what would be said of us. The very men-servants would cry shame on us as a mean-spirited family. The young English officers—don't I see the sneer on their faces as much as to say, ' How like those Irish beggars, with all their boasted hospitality, which is only a combination of vulgar plenty and shabbiness! positively shirking half a dozen bottles of wine!'"

The end of it was that there was not only a most liberal supply of wine, but also of the spirit for which the country is famous.

On these occasions Nora and Eveleen managed to secure the best partners, to the immense envy of many mothers who protested that it was all allowing to the well-filled hampers. I do not venture to pronounce how much truth there was in this, or whether there was any at all. Certainly the good things were eaten, and the good wine was drunk, and the dances were gone through, and there was an end of it; but there were many thorns hidden among the roses of the merry days at Dunless.

Dunless had not, as I have mentioned, the questionable privilege of a popular preacher, though unquestionably the Rector was an original. The Rev. Basil Floyd was the eldest of seven sons. Sorely against his will he was destined by his father to holy orders on the strength of the promise of a living by the Bishop of the Diocese, an old College friend. The youth's heart was bent on the army, but as the alternative lay between enlisting as a private if he must enter the army, and an early succession to the living of Dunless then held by an octogenarian, he made the prudent, if not congenial, choice of "going into the Church," and in due time he became Rector of Dunless. He never could quite forgive his father for the force which had been put upon his inclinations. In moments of confidence he would lament to his friends how unsuited he was both by temperament and tastes to the sacred profession which he had been induced to enter. He confessed how unequal he was to the spiritual ministrations of his parishioners; that he had no head for making sermons, and no natural gift of eloquence. Incapable of original composition, he gave his congregation the benefit of the compositions of others; when, however, he had to use the personal pronoun "I," he always supplied the correction,—"that is to say, the author." In figure he was portly and podgy; his clerical suits did not keep pace with his increasing proportions, and there appeared to be always the risk of their giving way in some quarter or other under the severe tension to which they were subjected.

When about fifty, he married a lady of forty. He had not contemplated matrimony—it was his fate—he had dropped into it, just as it had been his fate, not his vocation, to be a parson and to vegetate as Rector of Dunless instead of dying a hero's death on the battle-field. Fate, if it was fate, dealt kindly with him in giving him an excellent wife; and when Mrs Floyd gave hopes of his becoming a father, it might possibly have been some satisfaction to him to reflect that, owing to maturity of age, he would be spared the usual clerical lot of possessing a *too* fruitful vine.

The Rectory house was built on the top of a steep hill. It was a favourite walk of my father's; for from the summit the finest view of the bay and the open sea was to be obtained. One hot afternoon as he was slowly walking up he saw the Rector and his wife, arm in arm, coming down. Suddenly the husband dropped the wife's arm, and sprang from her side to her front, and somewhat in the fashion of a spread eagle held his coat-tails extended before her. Mrs Floyd, evidently puzzled by such extraordinary manœuvres, tried hard to regain her place by his side, while he, wheezing and snorting, twitched his head from side to side as a sign for her to keep in the rear. The reason of these mysterious antics soon appeared. The nervous husband had descried the approach of a well-known one-eyed noseless deformed beggar, and, fearful of the consequences to his wife in her interesting condition, he hit upon this expedient for screening the loathsome object from her sight.

"Only think what might be the after consequences," he bleated out when he saw my father coming up to him convulsed with laughter, "now, would not you have done just the same, Mr Rochford?"

My father always, deprecating any personal allusions to the ladies of his family, only courteously hoped that Mr Floyd had saved by his presence of mind any possible risk to his wife.

Shortly after, Mr Floyd became the happy father of a fine boy, who, in due course of time, was followed by another.

The close of Mr Floyd's history is a sad one. His two boys were the happy instrument in effecting a blessed change in his daily life and future prospects. He no longer regretted that a military career had been denied him. Mental stagnation gave place to activity when called on to undertake the education of his sons. Stores, long buried and scarcely even suspected to exist, came to the surface. The teacher and the taught beneficially reacted on each other. The nine months dead season at Dunless became the happiest portion of the year. And thus, in the loving work of training up his sons to be good and wise men, and in the fond hope of their achieving a brilliant career which he himself had failed in attaining, he passed usefully, calmly, and cheerfully through another dozen years of his mortal life. *The good wine had been left till the last.* One bright morning in May he promised his boys their first swimming lesson. The fond wife and mother watched them as they ran down the hill. It would be hard to say which of the three was the most light-hearted. Alas for the end! The sudden shock of the cold sea water was too much for a system no longer elastic. But for his grasping his boys round their waists he would have sunk below the surface. It was not a living father who clung to them; the heart had ceased to beat; the spirit had fled.

Book the Third.

CHAPTER THE FIRST.

PRIESTLY DENUNCIATIONS.

A CONTESTED election of more than usual importance was at hand. The Marquis of Landford had, ever since the Union, returned a member for the county. For some years his brother, Lord George Burchester, had been his nominee. A great political crisis was imminent. The Roman Catholic Association of which Daniel O'Connell was the mainspring, the Irish episcopacy and priesthood, the Roman Catholic gentry, and the Liberal (or, as they were called, the Radical) portion of the Protestant population, were united together for one great struggle. "Agitate, agitate, agitate, till the odious laws be repealed which bar out Catholics from the English Parliament House, as well as from their fair share of places and offices under Government." Such was the programme of O'Connell and the Association. As for the priesthood, they had their own special organisation and plan. Of every weapon which the armoury of their Church contained they made an unsparing and unscrupulous use. The task which they proposed to themselves was congenial, and not difficult of execution. Minds highly imaginative and excitable, and at the same time deeply impressed with the feeling of being a down-trodden and persecuted people—such was the soil on which the Romish priests had to work. From the altars of their chapels they thundered forth—"Boys, are ye going to vote for the accursed heretic—the scourge and oppressor of yer country? An' if ye do, I'll tell ye what every man, woman, and child among ye will have to pay for going against yer Church and ould Ireland. Now, boys, let me ax ye whether ye haven't souls as well as bodies? Ye know what yer bodies suffer from the famine-fever and the cowld of yer wretched cabins. 'Tis yer heretic landlords ye have to thank for yer hunger, and cowld, and nakedness; but ain't it a comfort for ye to know that ye are just like the blessed apostle St. Paul? The Haythen thrated him as yer heretic landlords and their griping agents are thrating ye; and sure and sartain 'twill be the Haythens' portion they will have in the next world; and it may be there will be still worse in store for ye. Hell fire is worse than purgatory, for when once in ye'll never get out. Not the blessed Lady herself, though she be Queen of Heaven, could drag ye out of them flames—no, not if she had all the saints and angels to help her. Boys, are ye willing to face that doom ? Do you want to see yer ould fathers and mothers and yer wives and children burning, and hear them cursing ye for it !"

To this terrible language there would be a running accompaniment of groans and half-suppressed shrieks from the congregation.

After a pause to take breath, the preacher would proceed—" Forty-shilling freeholders, to the rescue of bodies and souls ! Vote for Sturt. I'll head ye to the poll." And then, in a wheedling tone—" Boys, I promise ye the time will not be long in coming when ye'll have a good cottage, and a nice piece of ground, and a cow and a pig, and lashings for yerselves and families, and lavings for the poor beggar. An' it's straight ye'll go to heaven. It's a clear road ye'll have t'other side of purgatory ; and the blessed Mother of God, she'll have a welcome for ye ; and St Patrick, won't he be proud of ye ?"

Such were the threats and promises hurled forth with passionate declamation, and with a vehemence of gesture and gesticulation which had a most powerful effect upon the hearers—at once the most ignorant and the most superstitious population in Europe. With them the voice of the priest was the voice of God—" Sure, wasn't the priest the successor of St Peter, and hadn't he the keys of heaven and hell ? There's no going against him. Hard enough was their present state, but if they voted for the heretic, Lord George, it would be worse in the next world. An', anan, when the Catholics got into the English Parleyament, they would have the making of the laws, and they'd soon oust the heretics from the big houses and lands, and wouldn't forget them who had helped them by voting for Sturt; and it would all come true what the priest told them about the cottage, and the cow, and the pig, and the nate bit of land to boot."

The chapels could not contain anything like the numbers who crowded to the altar-denunciation services, to hear the priest explain the part which they were to take in redressing their country's wrongs. Those *without* generally far out-numbered those *within* the building. It was a wild picture presented by the motley crowd—some standing, some kneeling, some crouching. There were stalwart men of the small farmer class, with their frieze suits, knee-breeches, worsted stockings, and neat-fitting brogues; there were others with battered hats and tattered clothes—many of them shoeless. There were women, too—the better class with the national blue cloak. There were old crones, supporting themselves on sticks or crutches, muttering their prayers or telling their beads; and there were young girls, uncombed, ragged, barefooted. All throughout the churchyard, among the graves and monuments, a dense mass—old and young, well-clothed and ill-clothed—waited to receive devoutly the words of the priest, and to respond enthusiastically to his demands.

Just outside the chapel door there stood a burly form, who shouted out in stentorian tones the heads of the priest's address.

" He tells you, boys," the voice said, " vote for the heretic, an' it's a long lase of Purgatory ye'll have."

Groans, and shouts of " We won't, bedad we won't."

" Vote for Sturt, and maybe ye'll have a chance of going straight to Paradise."

Cheers—" We will, we will."

" If ye rats from the ould faith, an' sends Lord George to the cursed Saxon Parly-ament, it's a hotbed ye'll have for iver and iver."

" Ochone, groans and hisses for the bloody Lord. Was it not his own uncle who set up the cat and the triangle—curse him. The divil a one of us that will vote for him."

" Sturt for ever. Father Doolan says he's the boy."

The dense mass took up the cry, " Sturt for ever," yelling and screaming till they could scream no more.

The Marquis of Landford had not for years past resided at the family seat at Teranmore; but now that his political influence was threatened, it was considered desirable that the family should pay an immediate visit to the County. It was thought that the

Marquis' presence might serve as a wholesome check on the exertions of the priests, who were straining every nerve to prevent the return of his brother, Lord George Burchester.

The landlord appealed to the *temporal*—the priesthood to the *spiritual*—hopes and fears of the tenantry. It was a contest between the two, and promised to be a desperate one. The whole County watched with the deepest interest what would be the issue.

CHAPTER THE SECOND.

AN ESTATE AGENT.

Noi soli a noi stessi
Fabbri siam pur delle miserie nostre.

IT was the custom for the non-resident Irish landlords to be represented by an agent, who not only attended to the management of the estate, but who lived for the most part in the mansion. It was a necessity that the agent should be a gentleman by birth and education. A special training was also needed to enable him to take a leading part in all county business. He had besides to organise and preside at political meetings for the maintenance or advancement of his patron's interests. All applications for commissions or promotion in the army or navy, as well as for situations in the excise or the post-office, which it was believed the Marquis' great power and influence could obtain, had in the first instance to be submitted to the agent. It was his duty to classify the several suitors' claims, and to advise upon those which it would be most politic to satisfy or impolitic to refuse.

Mr Morgan Sullivan, the Marquis of Landford's agent, was an excellent man of business, having been carefully trained by his father who held the same office for many years. He was, however, excessively unpopular in the neighbourhood; for, while he was cringing to his superiors, he was arrogant to his equals, vindictive to those who he fancied had slighted or injured him, and tyrannical to his inferiors. His ruling passion was vanity, which had been fed by the deference which the Marquis always paid to his opinion and advice; so that in the Marquis' absence he deluded himself into the idea that he was the Marquis' second self, if not the Marquis himself.

When the electioneering movement in the county, as related in the last chapter, compelled the Marquis and his family to take up a temporary residence at Teranmore Castle, the agent's duties were greatly multiplied. He had to instruct the Marquis as to the history, social position, extent of property, amount of influence, of all the gentry for miles round; and never was he more in his element than when "coaching" the Marchioness as to those who were to be honoured by an invitation for the regulation three-days' visit at the Castle, and in fixing the boundary line beyond which it would not be prudent to extend the invitations to a ball. It was no easy matter at any time, but an especially delicate one when a contested election was at hand—a social grievance being as difficult to be smoothed over as a prejudice to be fought against.

Mr Morgan Sullivan's general arrogance of manner, and the airs of patronage which he assumed, raised great resentment against him in the neighbourhood. Those whose position in the County was too well established for them to be slighted or passed over, openly showed their appreciation of the man on every available opportunity. Those who were lower in the social scale, and were dependent on him for introduction to the Castle receptions, smothered their antipathy to him as long as the noble family were in residence. These were wounds to his vanity and stabs to his dignity, but they were forgotten in the society of the Marquis and the aristocratic circle collected at the Castle.

The web which is wound round the principal by the agent is a most difficult one to break through; and, if broken through, it would be only for the principal to find himself in a worse position than when he was held in bondage. Thus it came to pass that Mr Morgan Sullivan, though only an agent, was admitted to associate on almost equal terms with the noble family of Teranmore.

It was a sort of paradise to Mr Morgan Sullivan to mix with the very actors, and to hear from their own lips the scenes they had witnessed or assisted in—what horses were the favourites for the Derby and the Oaks—who had been cleaned out at Crockford's—what cases for divorce were likely to come on—the latest gossip at White's or Brookes'—piquant anecdotes of the exclusive lady patronesses at Almack's—the coquetry of the belles of the season—and naughty tales of actresses and ballet dancers.

To the tenantry Mr Morgan Sullivan was particularly obnoxious : " Shure an' wasn't it the griping agent (bad 'cess to him) who drew the hard bargains, and threatened to sell 'em up if they could not pay the rint? An' isn't he after making the farms bigger and bigger? Maybe small 'll be the hole he'll have in heaven."

" Whist "—an old crone would scream from out of the smoke of the turf fire—" the divil a bit of the likes of him gitting to heaven ! Aint he a heretic ? "

" If we could only get spake with the Markiss," said another, " maybe things would not be so bad ; he could aise matters a little, and 'twould be none the worse for himself."

When the Marquis died—he who had now come for a temporary residence at Teranmore—there was a long minority, during which Mr Morgan Sullivan reigned *de facto*. He resided at the Castle, and entertained the County, thus keeping up—as he maintained it to be his duty—the prestige of the family; so that when the young heir came of age, he would only have to place himself under the guidance of Mr Morgan Sullivan, and follow in his wake.

Matters, however, did not turn out exactly as the agent intended they should, when the young Marquis came of age and took possession of the estate. He had been advised by his English relatives to look into his affairs himself, to see with his own eyes, and to examine into the accounts not only of the property in general but of the domestic expenditure.

The estate had been excellently managed; but when explanations were required respecting the large amount charged for household expenses, and especially French and Barton's bill for wine, the agent replied, "Every bottle of wine charged for, your Lordship will find in the cellar."

And so he did, when he made a visit of inspection to the cellars with the old butler. But then the puzzle was, How could there be room for so much new wine, when (as he had always been told) the cellars had been always kept well stocked by his father? " Surely, Brindley, it was a pity you should have removed my father's old wine into another cellar to make room for all these new supplies."

" Another cellar, my Lord; there is no other cellar."

The young Marquis stared—"Where, then, is the old wine?"

"Gone, every drop of it, my Lord."

"How so? You always kept the key."

"So I did in your father's time; but ever since his death Mr Morgan Sullivan has had it. He demanded it of me, telling me that as he was responsible for everything, he must look after everything for himself. I did take it to heart, that, after I had been trusted so many years by my dear old master, the agent should not only take the key away from me, but never let me enter the cellar *alone*, though we were in it *together* pretty often."

"How so?"

"Why, what with luncheon and dinner parties, and breakfasts when the hounds met near at hand, and what with visitors constantly coming and going, bin after bin was soon emptied; for when you once begin on a full bin it don't take long for it to get empty, no more than when you once break up a guinea-piece, do the shillings give much account of themselves."

"At all events, you have accounted for the disappearance of the old wine, but did not Mr Morgan Sullivan give any reason?"

"O yes, he used to say that entertainments must be given, and hospitality must be shown, for the keeping up of the family influence."

The young Marquis knew well enough that, after the passing of the "Emancipation Bill," the political influence of his family was, as far as returning members for the county and the city of Landford, a thing of the past, not to be won back again by the agent giving entertainments to his own personal friends. On the contrary, he became fully convinced from the enquiries he made, that the favouritism and exclusiveness shown by the agent had operated in the opposite direction, and had alienated many who had formerly been zealous supporters of the political interests of his family.

One day the intelligence flew like wild-fire through the town of Landford that Mr Morgan Sullivan had been dismissed from the agency. People were unanimous in their satisfaction at the event, though, as to the causes of it, they differed widely. "The accounts not forthcoming," "the estate badly managed," "rents in arrear," "large sums wasted on the agent's extravagances," "French and Barton's bill frightful," "attempt to bully the young Marquis and keep him in leading-strings,"—such were the rumours, containing a grain of truth in a bushel of exaggerative chaff.

Mr Morgan Sullivan was complimented by the Marquis on his management of the estate during his minority, and was requested to retain his office as land-agent; but he was informed distinctly at the same time that, as far as related to the castle and the demesne, they would be placed in other hands.

It was a severe blow to Mr Morgan Sullivan. His social position would henceforth be a very different one to what it had been. No longer the great man he had assumed to be,—no longer the master of the ceremonies at the Castle entertainments, mingling familiarly with the aristocratic guests,—no longer indispensable to the *young* as he had been to the *old* Marquis.

Thus inordinate vanity met with its merited reward. Had Mr Morgan Sullivan had the good sense to know his own position, and tact and discretion to confine himself to its duties, he would have been spared both mortification and humiliation,—he would have remained the adviser and friend, instead of becoming the mere estate agent of the Marquis of Landford.

CHAPTER THE THIRD.

THE REBELLION OF '98.

" Long years ! yet has not passed away
The memory of that fatal day,
When all thy young and faded grace
Before me lay in Death's embrace.
A throb of madness and of pain
Shot through my heart and through my brain ;
I felt it then, I feel it now,
Though time is stamped upon my brow,
Though all my veins grow cold with age,
And o'er my memory's fading page
Oblivion draws her damning line,
And blots all images—save thine."
W. M. Praed.

MY father was a Tory of the old school. His political creed would now be regarded as narrow-minded, but then it was that of the Protestant landlords of Ireland with very few exceptions. He was as great a hero-worshipper, and as decided a partizan of William the Third, as Macaulay. In those days party toasts were the great feature of all official and convivial entertainments. My father's favourite toast was " The glorious, pious, and immortal memory of the great and good

King William the Third." His model prime minister was William Pitt; and his model king, if it were only from his hatred of Whiggery, was George the Third. Whiggery, with its logical development Liberalism and Radicalism, he attributed to the agency of the Evil One.

The great measure of the Whigs for the pacification of Ireland, " Catholic Emancipation," he scouted as utterly worthless for bringing about that result. The Roman Catholics would regard it only as the first concession wrung from the fears of the English government, to be followed by others. The Roman Catholic members, they admitted, would so hamper the Legislature by their votes as to be able in time to compel the passing of measures favourable to themselves and adverse to the Protestants.

My father lived to witness the fulfilment of some of his prophetic utterances. "Catholic Emancipation," as it was called, was soon followed, as a matter of course, by the removal of all civil disabilities,—by the appointment of Romanist judges, mayors, and other municipal officers,—and concurrently by the mutilation of the United Church of England and Ireland through the suppression of two Archbishoprics and four Bishoprics. We have already seen a Romanist made Lord Chancellor of Ireland, and consequently keeper of the Sovereign's *Irish* conscience; who can tell whether before long we may not see a Romanist installed at Dublin as king of independent Ireland? The *Ecclesiastical* Union which had been secured by the solemn sanction of the Coronation Oath has been dissolved—why should not the dissolution of the *National* Union follow?

Our grounds of Kilkreen sloped down to the river Dour; and as the view of the city of Landford was hidden by the fine old trees of the park, and the road by the plantations running parallel with it to a considerable distance, there was nothing to prevent our fancying ourselves far away from the haunts of men and the stirring sounds of city life.

The river was broad and deep; and on a calm summer's evening, when pleasure boats were passing up and down with their white sails like butterfly wings, the scene was enchanting.

When, however, I turned my eyes to the long stretch of meadow-land on the other side, the loveliness of the scenery was sadly marred. For some days rain had been falling, drenching the mown grass. No advantage had been taken of intervals of favourable weather for turning it over and gathering it into ridges and cocks,—there it lay, all brown and soppy.

Paddy, the spokesman of the haymakers, scratched his head—" Shure, yer honour," he said to my father, " there was St Anne's day (and wasn't she the blessed

Virgin's own mother ?) ; and thin, your honour, there was Dan Rourke to be waked ; and thin there was Dan's funeral "—

" And then," interrupted my father, irritated at the sight of the ruined hay crop, of which there had been such a splendid promise, " there were two days more for you fellows to lie about after your drunken revels."

Knowing that any remonstrances or appeals to the man's conscience would have not the slightest effect, he walked angrily away.

It had been a beautiful, breezy, sunshiny morning, and in the afternoon I put on my sun-bonnet and went, rake in hand, into the meadow to do a little amateur hay-making. I had also abstracted a volume of poetry from the drawing-room table, and when I became tired of my work I half-buried myself in one of my little grassy hillocks, and was soon absorbed in a tale of faithful but unrequited love. It was not long before I was brought back to the hard realities of every-day life by the excited voices of my father, my mother, and Miss Anstey Costello. Ireland was the subject of their conversation.

Tempted by the loveliness of the evening they had seated themselves on the terrace immediately above where I was lying hidden.

Miss Anstey Costello was a rigid adherent of her creed. Her forefathers had suffered and bled for it.

She was, however, a woman of the world, a pleasant companion, and a general favourite in society, never obtruding her opinions though quite capable of defending them when attacked. She was an adept in the teaching and tactics of her Church—ready to ignore or deny whatever told against it, or whenever historical facts were quoted which could not be gainsaid, to fall back on the "*Tu quoque*" line of defence—"the other side had done quite as bad, if not worse."

My father had been trying to prove that her Church had ever been a persecuting Church, instancing the massacres of St Bartholomew and the cruelties of the Revocation of the Edict of Nantes. She evaded his statements by the plea, "You know, Mr Rochford, that I am no historian."

"Then come to my library and read and judge for yourself."

She laughingly retorted, "Remember what your Saxon Prime Minister, Sir Robert Walpole, said, when a friend proposed reading history to him, 'O read me anything but history, for I know *that* is not true!'"

I wonder what that astute statesman would say of those historians of the present day who have transformed our traditionary historical scoundrels into saints and heroes.

"Surely you are not prepared to deny," said my mother, "that during the short reign of Mary, justly called 'bloody,' no less than four hundred persons, including four bishops, were burned at the stake, for the only offence of being Protestants."

"And are you prepared to deny," retorted Miss Anstey Costello, "that just as many Catholics were put to death by your Queen unjustly called 'good' Bess, including her own cousin, for the only offence of being Catholics?"

"Nay, nay," said my father, "we have the documentary proofs that there was not a single execution in Queen Elizabeth's reign which was not for political crimes."

"And may not the same excuse be made for the executions ordered by Catholic Emperors, and Kings, and Queens?"

"But," interposed my mother, "what do you say to the acts of the 'Holy' Inquisition, as it was called? Its victims were most of them so utterly insignificant that there could be no danger to the State from them, and they were never *questioned* about their political opinions."

"Every State is bound to take care of the faith and morals of its subjects, and bound also to suppress by strong measures those opinions which are subversive of either or both. Your Protestant Calvin burnt Servetus for what he called heretical tenets."

"He did, and all Protestants agree in condemning the act."

Miss Anstey Costello having nothing more to say, shifted her ground, and remarked deprecatingly, "All that we Catholics want now-a-days is our civil rights."

"That's just it," said my father, "but, unfortunately, *your* civil rights would be everyone else's civil wrong."

"God forbid," exclaimed my mother, "that the Roman Catholics should ever again have the upper hand. I shall never forget the horrors of the rebellion of '98."

Miss Anstey Costello had again recourse to her *Tu quoque*. "My dear Mrs Rochford, the Royalists were just as bad; even your side allowed that."

"Was it so?" my mother appealed to her husband.

"No doubt, my dear; savage passions inflamed Royalists and Rebels alike."

"The Royalists, as you call them," said Miss Anstey Costello, "burnt eighty of our country people in the Court House of Enniscorthy."

"And terribly the Rebels retaliated by burning a hundred and twenty-one in Scullabogue barn."

"Hardly less," said Miss Anstey Costello, "could have been expected from the poor, uncivilised, and ignorant Irish under the impulse of revenge, but your atrocities were committed by those who prided themselves on their superior education and intelligence."

"But why should the Irish be ignorant and uncivilised?" demanded my father. "Who have kept them in that state of ignorance but their priests? And the end of it is, they are led to the slaughter as in the rebellion of '98."

"What a time it was!" went on my father. "No one was safe. No one could tell who might turn out to be a rebel, traitor, or spy. I will give you an instance of what happened to myself. The militia force in which I held a commission was quartered in Waterford. The officers' mess was at the principal inn. Before sitting down to dinner we left our arms in a side room. A plot to murder us, while thus unarmed and unsuspecting, was discovered barely an hour before the time for its being carried into execution. The head waiter (a rebel) had given information of our habit to his comrades, who, after having slaughtered us, were to shoot down or pike the men, and make themselves masters of the town. I was warned of it by a faithful servant of mine, who had somehow—he would not tell me how—discovered it; but before he revealed it he made me swear on my knees never to take a step or say a word which might by the remotest possibility betray him. Were he even suspected, there would be, as he said, a ten feet long pike through his body before the night was over."

"I had my experience also," said my mother. "I was in Waterford at the time, staying with Uncle and Aunt Leslie, and we were holding ourselves in readiness to escape any day to England. Two whole days were my aunt and I occupied in quilting a number of guineas into our stays, as the securest and least suspected place. At last it was decided that it was no longer safe to remain, and with a party of friends we got on board a sailing vessel which had been provided against the emergency. It providentially happened that we had a Naval Lieutenant on board, who remarked that our vessel was out of its right course; in fact, instead of making for Milford Haven, we were fast approaching Wexford Harbour which was then in possession of the rebels. With a spring the Lieutenant was upon the Captain, 'You are a traitor; order the steersman to put the ship round, or by G— I'll blow your brains out,' and he held a pistol to his head. That bold and rapid step saved us; but it was an anxious voyage to Milford Haven."

"Wexford!" said my father. "Why, I was engaged in re-taking it from the rebels. What a bloody battle it was! And yet, I do not know whether afterwards it was not more harrowing to my feelings to witness, as part of my duty, the execution of the rebel chiefs and the fixing of their heads on spikes over the Court House."

Suddenly Miss Anstey Costello sprang from the side of my father and mother, ran down the terrace steps, and—catching sight of me—threw herself down by my side, and wept and sobbed convulsively.

"What is the matter?" I exclaimed in alarm.

"O my God, can I ever forget? Shall the dreadful sight be ever coming back before my eyes? Kathleen, they did not mean—they are too good, and kind, and considerate to give pain to others. But O, if they only knew what I have seen and suffered! How often, in my frenzy, have I called on my Maker to take the life He had given me, since He had allowed cruel hearts and ruthless hands to rob me of a life so precious to me! I looked at every thing through *him*—he crept in to my every thought—he was this world to me, nay, he was heaven itself—at least earth became heaven when I looked forward to the time when we should be made one."

She covered her face with her hands.

I stole my arm round her waist and drew her closer to me. It was my way of showing that I sympathized with her in her great grief. Though I must confess that, in the pride of my girlhood, and in my simple ignorance of the ravages which time and sorrow can work, I wondered—while looking at her lank and graceless figure, and her worn unattractive face—how she could ever have been an object of passionate attachment to any one. She must have divined my thoughts, for she said sadly, " Ah, Kathleen, thirty years have left their mark on my face and figure. A blight came and withered my early bloom, and grief has done the rest."

" Do tell me your story."

" I cannot, it is all too painful."

I was dying to hear from her own lips a personal love-story, and I thoughtlessly asked her why she rushed away when my father spoke of the execution of the rebel chiefs.

" Don't press me, Kathleen. O the merciless butchery in cold blood! The cruel deaths men were condemned to, whose only crime was the love of their country!"

I felt as if I could not let her go, without drawing from her the cause of her terrible emotion. Thirty years ago! why, to me it seemed an age—at any rate quite time enough to have obliterated every remembrance, deadened every emotion, buried every grief.

" Does papa know?" I asked.

" Yes, but he has evidently forgotten, or he would never have alluded to those dreadful executions. But, Kathleen, I see you are determined to know, and so it is better you should hear it from myself."

"I was engaged to be married to young Gerald Sherard. When the rising took place he could not desert his party, which had taken up arms to free their country from the tyranny of an alien power. Colonel Walpole was in command of a body of troops. On their march to Gorey, a detachment of our men, commanded by young Sherard, suddenly came upon Walpole's force in a defile, defeated them, and captured their cannon. Colonel Walpole was shot through the head. When the fortune of war turned, and our side was the losing party, there were some who swore falsely that it was by Sherard's hand that the shot was fired which killed Colonel Walpole. By General Lake's order he was beheaded and his body hung in chains. They would not tell me where they had hung him; but I knew that neither cruelty nor indignity would be spared, and that it could be only *at his father's gate* that the gallows would be fixed. One evening—just such an evening as this—I stole out. I hurried towards Sherard Castle; and there—right in front of the house, of which every shutter was closed — hung in chains the headless body of my beloved Gerald. Merry children were playing about the very gallows, and some were gathering wild strawberries under it. As I came near, I heard a sad and broken voice—

"'Children, you must not eat those strawberries;

they have been nourished by the blood of a murdered man."

"It was Gerald's father who spoke. He saw me, and tenderly led me home again."

Then, evidently making a strong effort to break away from these horrible recollections, she asked me what I was reading. I thought the beautiful lines so appropriate, that I could not help reading them to her.

"O lady, twine no wreath for me,
Or twine it of the cypress tree.
Too lively glow the lilies light,—
The varnished holly's all too bright,—
The May-flower and the eglantine
May shade a brow less sad than mine;
But, lady, weave no wreath for me,
Or weave it of the cypress tree.

"Let merry England proudly rear,
Her blended roses bought so dear;
Let Albin bind her bonnet blue
With heath and harebell dipp'd in dew;
On favour'd Erin's crest be seen
The flower she loves of emerald green;
But, lady, twine no wreath for me,
Or twine it of the cypress tree.

"Strike the wild harp, while maids prepare
The ivy meet for minstrel's hair;
And while his crown of laurel-leaves
With bloody hand the victor weaves,
Let the loud trump his triumph tell.
But when you hear the passing-bell,
Then, lady, twine a wreath for me,
And twine it of the cypress tree."

I had hardly finished when the bell of the Convent, on the opposite bank of the Dour, rang out the Angelus.

"Kathleen," she said pensively, "I often wish I had taken the veil; I should then have had the peace of forgetfulness, and the certainty of heaven."

"They tell me," I replied, "that—wherever we go—thought and memory go with us."

"I know that we Catholics and you Protestants differ on that point: the Convent seclusion, and meditation, are with *us* the nearest approach to divine life on earth."

"How do you reconcile this with our Lord's prayer for his disciples—'I pray not that Thou shouldest take them out of the world, but that Thou shouldest keep them from the evil?'"

"The world has been my battle-field, and must be so to the end; but before I leave it, I hope to have the grace given me to pray that *his* murderers may be forgiven."

CHAPTER THE FOURTH.

DANIEL O'CONNELL.

"He that goeth about to persuade a multitude, that they are not so well governed as they ought to be, shall never want attentive and favourable hearers."
Hooker. "*Ecclesiastical Polity.*"

ON account of the high pitch of fanatical excitement to which the peasantry had been wrought by itinerant demagogues, priestly dictation, and altar denunciations, it was thought advisable that we should leave Kilkreen when the canvassing commenced, and not return till sufficient time had elapsed for the subsidence of the evil passions raised by a contested election.

Personally, my father was extremely popular; he was courteous in manner, kind-hearted, hospitable, and knew no distinction of creed in the distribution of his charities. Nevertheless, he knew that his life was not safe; for religious bigotry might any hour inflame the mind of an ignorant zealot, who might think that it would smooth his own path to paradise by sending to hell an influential supporter of an heretical candidate.

Indeed, my mother's fears very nearly brought on a brain-fever. She passed the hours of his absence from home in a state of violent agitation, or, what was more trying, of prostration of body and mind, from the dread which never left her that he would be shot down by some unseen assassin from behind a hedge or wall, or that his head would be fractured by the bludgeons of a furious gang.

As the business of the election compelled my father to be away from home from early dawn till late in the evening, my mother's terrible anxiety on his account soon communicated itself to the rest of the family, and right glad were one and all of us when we left Kilkreen, and moved into a furnished house in Landford.

The windows of our principal rooms commanded views of both the Tory and the Liberal committee rooms, while the street in which our house stood was the great thoroughfare of the town of Landford.

Many an incident characteristic of an Irish election took place almost under our very windows. Here a knot of staunch Tories would be discussing in loud tones and excited gestures the probable result of the election; there a troop of trimmers would be speculating on the probability of the Liberals coming into power. It was the common talk that Lord Anglesey —the Lord-Lieutenant—was openly countenancing the

Liberal party, and that two of his sons were members of the Roman Catholic Association.

Shoals of country people flocked into the town on market-days and thronged our street, roaring with laughter at the tale of some clever trick played off on the Tory agent, or raising groans when some well-known opponent of the Liberal side passed by.

A contested election was a costly affair. It was obligatory on the candidates to keep the public-houses open, not only while the polling was going on which lasted for a fortnight, but also for weeks before it commenced. Men and women, in various stages and degrees of intoxication, were, day after day, and all the day long, to be met with at every turn and corner of the town, screaming "Sturt for ever," "Down with the heretic Lord."

It was rare fun when some burly fox-hunting squire pounced down upon a suspected tenant, and dragged him into the Tory committee-room, where he would be badgered for half an hour—threats and promises being alternately resorted to, in order to make him pledge himself to vote for his landlord.

"Shure and sartain I will, gintlemen," said the captive.

"Mind you do, Terence," said the captor, looking sternly at him, and shaking his riding whip in his face.

"Aye, yer honour, Terence is a man of his word. An' how could he go agin the Markiss? Didn't the agent promise to add a couple of fields to his bit of farm, and would say nothing agin his building a cabin for his boy Mike, who was only waiting for a roof an' a pratie garden afore he axed pretty Moll Slater, whom he had been courting ever since she was sixteen, the crater, to marry him?"

All the time this was going on, one of the spies of the other party had been lying in wait for the man; and no sooner was he clear of the committee-room than he was down upon him—"Halloa, Terence, ye rascal, have they made a traitor of ye?"

"Any how they thried; bad 'cess to them."

"But, Terence, ye blackguard, by vartue of your oath, didn't they make ye go down on yer knees and swear ye'd vote for the heretic?"

"The divil a bit; them gintlemen wouldn't make a poor fellow like me swear."

"May be they promised ye something?"

"Arrah, thin, go an' ax them yerself, if ye want to know; an' that's all ye'll get out of me, I'm thinking."

However, poor Terence was in the meshes of a net from which none of his class could extricate themselves. It was not long before his wife had a visit from the priest, who soon extracted from her the story of the two acres of land, the cabin, and the potato garden.

"An' it's not me that's going to give the sacrament of the Holy Catholic Church to the likes of him, I can tell ye, Mrs Donehan; and ye can tell Terence that I told ye so. An' there's worse in store still for him if he's going against his religion. It's soon he'll be down with the fever, and maybe he'll be long waiting for the last rites of the Church afore they come to him."

So, what with the threats of the priest, the entreaties of his wife, and the scowls of the neighbours, poor Terence was obliged to give in. He "niver meant to go agin his conscience and his religion—he wasn't the boy for that; he only said what he did, to palaver the big man with the whip; an', anyhow, going back from your word with a heretic was no sin at all, at all."

The Terence-O'Donehan scene was one which was constantly repeated, and always with the same result.

The candidate brought forward by the Liberal party for the purpose of wresting the representation of the county from the Landford interest, was William Leslie Sturt. He was of an old family, had large landed property, and had lately attained his majority.

Every effort was made that his first public entry into the town of Landford should be an imposing one, and it was a perfect success. The procession extended as far as the eye could reach. It was headed by a band playing national airs. Then came an open landau, in which were seated Mr Leslie Sturt and his proposer and seconder, acknowledging with smiles and bows the cheers of the mob, and the waving of handkerchiefs by many a lovely occupant of windows commanding the line of route. There were, too, many glances of admiration even from fair political opponents; for Mr Leslie Sturt was handsome as well as young, while Lord George Burchester was plain middle-aged and uninteresting. Daniel O'Connell came next in the procession. He stood up in the carriage, his right hand waving his cap, his left placed on his breast, across which was a broad green sash. There were vehicles of all sorts and descriptions, from the well-appointed carriage (very few of these) down to the miserable jingle; the horses, drivers, and occupants were decked with rosettes, bows, and streamers of green ribbon; the progress was the very slowest—a dead halt occurring every now and then, caused by the dense throng of men with shamrocks in their hats and shilelaghs in their hands, all shouting, screaming, yelling, "Sturt for ever," "Down with the heretic," with other mob cries, some not fit for ears polite.

To our dismay, the evening before this public entry

of Mr Sturt, my father gave peremptory orders that all our blinds should be drawn down and the window-shutters closed. But, as his orders extended no further, my mother, with Nora and Eveleen, slipped out by the back door as soon as her husband was off to the committee-room, and was seated at a window of a friend's house, whence a good view could be obtained of the balcony whence the speeches were to be delivered. Our governess and her pupils were equally fortunate in obtaining similar accommodation at another window.

A large balcony had been erected in front of the windows of the Liberal committee-room.

Mr Leslie Sturt was the first speaker. In a short fluent speech he thanked the constituency of Landford for the enthusiastic reception they had given him that day, and for the high honour they had conferred on him in choosing him, a young and untried politician, for their candidate to represent the great county of Landford. In return for such proud distinction, he could only say that such powers as he possessed should be devoted to the interests of his native country, and consecrated to the task of raising her from the degradation to which she had been brought by unjust laws and partial government.

Then O'Connell came forward.

The cheering, the shouting, the throwing up of

caps, the brandishing of shilelaghs, from the dense, surging mass below, lasted for full half an hour; then came that deep, hoarse, subdued roar, so peculiar to an Irish mob, which I can compare only with the rumbling noise preceding an earthquake. And when this died away, then there burst forth from the lips of the "Liberator" such a flood of eloquence as I have never since heard equalled. His wonderful voice penetrated through, around, above the vast multitude, who hung upon every word he uttered as if he were an accredited messenger from heaven.

O'Connell was a man marked off from his generation. There was power in the ample intellectual development of his massive head. The strong force of a determined will to break through all opposition, and trample down every barrier which stood in the way of Ireland's political and social enfranchisement, was stamped upon every feature of his broad and expressive face. To the last he retained the affection and gratitude of his countrymen. He still lives in their memory. He had no rival during his life nor successor since his death. A foremost place among Ireland's great men will always be awarded to Daniel O'Connell.

"Fellow-countrymen and countrywomen," he began, "you have this day shown yourselves worthy of the land which gave you birth."

Then he went on to describe in glowing terms Ireland, *what it had been*—the island of saints; the sanctuary of devotion; the cradle of civilization; the nursery of kings and heroes, of poets and orators, of brave men and virtuous women.

Then with deep pathos he proceeded to contrast the Ireland of the *past* with the Ireland of the *present* day—no longer "Ireland great, glorious, and free," but fallen, debased, enslaved, pointed at by Continental nations as having reached the lowest depths of wretchedness, destitution, and misery.

Then he entered into the causes which had wrought her social degradation—her religious subjugation—and her political extinction.

"What has the Union done for you? Drained the resources of your country.

"What is Saxon rule doing for you? Depriving you of your liberties.

"What are your landlords doing for you? Do they live among you? do they lighten your burdens? or do they leave you in the pitiless grasp of griping agents, who wring from your bowed backs and tottering limbs even to the very last farthing, that in another land they may clothe themselves in purple and fine linen and fare sumptuously every day?

"Up, fellow-countrymen and countrywomen. Rest not till you have expelled from the representation every

Saxon nominee. Begin with Lord George Burchester, the nominee of the Marquis of Landford, one of the venal aristocracy, who, for the bribe of place and power, sold your liberties at the accursed Union."

Raising aloft his arms he finished with this passionate apostrophe,

" O my poor Country, trampled beneath the iron heel of despotism, quivering in every fibre, bleeding from every vein, who will bind up your wounds and raise you from the dust ? "

He stopped—his arms still raised up ; the silence throughout that great multitude, lately so tumultuous, was something quite awful ; after a pause—I cannot tell how long—he burst forth,

" Hereditary bondsmen, know ye not
Who would be free *themselves* must strike the blow."

CHAPTER THE FIFTH.

BEHIND THE SCENES.

GREAT excitement was created in our family circle by an invitation from the Marquis and Marchioness of Landford to Mr, Mrs, and Miss Rochford, to spend three days at Terenmore Castle.

Nora immediately opened the campaign on the question of her dress, protesting that she had not a single one in which she could possibly appear at the Castle.

"You have only worn your last ball dress but once, my dear," said her mother.

"That was two months ago, mamma. It's freshness is quite gone; it is limp and tumbled; besides, it is not fashionably made."

"Made by the best dressmaker in Landford, Nora."

"Well, I know it was; but I do object to a provincial cut, especially when I am to appear in company with the fashionable—and no doubt fastidious—Lady Constance Burchester. Really it is a severe ordeal, and there will be, of course, a number of their fine English friends staying in the house, who will amuse themselves in criticising the Irish costumes."

"I always observe," said my mother, "that extraordinary expenses are like a certain class of troubles— they press on us at the same time in an aggravating sort of way. There's the rent of this house; then we must have Lord George Burchester to stay with us during the election, besides keeping open house for his friends. And now there is this expense of a visit to the Castle."

"I say, mamma," said Nora, coming to the point at once, " had I not better write to Mrs Murray, in Dublin, to send patterns of silks and transparent materials?"

"Goodness, Nora, what will your father say?"

"I am sure papa would not wish his daughter to disgrace him; and, remember, it is the first year of my coming out."

Just at this moment my father entered, and my mother remarked to him—" Here is Nora wanting to have dresses from Dublin."

"You know, papa," said Nora deprecatingly, "we are going into quite a different society, and if I am not properly dressed what remarks I shall be subjected to."

My father set Nora down at once; "Worse remarks will be made if we try to vie with people who can count off a thousand to each hundred of our income."

"But, papa," pleaded Nora, "somehow in a room, how it is managed I cannot tell, but people do resemble each other in their dress."

"Not in their diamonds," sighed my mother, whose special grievance it was that her father-in-law had gambled away the family jewels—a charge which my father always hastily escaped from, never resenting it further than by a "Tut, tut," under his breath. He could be sufficiently roused by some piece of arrogant pretension on Nora's part to place her in her proper position, yet he had not the strength of will nor the energy of character to keep her there. He had shown a resolute opposition to any member of his family appearing at the windows of his own house and thus giving countenance to the liberal candidate, yet he made no opposition to their joining his presumed supporters at the windows of other houses; and when he heard Nora and Eveleen maintain that Mr Leslie Sturt took particular notice of them when his carriage came to a standstill beneath the window they occupied, he made no remark. As to women's dresses, however, he would have nothing to do with that,—let the mother manage that; and taking up the newspaper he was soon absorbed in the pompous description of Mr Leslie Sturt's public entry into the town.

As soon as the time came for his being due at the committee-room and he had left the house, the wrangling between my mother and Nora recommenced.

"I have made up my mind, Mamma," said Nora peremptorily, "to stay at home, if I cannot have dresses from Mrs Murray."

From her knowledge of her husband's character she was sure that any further appeal to him would only be met by,—" Cannot you arrange matters better than by driving the girl to act like a simpleton, and make herself and her family appear ridiculous?" Besides, she was proud of Nora's beauty, and there were certain vague ideas floating in her brain of the possibility of the fresh, fascinating, unsophisticated Irish girl (Nora unsophisticated!!!) making an impression on the heart of some *blasé* English nobleman, or of some commoner of ancient lineage and large landed possessions. No, it would never do to spoil Nora's prospects; nevertheless, she would show a little fight first.

"There is a large bill already owing to Mrs Dermott (the Landford dressmaker); when she hears that Mrs Murray is furnishing you with dresses, she will be sure to press for immediate payment."

"If she does, she must wait, that's all."

"But *I* must have a couple of dresses from her, and you know how she will pester me about you."

"O yes, I know;" and (mimicking Mrs Dermott),

'I have such sweet gauzy materials, Ma'am, quite the thing for young ladies' wear, Ma'am.' Really, if that is all you have to face, Mamma, it is not so very much after all," saucily remarked Nora.

"It is a great deal to me, however, though you make little of my feelings."

"O Mamma, have you not been cultivating my feelings ever since I was a small child by telling me that a girl had far better never appear in society unless she was well dressed? and now you turn upon me when I ask you to allow me to order a few dresses from Mrs Murray for a visit which may never come in my way again."

This plausible reason seemed a sort of loophole for my mother to escape from the unpleasant reflection that Nora had flouted her and carried her point against her, so she agreed to her writing to Mrs Murray for patterns and prices, but added,—"Yes, it will be your only opportunity, so make the most of it; for whatever may be the result of the election, as soon as it is over, the Landford family will take flight to England, and leave Terenmore Castle to be occupied as before by Mr Morgan Sullivan."

Looking back through the long vista of past years, a painful remembrance is forced on me of this and similar domestic episodes, of the excited feelings about trifles, of the heated altercations about unimportant matters, and the frequent mortifying concessions my mother had to make to a selfish and exacting daughter.

Alas, poor human nature!

With the exception of my sister Nora who since that time has had to face terrible sorrow and suffering, and of the Lady Constance Burchester—doomed to the living death of mental decay, all the actors in the busy scene I am describing have found their habitation in the grave, and in the language of the patriarch " have said to Corruption, thou art my father; and to the Worm, thou art my mother and my sister."

CHAPTER THE SIXTH.

TERENMORE CASTLE.

"Dulce ridentem Lalagen amabo
Dulce loquentem."
Hor. Od. i., 22.

THERE was an expression of mingled satisfaction and relief on the faces of mother and daughter upon their return to the hired house at Landford after the three days' visit to Terenmore Castle. My father was in excellent spirits. For years he had been on terms of close intimacy with the Marquis of Landford. During the morning hours he had been closeted with him in his private room discussing the steps to be taken against the coming election. The Marquis candidly acknowledged that the loss of this seat would be the knell of his political importance, and would be followed by the defection of other constituencies which had hitherto been under his control. The Liberal party were quite alive to the value of the stakes they were playing for, and were straining every nerve to annihilate the Landford influence in the County.

"Rochford," said the Marquis ruefully, "I shall lose my influence with the Ministry when I can no longer command some five or six votes in the Commons. Just look at this pile of letters containing requests for things possible and impossible,—for commissions without purchase for raw youths, promotions for those who have seen no service, government livings for unheard-of curates, and appointments from the judges' ermine down to the exciseman's gauge. One comfort however,—if they unseat George, there will be an end of these pestering applications."

My mother's impression of the visit was not so favourable as my father's. "Though no one could have been more attentive than the Marchioness," she remarked, "yet the evident solicitude of her manners betrayed the effort of an imposed duty." To any one with a less keen insight into character than my mother had, her ladyship would have appeared as a perfect model of high-bred unstudied demeanour. It was not her overacting her part that gave an unreal air to her intercourse with her guests, for she was naturally a simple-minded woman, she was a good wife and mother, and she worked with heartiness and energy to promote the popularity of the family; but it was the tone of her high-born English guests, who—being only uninterested spectators of the political game which was being played out—could not be expected to wind themselves up to any particular interest in Irish families whom they had neither known nor heard of, and whom they considered as a distinct species from themselves. After contributing a certain amount of general talk, they considered that they had done all that politeness to their hostess required, and drifted off to the discussion of their own affairs,—and the Marchioness too often drifted off with them. The arrival of the post-bag was always the special occasion of such clique intercommunications, such as allusions to secret marriages and elopements,—the probable breaking-up of some old family establishment,—the strange proceedings of the Duke of —— of which the Duchess seemed to take no heed,—the fact of Lord —— leaving his young wife to entertain a large party at the country-seat while he was yachting in the Mediterranean,—some Ministerial embarrassment or Cabinet fracas,—compared with any one of which matters the great struggle then going on in Ireland seemed to be of infinitesimally insignificant importance.

There being no other young lady visitor, Nora was taken at once by the Marchioness and introduced to Lady Constance,—" I expect you to become great friends, my dears," gracefully conveying the idea that it would be for her daughter's advantage to have such a companion as Miss Rochford.

As it was time to dress for dinner directly after such a cordial introduction, the advances towards the proposed intimacy had to be postponed. Nora possessed the requisite qualities for adapting herself to those among whom she was thrown, when either taste or self-interest called forth her powers of pleasing. She passed through the ordeal of dinner with much ease and self-possession. The Marchioness sent her in with her nephew, Colonel de Lisle Arbuthnot, of the Life Guards. Though he was a spendthrift, a gamester, and dissipated in his habits, he was—when in the companionship of a lively and pretty girl, and in the enjoyment of a good dinner and good wines—indisputably fascinating. His amusing small-talk, droll anecdotes, cynical and sarcastic remarks, had the effect of drawing out Nora and making her appear to the best advantage: she never was deficient in smart repartee and quick rejoinder, and now her coming-and-going blushes, her expressive dimples, and her pearly teeth, gave additional grace to all she said.

She was quite as much at her ease during that interval which is sometimes spoken of as pleasant and sometimes as Purgatory—that interval, namely, during which the ladies are left to their own resources in the drawing-room before being joined by the gentlemen. Had none of them spoken to her, she would have put it down to envy, being fully conscious in her own mind that she was not one to be overlooked or treated with indifference.

French Modistes had not then usurped the position of arbiters of taste, elegance, and fashion. Nora's equipment—fresh from the hands of Mrs Murray—was very nearly on a par with that of Lady Constance. Indeed, what the London-made dress gained in superior finish, the Dublin one gained in freshness. Lady Constance had worn hers at many a party during a season in Town, while Nora's had been put on for the first time. It was a satisfaction, too, to feel that her tulle dress had been trimmed with French blonde, and not with vulgar imitation—as it would have been had it been turned out by Mrs Dermott, the Landford dressmaker.

Though her voice was neither powerful nor well cultivated, Nora sang with expression and feeling, wisely confining herself to ballads. Italian bravuras were only for practice, and for giving flexibility to her vocal organs,—these she never attempted in public. Satisfied with the effect produced by her singing one of her national melodies, she did not attempt to vie with Lady Constance's elaborate vocalisation of "Una voce," by acceding to Colonel De Lile Arbuthnot's request that she would sing some Italian song—as "he was sure she would sing it divinely."

She did—for the time—make an impression on the *blasé* Lifeguardsman,—according to her own account.

The next morning, on going down before any of the rest of the family into the drawing-room, my mother and Nora heard voices in the adjoining conservatory, of which the door was open : " There is something wonderfully fascinating about this petite piquante Irish girl," said one voice, which Nora instantly detected as that of her Lifeguardsman,—and then it went on to hum—

" And given the saint one rosy smile,
She ne'er had left his lonely isle."

" O, hang it, Dick," said the other voice, " you are not going to make yourself out to be a saint."

" Her saint must have been a muff and an idiot. She gave me more than *one* rosy smile. And how she acted the lines ! Such glances from her brilliant black eyes ! "

" When you leave this lonely isle, you may perhaps carry off the little syren with you."

" She is a regular bud of beauty, and I should be proud of introducing her to the most fastidious of my family ; but unfortunately I am not a marrying man, unless I got a pot of money ; and as to an Irish girl with a " dot," she is about as likely to meet with as a sea-serpent when cruising in a yacht."

There is no telling what further revelations mother and daughter might not have been made privy to, had not the breakfast bell rung, and several of the family entered together into the room.

CHAPTER THE SEVENTH.

IMPOLITIC CONFIDENCES.

"And, all Hibernian though she be,
As civilised, strange to say, as we."
Moore.

AN intimacy was soon established between Lady Constance and Nora. Had the Marquis and Marchioness foreseen the possibility of their daughter making a confidante of my sister, and confiding family secrets to her, they would neither have proposed nor countenanced the intimacy. There was an elderly French woman, who had been the governess, and was now the companion, of Lady Constance; and as "Miladi" had expressed her wish that the young ladies should become great friends, and as Madame did not understand but very little English, she could have no reason to suspect that her young charge's communications with her new friend would be of any kind different from that between the Marchioness and Mrs Rochford.

Lady Constance was not disposed to pass the greater part of the morning in displaying her accomplishments, which were of far more than average standard. She wanted to talk to a girl of her own age, who could sympathise with her. Her lady-like instincts restrained her from rushing at once into her family and special grievances, which she would long to confide to her companion; and so she opened the conversation with some personal preliminaries.

"How very effectively you sang that national air, last evening, Miss Rochford."

"If I could sing as you do, Lady Constance, I would throw aside all my simple lays."

"Yet with your simple lays (as you call them), you won over such a fastidious man as my cousin De Lisle. Why, I heard him this morning before breakfast humming over and over again in the conservatory,

'And given the saint one rosy smile,
She ne'er had left his lonely isle.'

I suppose, Miss Rochford, you have heard Pasta sing 'Una voce?'"

"I have never heard her, Lady Constance."

"You have heard Sontag?"

"No, Lady Constance."

"You astonish me, Miss Rochford; I should never have set you down for a Puritan."

"I am no Puritan, Lady Constance, but as neither

Pasta nor Sontag has visited Landford, I have had no opportunity."

"Why, have you never been in London?"

"No, nor ever crossed the Irish Channel, nor visited the Lake of Killarney, nor the Giant's Causeway, nor the Wilds of Connemara."

Lady Constance clapped her pretty hands in astonishment; "I never thought"—and she stopped.

"Never thought what, Lady Constance?"

"O, I never could have taken *you* for a—a—a wild Irish girl."

Nora reddened with anger, but restrained the savage retort which rose to her lips.

"I have heard, Lady Constance, that the English consider themselves the civilisers of the native Irish. Nevertheless, permit me to assure you that there are many Irish ladies and gentlemen who would not disgrace England, though they know no other land than their own."

"I am sure I can quite believe it," Lady Constance replied heartily, looking Nora all over admiringly, thus gracefully and unconsciously escaping out of the little blunder which she had unconsciously made.

"How I wish," she went on, "that this horrid election was over. Mamma is urging papa to return to our place in —— the very day it is decided, but papa will make no promise."

"Would it not have an ungracious appearance, such a hurried departure?"

"So papa says; it would look ungrateful if Uncle George wins, and revengeful if he loses."

"If I were the owner of such a castle and domain as Terenmore, I should delight in spending the greater part of the year in it."

Nora had yet to learn that places and people are not always as they appear outwardly.

"No; you would not, Miss Rochford, if you were to change places with me."

"Lady Constance," said Nora in astonishment; "what can you possibly want that you have not got here? A grand house and extensive grounds, carriages and riding-horses at command, and any amount of visitors you please."

"The castle is spacious, no doubt, but it is dreary and uncomfortable and miserably furnished. Mamma says that for the short time we have to remain in it, it would be folly to spend money in furniture and decoration, as it would only be for the benefit of Mr Morgan Sullivan and his friends. And as to a party in the house—a regular list made out, visitors coming and going, a constant succession of guests such as we have at Idleworth Park, is quite out of the question. Here we can have only the odds and ends of society— guests of necessity, not inclination; not but there are charming exceptions," and Lady Constance smiled meaningly on Nora. " Besides, it is not safe for mamma to drive, papa has had such threatening letters. I delight in a good gallop and companions to enjoy it with me ; but I have no one but my cousin De Lisle, and he will not ride with me, as he says the roads are ruin to the horses' legs and fatal to their riders' necks."

" What are you taking my name in vain for ? " said the person spoken of, stepping in through the open window, glad of the excuse which the sound of his name gave him for killing the time which hung so heavy on his hands, by a flirtation with Nora, which he knew could have no further result than the amusement of the hour.

" I was just telling Miss Rochford your opinion of our roads."

" Execrable. I wish Terenmore was built on a small island, Miss Rochford ; it would be so romantic to see you steer your bark up to the very castle walls."

" And be ordered off by the chaplain," said Nora laughing.

" Not, by heavens, if I knew it. Was there never a creek or cove for your maid to have steered into for the night ? And in the morning when the old gentleman was taking his constitutional she might have seized the opportunity of shooting right in front of him, and then,—giving him one rosy smile, she ne'er had left his lonely isle."

"His wife might not like such an arrangement," said Lady Constance, who was no hagiologist.

"Wife! why he was a monk, a saint," exclaimed Nora.

"I am glad," said the Colonel, "for the honour and chivalry of England that St Senanus was not an Englishman."

"And I am glad," said Nora, "for the self-denying saintliness of Ireland, that he was an Irishman."

After the conclusion of the visit, its incidents were freely discussed in our family circle. All had not been sunshine, and the shadows were quite as much talked over as the lights. Nevertheless, when visitors poured in upon us, not one of them would have suspected, from the conventional description which they heard, that there had been a single cloud during the whole visit — "Everything so charming, the Marquis so courteous and benevolent, the Marchioness so unaffected and so interested in all relating to Ireland and the Irish; and as to Lady Constance, though she had been the reigning belle of the London season, she was perfectly happy and contented at Terenmore."

Such varnished pictures are the shameless shams of society; it is little short of putting in circulation debased coin. Who does not know by painful experience the dulness and heaviness of many a country-house visit, the wearisome tediousness of most dinner parties, the physical discomfort and mental irritation of the crowded staircases and dancing-room at a fashionable ball?

CHAPTER THE EIGHTH.

PARTY SPIRIT RUNS HIGH.

How the viragos of Landford disagreed with Colonel Grainger, and how he disagreed with them *in toto.*

WERE a future Virgil to conduct a future Danté through the Inferno, and describe the several circles of punishment allotted to the several classes of sinners, would he not have to point out to his companion one special circle appointed for contested-election-sinners?

Bribery and corruption, lying and drunkenness, low cunning and loud cursing, the passions of hatred and revenge lashed into furious outbreaks by political excitement, would surely doom both tempters and tempted to pains and penalties not inferior to those depicted by the Florentine poet.

The Liberal party had high hopes of carrying the election for the county of Landford. They were supported by the whole force of the Roman Catholic priesthood; Dublin Castle gave no uncertain sound,— the Lord-Lieutenant, Lord Anglesea, openly siding with them, and his sons enrolling themselves as members of "The Catholic Association."

Still the Tories were not disheartened. Most of the country gentry were with them, and they were slow to believe that the tenantry could turn against their landlords when they came to the poll. They were up and doing as well as their opponents. Their agents watched every opportunity of circumventing the Romish priests and their emissaries; they hung out liberal promises for such tenants as voted for Lord George Burchester; they hinted at eviction, demand of full payment of arrears, and no more 'running gales,' for such as voted against him. It was well known, that if the tenants were true to their landlords, Mr Leslie Sturt would not have a leg to stand on.

The small farmers and the forty-shilling freeholders had not an easy time of it. There were some who had made up their minds but would give no sign, generally men of brutal force and determined will; though they were under suspicion and surveillance, yet after a time were left unmolested : "Did they not belong to a clan ? had they not powerful frames, and heavy fists, and bludgeons which would smash to smithereens those who meddled with them."

Others, who had succumbed to the spiritual power of their Church against their will, were perhaps the noisiest in blurting out "they warnt the boys to go agin their priests and their counthry;" things went very smooth with them, "barring the threats of the cursed Tory agint;" and they had no fears before their eyes of being nagged by the women at the priest's instigation, or of the interruption of the blazing turf-fire, the hot potatoes, the savoury red herring, and the butter milk; and if they did get a little the worse for the drop, it was not flung in their faces.

It was far otherwise with the vacillators, or, as they were called, the skulkers or slieveens. Poor souls! many did not know their own minds; and many had not the courage to fly in the face of their landlords, when they looked round the four walls of the cabins which had sheltered their fathers, and on the old mother crouching beside the embers, and on the wife whom, years ago, they had brought to live and end her days—where the old crone was then ending hers —and where the children had been born and reared, or else had died and been waked :—

"Were they to be driven to go agin their landlords, who could turn them adrift without a roof to shelter them, and without food or clothing to keep body and soul together?"

Yet, on the other hand, it was very hard to meet with only scowls and black looks from the women who had been set on by the priests,—to have their food thrown down before them as if they were dogs, cold potatoes and sour milk, and a running accompaniment of threats and curses if they went against their Church and Country.

Almost facing our house in Landford was a pastry-cook's—or, as it was called, a cake-shop—kept by Mrs M'Cann. The jam-tarts and apple-puffs are delicious remembrances of my youthful days. Since then I have often revelled in the refined and artistic patisserie of Gunter of Berkeley Square, Guer of the Rue de Rivoli, of Donay of Florence, and Sempronij of Naples,—yet Mrs M'Cann's jam-tarts and apple-puffs have never been effaced from my remembrance.

The shop had a great reputation, and was the rendezvous and the afternoon lounge of the idle fashionable men. *There* most of the gossip was manufactured, and all the events of the town and neighbourhood were discussed. Mrs M'Cann, in her brown silk dress and mob-cap—her elbows on the counter—was always to be found at her post in the afternoon. She was a general favourite, and was privileged to share in any conversation that was going on, in which she was quite competent to take her part, being familiar with the concerns of her customers who consisted of all the principal families. She was a politician; but, having a steady eye to the main chance, she was too shrewd to injure her business by offensively obtruding her opinions. She was a devoted adherent to her Church. Why, was not one of her nephews a coadjutor to Father O'Flaherty? and was not another in training for the priesthood at Maynooth—all at her expense? and was she not on friendly terms even with the very bishop himself?

The marriage of a niece, to whom she had given "a tidy bit of money," took place shortly before the election. We watched the bridal procession from our windows. The bride was conveyed to the chapel in a sedan chair, followed by jaunting cars and jingles containing the family and friends. The wedding supper, as we heard from some who were present, was magnificently got up. The Bishop honoured it with his presence, and was honoured in return by large sums deposited in the plate which was handed round, all the guests being expected to contribute towards the fee required for the holy sacrament of marriage.

"No wonder," my father remarked, "the priests prefer the free-will liberality of their flocks to the paltry endowments which the State would bestow."

It was evident to those whose political creed was influenced by self-interest that Tory ascendancy was on the wane, and they prepared to trim their sails and be guided by coming events which were already casting their shadows before.

"The Duke might overcome the scruples of the King, and drill the Cabinet into passing the Emancipation Bill," they argued; "he might explain to their conviction, that among the provisions of the Bill there were quite sufficient safeguards against any injury to the Constitution; he might persuade them that the country would be quieted, and that no further demand would be made upon the Imperial Government;" but they knew well enough that the Country would *not* be quieted; that the Bill, once passed, would only be the opening of the door to further demands,—and that Roman Catholic members would soon be returned who would never cease their agitation, both within and without Parliament, until these further demands were conceded.

Long and warm were the discussions which were carried on in Mrs M'Cann's shop between the Tories and the Trimmers; and it was a wonder, considering how high party politics ran, that neither bones were broken nor blood shed on these occasions.

Mrs M'Cann had always a word of encouragement for the Trimmers whenever the other party were not within hearing distance.

It happened, however, that on one occasion my father overheard her saying, "Look at what Dublin Castle is doing for you; it won't be long before, with a little more of the like help, the Irish foxes will exterminate the English foxes"; and he startled her by at once coming down on her: "I tell you what it is, Mrs M'Cann, your priests are the huntsmen, and it is they who are setting the ignorant peasantry to run to earth the good old Tory foxes."

Morning after morning the Radical newspaper was filled with the most inflammatory articles, as well as with the lowest and most scurrilous personal allusions: there was not a scandal, with or without foundation, which was not raked up and grossly exaggerated.

The whole interest of the contest lay entirely between Lord George Burchester and Mr Leslie Sturt. It had been arranged that the seat of the other member, Mr Bryan Mansell, was not to be disturbed. He was an elderly and universally respected man, who had represented the County for many years; latterly his opinions had veered towards the Liberal side, and it was suspected that he would vote for Catholic Emancipation. All the second votes of the Liberal, as well as of the Tory party, were to be given to him.

The writs were out. The election was approaching. Lord George, Colonel Grainger, and John Burnard, Esq., became our guests. The day after their arrival was the Nomination. The proposing and seconding of Lord George Burchester were performed by pantomimic dumb-show. Mr Leslie Sturt's proposer and seconder had a fair hearing, the other party not being strong enough to retaliate by drowning their voices in choruses of yells, hisses, and groans.

The election lasted a fortnight; and as there was but one polling-place for the whole county, it may well be imagined what a pandemonium Landford became. All the county gentry crowded into the town; the private houses, the inns, and such lodgings as were to be had, were literally crammed. The public-houses drove a roaring trade; they and every crazy tenement harboured the voters who came from a distant part of the County.

Lord George had to be guarded all the way from our door to the hustings by a body of police. A large party of his friends formed a lane for the protection for the more aged and timid of his voters on their way to the poll, without which they would have been exposed to the violence of the mob, who not only *threatened* but *meant* mischief. Whenever a Tory voter came in sight there was, on a given signal, a rush to hustle, knock down, and trample on him, and when the assailants were foiled in the attempt they took it out in curses and threats.

It was hardly possible for a country gentleman to mount his horse and ride to the town to record his vote, without being stopped on the road by a band of patriot Pats; and, if he escaped being treated to a taste of the shillelagh, his horse's head would be turned, and he would be ordered to "go home and look afther his wife and childer till he larned better manners than to vote against his counthry."

Both organization and brute force were called in play by each party. Agents for each side were engaged who were most skilled in the art of evading detection and conviction for bribery. Conveyances were provided for bringing the voters from their distant homes. Parties were told off for escorting them on the journey, and setting them down at the doors of the public-houses or other abodes which had been hired for their reception, where they were supplied with food and unlimited drink, and were watched day and night against any attempts at assault or abduction.

We used to observe the outside cars closely packed with live cargoes of Tory voters, most of them wearing a dogged scowling expression on their faces, very few of them having that jaunty devil-may-care air which is so common to the small-acred farmers. Running behind and beside the cars were yelling screeching mobs of women and spalpeens, who did not always confine themselves to curses and execrations, but used mud and dirt to give force and point to their words.

In the square fronting our house the police force was drilled every morning.

The words of command would sound strange to English ears. For instance:—

Officer. " 'Tention, boys.

When I say 'dhra,' don't dhra ;
When I say 'surdes' (swords), don't dhra,
But when I say 'dhra surdes,' then dhra surdes."

The soldiers, though strictly confined to barracks, were still kept in readiness to march immediately to any point to which they might be summoned by the mayor or chief magistrate. Their orders were, that if the rioters refused to disperse after the Riot Act was read, they should fire blank charges in the first place. It was very questionable whether such a proceeding did not encourage rather than discourage the mob, as an idea of personal invulnerability was raised, which led to renewed acts of violence; and when at last the extreme measure of firing bullets had to be resorted to, many who had only been brought together by curiosity were killed or wounded, while the ringleaders escaped.

Prominent on these occasions were the women, who in language and behaviour were worse than the men. One day, on his way to the hustings, Colonel Grainger found himself surrounded by a troop of female furies. He was well known as the proposer of Lord George Burchester on the nomination day, and easily distinguishable by his great height and size.

Instantly he became the object of loud cursing and obscene epithets. One vigaro was particularly active in hounding on her comrades. She spat in his face, and called on the others to do the same. In a minute he was covered with defilement. In elbowing his way out of the throng, he brought his iron-heeled boot with full force down upon the virago's naked foot. The howl of agony she raised caused a diversion in his favour, and he extricated himself without much exertion from a position which might have been one of danger.

"Served her right, the she-devil," as he said when he rejoined us. "She has cost me a suit of clothes."

CHAPTER THE NINTH.

WE ESCAPE WITH OUR LIVES.

"Hi motus animorum atque hœc certamina tanta
Pulveris exigui jactu compressa quiescent."
Virgil, Georg. iv. 86.

"Yet all these dreadful deeds—this deadly fray—
A cast of scattered dust will soon allay."
Dryden's Translation.

"These risings of [rebellious] spirits, and such [street] fights as these, quelled by the discharge of a little [gun] powder, will be set at rest."—*Prose Translation.*

DURING the progress of the election our house used to be thronged with visitors of all sorts to hear the numbers polled, of which notice was sent to us every hour. From three till six o'clock the great muster took place of our friends, especially of young men from the Country, and of officers from the barracks who, happily for the young ladies, were not confined to quarters like their men.

Nora alone had been regularly introduced. Eveleen was supposed to be in the school-room. But Eveleen could not or would not understand why, having been allowed to join in all the gaieties last summer at Dunless, the same liberty should not be granted to her at Landford.

"My dear," replied my mother, when Eveleen appealed to her, "it was quite a different matter when we were at the sea-side."

"I cannot see how, Mamma."

"You do not comprehend these things, Eveleen. The amusements you entered into at Dunless did not stamp you as being 'out;' but here in Landford, if you are to be in the drawing-room, receiving visitors and dressed like Nora, it would be a positive disadvantage to you, as in a few years—should you not be married in the meantime—it will be said, 'O, Eveleen Rochford, let me see, I remember she was grown up and introduced in the year of the great election for Landford County.'"

"It is not balls I want to go to, Mamma; I know well enough that it is her first ball which fixes a girl's age."

"Other events do the same. All the girls born in '98 have even now the soubriquet of 'rebellion birds.' Some mothers were silly enough to have their daughters named Horatia on account of their being born on the day of the victory of Trafalgar; there was never any dispute about their age—were they not 'Trafalgar girls?' Besides, Nora is always at me;

L

she says I am not doing fairly by her in allowing you to come so forward as I do."

"And am I to be confined to the school-room, dressed like a school girl, and to hang down my head and shut my eyes and not open my lips when I am addressed by the young men who walked and danced with me, and were so kind to me when we played our round games at Dunless?"

"You should remember, Eveleen, that you are not seventeen."

"I shall be at the end of this month; and I don't see why I am to be hid away merely to please Norah. But, Mamma, have you ordered my dress and bonnet at Mrs Dermott's?"

"Yes, my dear."

"And what have you chosen?"

"Mrs Dermott advised a blue muslin, and a straw bonnet trimmed with white ribbon, as the proper thing for you, as you were not out."

"And what for Nora?"

"I had my own design for her which she readily fell in with—lavender silk for the dress, and pink watered silk for something between a hat and a bonnet."

Eveleen was a most lovely girl. Her beauty was of the Saxon type, which she inherited from her grandmother, who was an Englishwoman and a celebrated beauty. Her figure was tall lithe and pliant, her head small and well-placed on her shoulders, her complexion fair with a tinge of colour, her features delicately classical, her eyes blue, her hair light and worn in the fashion of those days, rippling over her forehead and descending in ringletty cascades down her shoulders.

Nora was small, with a well-rounded figure; her hands and feet were models, her eyes and hair were black, her complexion clear and pale. The sisters were contrasts to each other, but Eveleen was far the lovelier of the two.

Eveleen rejoiced in her beauty. It was her great occupation how to set it off to the best advantage, so as to obtain for it its full value of notice and admiration. Conscious of her charms, without a particle of shyness or diffidence, full of life and spirits, and craving for attention, you might just as well expect a young race-horse, which has once tasted the excitement of a race, to keep from fretting, fuming, and chafing within view of the race-course, as Eveleen— after experiencing the delights of society at Dunless and being now in the very centre of the sights and sounds of gaiety—to settle down calmly and contentedly within the four walls of a schoolroom, with only younger sisters and a governess for companions.

So she took counsel with herself how she could be

placed on a par with Nora—so far as being dressed like her and admitted to the drawing-room receptions. In regard to equality of dress she must call in another to her aid—and to that other she speedily betook herself.

My father had a maiden sister, a lady of independent means, who resided in the town of Landford. She was warmly attached to her brother, and she liked my mother in the usual sister-in-law style. She disliked Nora, who was pert and flippant: Eveleen, who was her god-daughter, she both loved and was proud of: of the rest of the family she was fairly fond. "Aunt Evie" (as we called her), like most single ladies who live alone, was well pleased to be told all that was going on.

It was to "Aunt Evie" to whom Eveleen looked for help in her dilemma, and hastened to call on her. She was crafty enough not to let out the real motive of her visit; so she began to tell all the latest news about the Election,—how the leaders of the Tory party had a sort of East-wind look, as if things were going wrong,—how her mamma was worried at so many meals at irregular hours,—how the servants were turning runty and inclined to be disorderly, for it was no easy matter to keep them in good humour while trying to keep down inordinate waste,—and how Lord George's valet was the plague of the house, always in every one's way, and full of airs which the servants were beginning to copy.

Then Eveleen went on to describe Nora's dress, and wound up with a piteous appeal to her listener's sympathy—" O, Aunt Evie, is it not too bad that I should be dressed up in a muslin frock and straw bonnet?"

" It is hard," said the aunt, consolingly; " and how set-up that minx Nora will be! Yet, at the same time, I admire your mother's taste—lavender silk dress and pink watered-silk bonnet."

Tears of disappointment were slowly gathering in Eveleen's eyes, for her aunt made no sign; indeed, a fit of absence came over her from which she awoke after a time with the remark—" blue muslin! why, I always thought that blue was your favourite colour."

" It is not the colour I object to, dear aunt, but the material. Muslin! and Nora is to have silk."

" Silk—muslin," muttered my aunt. " Perhaps the Landford public may say—' those Rochfords, though they are so grand, can afford to dress up only one daughter at a time.'"

" A sky-blue silk dress," she went on musingly, " a white watered-silk bonnet; no, that won't do—it's too heavy; a chip hat, with blue forget-me-nots."

I was my sister's companion in this visit, but my aunt had not honoured me with much notice. " I hear," she said, "that Mrs Dermott has got in her Summer stock, so I shall just step in and have a look at the novelties of the season. We can leave Kathleen at home on our way; you will go on with me and help me to choose a bonnet and dress in case I should want one."

Most afternoons Eveleen contrived to make her way into the drawing-room at the hour when it was crowded with visitors, always taking good care to dress herself in the best that her limited wardrobe allowed, and to roll out the rich masses of her hair in the most studiedly-unstudied fashion.

Nora used to be very vicious, and to upbraid her mother for allowing Eveleen to take such liberties.

"Would you have me draw on myself the remarks of our visitors by turning Eveleen out of the room?" asked my mother.

"Eveleen would not dare to smuggle herself in, unless you secretly connived at it," was the dutiful rejoinder.

There was some truth in Nora's charge. Eveleen was one of whom any mother might be proud; her manners were so winning, and she had such a fond and engaging way of throwing her arms round her mother—when she began to scold her for disregarding her commands—as effectually to silence and disarm her. Besides, the father loved the second much more than the elder daughter; and — had repressive measures gone too far—he would have interfered, and have prevented Eveleen being kept in the back ground to the encouragement of Nora's selfishness.

So Eveleen triumphed; she had the full run of the drawing-room, and came in for more notice, and I fear more flirting, than was good for her.

The Saturday in that particular week, in which all these family political movements took place, was a busy day to every one.

Domestic arrangements engaged my mother—there were the supplies for two days to be calculated and procured. More serious and important measures occupied the whole attention of my father and the heads of the party. Steps had to be taken in order to prevent the voters being tampered with during the Sunday—such voters at least as were not too intoxicated to be in danger of being tampered with. The great point was to stop—by hook or by crook—all of them from attending mass; for once within reach of Father O'Flaherty and his coadjutor, small chance would there be of a single one of them voting for Lord George Burchester.

The whole of that Saturday evening Aunt Evie was closeted with her favourite niece. Bridget looked conscious and important, as if entrusted with the conduct of some great matter: " That's *only* for Miss

Nora," I heard her say superciliously, as a boy came upstairs carrying a wicker basket; but when, just after Mrs Dermott's "first-hand" appeared, followed by a young woman with a couple of boxes, they were hurried without a word into the room where aunt and niece were. Nobody but myself suspected that anything was going on there; indeed, there were such streams of people coming and going all day long that nobody had any time to think of any one's affairs except their own.

It was a beautiful summer's day that Sunday which followed.

The family and the guests were all assembled in the drawing-room preparatory to starting off for the Cathedral service, all with one exception, namely Eveleen. My mother had taken a satisfied survey of Nora's dress, and was beginning to show symptoms of uneasiness at Eveleen's absence. Had she sulked at the last moment? Was the trial too great of the disadvantageous contrast her dress would form to that of her sister's?

Suddenly the door opened, and Eveleen, with a flush of mingled modesty and mischief on her beautiful cheeks, stepped lightly across the room, and with an appealing look to her father as if she needed his protection she placed her arm within his. Instead of the muslin dress and the straw bonnet, she appeared in the glories of sky-blue silk, and hat of white chip with detached bouquets of forget-me-nots. She did look excessively lovely—her long eyelashes half veiling her eyes which were cast down as if dreading to encounter a glance of disapprobation from her mother.

My father, knowing nothing of the secret of the dress-transformation, nor whether there was any transformation at all, looked fondly and proudly on his clinging daughter. My mother at once guessed through whose agency it was that Eveleen had contrived to defeat her and eclipse Nora. I fear that Eveleen disturbed the devotions of some of the occupants of our pew that morning.

For the first few days the numbers polled for the three candidates were pretty equal; if one day one candidate headed the others, the others were sure the next day to come up to him at least. Those who were not behind the scenes considered Lord George Burchester's success as certain—even with a large allowance made for defections from the ranks of the tenantry of the Tory landlords. Those who worked the election were far from sanguine. Every staunch supporter— every one who could safely be counted on—had been polled. There still remained a great mass of voters who had not yet gone to the poll, and on the side which *they* took the issue of the contest depended. It was known that they had been tampered with during the time they were supposed to be in the safe keeping of friendly (treacherous?) publicans and lodging-house keepers. The priests had managed to get access to them. What publican would run the risk of the loss of his custom by refusing them admittance? or what owner of a tenement would incur the loss of lodgers by a curse being solemnly pronounced upon his habitation?

Outside every such house were organised gangs awaiting the sallying forth of the voters. As soon as they appeared, they were surrounded by men flourishing sticks, and shouting, "These are the boys who are marching to the rescue of their counthry;" almost to a man they voted for Sturt and Mansell.

It was a terrible period,—the ferocity of the mob—the triumph of brute force—the breaking up of all kindly relations between landlord and tenant—the overwhelming odds of the winning party—the total discomfiture of the losing party which comprised seven-eighths of the owners of the land, who suddenly found, what they had always regarded as their legitimate rights, snatched from them by priestly influence and mob intimidation! What was it leading to? What would come next? What would be the end? Such were the anxious enquirings of men of property and station.

The chairing of Mr Leslie Sturt—for Mr Bryan

Mansell declined the honour on the score of ill health —wound up with a regular Irish shindy. Flushed with their victory over "the oppressors of their Country," and maddened with drink (for they had broken open the public houses and rifled the cellars), there was no act of violence or brutality for which the mob was not perfectly ready. Every person, though only suspected to be a Tory, who had the misfortune or imprudence of being abroad, was savagely beaten. Life was not safe any more than property.

Our house was a special mark for their vengeance. We had scarcely finished barricading the windows, and putting additional fastenings on the front door, before a dense crowd appeared before the house, uttering fearful threats. In a moment there was not a window-frame or pane that was not smashed. And then came the thundering of bludgeons and hammers against the shutters and door, which we expected to give way at every successive stroke.

The gentlemen of our party were below in the hall, prepared for a desperate—though it might be an unavailing—resistance. We women and girls were assembled in the drawing-room, anxiously awaiting our fate,—for how could our gallant little garrison, with no other weapons than their walking-sticks, hope to protect us long? Yet there was no fainting nor screaming among us. Silent and pale we stood, but calm and resolute ; not an exclamation broke from the lips of any one of us, even when the mob—apparently despairing of forcing an entrance—shouted out, " Set fire to the house !"

Just then there was a distant hollow tramp, tramp, tramp,—the measured tread of a body of soldiers ; it came nearer and nearer, and stopped within a few yards of our house. Help had come at last—not a moment too soon. There was a short pause, and then we could hear a single voice either speaking or reading. Sure it must be the reading of the Riot Act. There followed jeerings, hisses, and hootings, above which rose the short, sharp, word of command, " Ready, present,—fire." A volley of musketry,—half a minute's silence,—and then yells of defiance, cries of " Down with the sodgers," and a whistling and rattling which we knew could only be from a discharge of stones.

Again the short, sharp, " Ready, present, fire,"— and again yells ; but this time they were yells of agony and terror. A hoarse, confused noise of the rushing of feet,—then the tramp, tramp, tramp across the square and down the next street, till it was lost in the distance.

All was now silence, broken only by low groans. Stealthily, and by degrees, we opened first one and then another shutter, and peeped out at the scene before us. Of all that seething, surging human mass which had thronged the square only a quarter of an hour before, none now remained but the wounded and the dead stretched upon the ground.

Thus ended, in storm and slaughter, the memorable contested election for the representation in Parliament of the County of Landford.

Book the Fourth.

CHAPTER THE FIRST.

ONLY A LETTER.

" Some are so curious in this behalf, as those old Romans, our modern Venetians, Dutch and French, that if two parties dearly love, the one noble, the other ignoble, they may not by their laws match, though equal otherwise in years, fortune, education, and all good affection. In Germany, except they can prove their gentility by three descents, they scorn to match with them. A noble man must marry a noble woman; a Baron, a Baron's daughter; a Knight, a Knight's; a Gentleman, a Gentleman's; as slatters sort their slats, do they degrees and families. *But these are too severe laws and strict customes.*"

Burton's Anatomy of Melancholy, p. 375, Ed. 1660.

ANNO MUNDI 1° it was decreed that "It is not good for man to be alone."

Anno Domini 58° it was advised, "I will that the younger women marry."

Among all the changes and revolutions which have taken place among the civilised nations of the earth, marrying and giving in marriage has been honoured in the observance by all ranks and classes.

Has not a change of feeling and practice come over the present generation?

Instead of an *unanimous consent*, is there not *a merely sectional obedience* to Divine decree and Apostolical counsel?

"It is not good for man to be alone."

True, say those who can afford the luxury of a wife, and who desire an heir to their property or title,—and straightway they ally themselves with *Beauty*.

True, say the successful miner, engineer, speculator, financier, merchant, who have realised more than princely wealth, and who desire to graft an artistocratic shoot upon their plebeian stocks; they ally themselves with *Rank*, choosing a high-born maiden whose minimum of good looks would bar her from marrying in her own set.

True, say the penniless men of rank; they must live and maintain their position; they therefore ally themselves with *Money*.

True, say they who regard matrimony as a "holy estate,"—who regard a good wife as the best of God's good gifts,—who feel that man and wife cannot be "one flesh" unless they be of one heart and one mind—bound together by mutual love, sympathy, and respect,—who look not out for beauty, rank, or money, but to find and secure a "help meet" for them,—these marry for *Love*.

As for the rest, they are independent of the matrimonial law ecclesiastical or civil, of priest or registrar.

"I will that the younger women marry."

How many would gladly and thankfully undertake and fulfil the duties and obligations of woman's appointed mission! If the woman was made for the man, and the man repudiates the alliance, the woman is utterly powerless to enforce it. The male defaulter has his ready and specious excuse,—" it is the women's own fault,—look at their extravagance in dress, their passion for amusement, their craving for excitement, their want of feminine manners!"

Granted, for argument's sake. But who made them so? If there were no horsey men, there would be no horsey women. If men had not elevated the Thais' and Phrynes of the demi-monde into models of taste, there would have been no opportunity for women to copy their dress, talk, and manner; they would have retained their gracious inheritance of modesty, delicacy, and purity; they would have shrunk with horror from crowding to witness the unmanly sport (sport!!!) of pigeon-shooting,—they would never have thronged the boxes of a theatre, and listened with unblushing cheeks to the filthy allusions and the *sous-ententes* of an immoral and indecent French play.

A few years ago there arose a wail of distress from Belgravian mothers that no suitable proposals were made for their daughters. It was answered by the rational remark, that if they must marry, and if there were none in their own rank to marry them, they had better lay themselves open to the addresses of suitors belonging to a lower rank. An example has been given of Royal wedding with Subject blood, and Ducal with Legal; the next step will be for the Gentry to wed with Retail blood.

In the days of my youth things were, happily, different. There were not then the shoals of single ladies we now see. Spinsterhood was the exception, and not—as now—the rule in families. It was a thing unheard of that a marriage should be broken off when the trousseau was actually complete, the bridesmaids prepared, the wedding presents on exhibition, the wedding guests invited, the wedding breakfast ordered, and even the wedding tour planned. Matrimony was not then a commercial affair. Parents expected, and daughters expected, that, as a matter of course, a lover would appear at the proper time and be duly transformed into a husband in the sight of God and man.

Nora and Eveleen had been married. Mildred and Aileen had been introduced. And I was seventeen. I was in an anomalous position. I was in the way. No one wanted me, except my father, and I could not be with him the whole day. The greater part of my time was passed in day dreams, in building castles in the air, or in desultory and miscellaneous reading.

M

My mother had told me that I was not to expect to be introduced into society until Mildred was married. I well remember the day she told me; we were walking in the garden, I saw a caterpillar crawling along the ground in our path, and I wondered whether it had an elder sister, and if so whether it would not be a merciful act to crush it with my foot.

However, it was not very long I had to wait for making an appearance on the stage of our little world.

Our usual Christmas guests had departed: and we felt a sort of relief that there was an end to the heavy monotonous meals peculiar to the season, and to the burden of having to find in-door amusements at the most dreary time of the year.

There had been an unusual amount of rain; it poured in torrents every day in unbroken succession for a fortnight, and then came a heavy fall of snow with sharp frost. The windows looked as if paned with ground glass; the icicles hung in long stalactites from every projection; the terrace walk was a white slippery pavement; the boughs of the fine old trees of the park were weighed down with heavy masses of snow, and scattered all around showers of sparkling gems with every passing breath of wind. Timid hares crouching under ferns in some sheltered nook, their ears alternately raised vertically or depressed backward to catch the earliest sounds of an intruder's step,—rabbits hopping out from their burrows to make their mischievous browsings on the barks of young trees,—squirrels leaping from branch to branch as if playing at hide and seek with each other,—birds uttering faint melancholy notes as if in despair of finding their daily food,—the shrill cry from a distance of some victim of stoat or weasel; such were the sights and sounds I encountered upon throwing up the window for my father to scatter abroad the usual morning dole of crumbs from the breakfast table to the robins and sparrows.

A wicked desire took possession of me of witnessing how birds would behave in a state of intoxication. I had seen men and women in that state,—now for the birds. I went and got a little whiskey from the butler, in which I steeped some crumbs and threw them on the terrace, and waited for the effect with some curiosity. At first the little creatures seemed shy, but soon greedily swallowed the drugged morsels. It was not long before they went round and round as if pirouetting for very pleasure; then they turned somersaults, then they tried to fly, but their wings were evidently not in working order, for their owners did not rise above a foot from the ground before they came down headlong, only to repeat the experiment with the same result.

"Them birds be bewitched," I heard the postman remark to himself as he crunched the snow with his feet; " it's a purty male the cat'll have of 'em."

But the cat had no such meal, as I carefully watched over the victims of my treacherous hospitality until they recovered from their involuntary intoxication.

In those days when every letter was paid for in silver, young ladies in general had few correspondents, and I had none. So the sight of the shivering postman with his blue nose and red cheeks excited neither my curiosity nor interest, nor withdrew me from my post of guardian over the birds' safety.

I was startled by hearing my name mentioned. On turning round I saw my mother standing by my father with an open letter in her hand, and that both their eyes were fixed on me. Somehow or other, insignificant I had become an object of extraordinary interest.

"Read the letter," said my father.

"It is from your aunt Haughton," said my mother; and then she read aloud the letter. In my case, as in that of many others, a letter (ONLY a letter) entirely altered the current of my life.

"MY DEAR SISTER,—I suppose you, like ourselves, are in the midst of frost and snow. The Canon is rheumatic, and wheezy in the chest; so I have persuaded him to keep within doors, and to put on his great-coat and velvet cap. He says the coat is so tight-fitting that he feels like a hog in armour. His spirits are low, and so are mine. The departure of an only daughter from us is a serious loss to us, though, from one point of view, we rejoiced at Geraldine's marriage, as it was a most advantageous one; and we encouraged it in every way. Still, we bitterly regret it, on account of the great difference it has made in the happiness of our daily life. We may be described as travellers who have reached the top of a hill, and now their carriage has begun to descend on the other side, with no drag to moderate the rapidity of its downward course, and with no cheerful companion to smooth the roughnesses of the road. We dine out as often as usual, and have the same number of dinner parties at home; and I have no lack of gentlemen to escort me into the supper-room at the balls and routs, as often as I wish; but never do I see the face of a young man at the conventional afternoon hour. Plenty of cards after a dinner party, which are ignominiously consigned to the waste-paper basket; and I wish the coxcombs could see the value entertained of their pasteboard. How different it used to be before our Geraldine's marriage! Then my fine fellows were always calling, and never knew when to take leave, barely leaving us time for dressing for dinner, and keeping us in a fever about the Canon's displeasure at our unpunctuality. Our present style of society is rather of the hum-drum order—middle-aged and septuagenarian. And now that I have no daughter to dress and take into society, and have no longer a share in those many small interests which a young girl creates around her, I can almost say that my occupation is gone. What will you say to the proposal I am going to make to you — that your Kathleen shall occupy the place left vacant by Geraldine, and that I shall introduce her, and do the best I can for her? Three girls are an awkward number for you to chaperone. As Mildred is little more than twenty, it must be some years before she will yield to be put on the shelf, unless married in the interim; and it will be hard for Kathleen to lose the opening and ripening years of girlhood. The advantage will be mutual. I shall have an object in life still,—the Canon will be cheered by the sight of a bright young face,—and Kathleen, being as a daughter to us, will immediately enter the best society which the town and neighbourhood afford. There is only one proviso: Geraldine— though of the most amiable and unselfish character— might feel hurt at Kathleen replacing her *in all respects*. I suggest, therefore—in order to obviate any such feeling she might entertain, as well as

remove any delicate scruples on your part—that her father supplies Kathleen's dress. The Canon unites in wishing you and your's many happy new years.— Your affectionate sister,
"MARY ELIZA HAUGHTON.

"*P.S.*—We had quite a scene last night at Mr Beattie's ball. He took Lady Brindley in to supper. Madame Bonaparte Wyse, who was there, flew into such a rage, and screamed—so as to be heard by every one—that she ought to have precedence of every one in the room, as she was of royal blood and a princess in her own right. Her husband had great difficulty in getting her to take his arm, and be conducted to her carriage. She is a splendid woman, but she has, O such a voice!—and such a temper! There are rumours of a separation."

The postscript, which would have been the most interesting part of all to anybody but myself, I scarcely heard. My aunt's invitation, would it be accepted for me? How my heart beat! I could hear it as distinctly as the hall clock. Had an immediate refusal been given, I believe I should have fainted. Yet I never uttered a word. I felt as I could fancy a prisoner would do who was waiting for the verdict of a jury.

My mother had already made up her mind. "Do

you think you can get on without Kathleen?" she asked my father.

"I must," he answered huskily, "since it will be for her advantage."

He crossed the room, and caught me up in his arms; then releasing me, he looked into my face with a concentrated expression of love and sadness, and, kissing me tenderly, he quitted the room without another word.

I understood only too well that look of my father's. I had been his companion in his walks and rides; I had written most of his letters for him; I had often read aloud to him (he would let no one read to him but me). Never were father and daughter more fondly attached to each other.

CHAPTER THE SECOND.

A BRUTAL MURDER.

> Dost thou desire to contemplate
> A band of faithful witnesses
> Of truths high, holy, and sublime?
> Behold them in the Sister Isle,
> God's heroes, stewards—ministers
> Of holy mysteries divine,
> Once owned as such in other years.
> This century, into life scarce warmed,
> Has seen them robbed, or starved, or slain;
> Abandoned—not by open foes,
> That were less bitter, but by those
> The sworn defenders of their order,
> Of contracts, coronation oaths,
> And treaties, all oblivious.

WITHIN the hour, my father's attention was painfully diverted from me, and from his regrets at my coming separation from him.

A horrible tragedy had been enacted in the parish: For some months past the anti-tythe agitation had been so effectively carried on, that it had become necessary to employ Process-servers throughout a great part of Ireland.

There was such an unusual uproar in our hall, and such loud voices, that we were all attracted thither.

Policemen had brought two prisoners whom they arrested on suspicion of having been engaged with others in a brutal murder, and they were accompanied by such witnesses as they could collect to support the charge.

The murdered man was a process-server. He had been engaged to serve a notice upon a farmer in our parish. It had transpired that the notice *was to be served*, and *when*. On his proceeding to execute his task, a number of labourers at work in the adjoining fields, on a preconcerted signal, rushed on him, and beat him with spades, forks, and bludgeons till his head was a smashed mass of flesh, bone, blood, and brains.

The wife's grief was terrible to witness; her eyes were fixed and glassy; her face whiter than any sheet; her hands clenched, as if no force could ever separate them; she did not speak—she did not seem to hear or understand when spoken to.

Poor thing! she had been brought in order to give evidence as to the identification of the body. Identification! why, there was nothing to identify him by but such fragments of torn and blood-sodden clothes as still stuck to him, and his watch—even that was battered to a metal lump.

My mother saw in a moment that our hall was no place for her, and taking her by the arm she led her unresisting into the morning-room, in the hope of being able to soften and console her.

As for me, I crept quietly back into the hall, which had a strange fascination for me—with those policemen and those two hand-cuffed prisoners.

The hall was always used by my father as the place for magisterial business. I never before had the curiosity to be there, and I should never have been allowed. Now, every one was too occupied, and too awed, to notice me.

While my father was making out the commitments, our Rector, Mr Ingram, rushed in; he was in great agitation; his first words were, " It's my doing; I am the murderer."

Every one must have been as electrified as myself, —our gentle, kind-hearted, truly Christian clergyman a murderer !

My father only said, " Be calm, Mr Ingram, and explain yourself."

" Sir, if I had not given the order to serve the notice for driving the land, the man would not have been murdered. Whatever it may be in the eye of the law, I feel that, in the sight of God, that man's blood is on my head."

" I do not know that you could have done otherwise," said my father, " still it might have been better to wait a little."

"Despair drove me to it; no, it was a wicked distrust of God's providence,—*how wicked* I now see. Wait? Mr Rochford. Why, I have waited and waited. There are three half-years' tithes now due to me. I have nothing but the tithes to subsist on; they are our whole support. For weeks and months past we have been little short of starving; and we have carefully concealed it from every one. Do I look the man I was a year ago? Do my wife's and daughters' pinched faces and shrunken figures tell no tale? But O, if I could have foreseen this,—if I could but have dreamed of it,—we would still have gone on waiting, and would have committed ourselves to Him who feeds even the young ravens which call on Him."

CHAPTER THE THIRD.

EXTENUATING CIRCUMSTANCES ! ! !

"Ille meos primus qui me sibi junxit amores
Abstulit: ille habeat secum servetque sepulcro."
Virgil, Æn. iv.

"Ubi idem et maximus et honestissimus amor est, aliquanto præstat morte jungi quam vita distrahi."—*Valer. Max.*

WAS I hard-hearted? I hardly think so; for I sobbed so bitterly while Mr Ingram was speaking, that my father at last turned round, and finding who it was, ordered me rather sternly to leave the hall.

But was I not light-hearted? I fear I was. For I had not closed the door two minutes before I quite forgot the painful scene I had witnessed—forgot the policeman and the prisoners — forgot Mr Ingram's miserable tale of distress, of which we had not the least suspicion. I even forgot all about my mother, and never went to see whether she had succeeded in calming the murdered man's widow.

All my thoughts were engrossed by the prospect of the great change in my position. Visions of beautiful dresses, and of balls, and of the delights of society of which my sisters were for ever talking, and of the sensation I should create, and of the attentions which would be paid me, swept across my silly mind. I was so full of happy expectations that I felt I could not keep them to myself. Mildred and Aileen had never admitted me to any of their confidences; they always called me a child, and they treated me as such. I verily believe I should have set up my cat on a chair, and opened my heart to her, and accepted her purrings as genuine congratulations, had I not suddenly recollected Miss Anstey Costello. There was a sympathetic feeling between us, spite of the disparity of our ages: she had confided her griefs to me, why should I not my joys to her?

She and her brother lived together in a pretty cottage about a mile off. During the whole way I was full of my happy lot—not one single thought of the dreadful events of the morning.

"You have come to tell me," said Miss Anstey Costello, "of this affair about which every one is talking. They say that some men have been taken up to Justice Rochford's."

A sudden pang struck through me. How could I, in my selfish gratification, have forgotten the miseries of others?

"Indeed, Miss Anstey Costello, I am ashamed to

confess that it is only about something concerning myself I have come to you."

"Tell me first about this event which some will call murder, and others the wild justice of revenge."

I gave her all the particulars as I had been able to gather them from the proceedings before my father.

"It is very shocking, but still there is something to be said on the other side," remarked Miss Anstey Costello.

"On the other side!" I exclaimed in indignant surprise. "Why, what *can* be said for those who commit a horrible murder of an innocent man, or for those who hound the murderers on?"

"Is there nothing to be said for the poor farmers who have their hard earnings wrung from them in order to enrich a heretical church?"

"It is not the farmers who pay, but the land which they hire on the condition of paying the tithes; and our Rector has as much right to the tithes as my father has to his rents."

"It does not matter much whether it is they who pay or the land: it comes to the same thing—the money is wrung from them."

"Oh, Miss Anstey Costello! just remember the language which was used before the passing of the Emancipation Act. Did not your Bishops say that such a measure, once passed, would put an end to all agitation, and that all classes would be bound together by the bonds of peace and good will?"

"All I can say is this—if they did say so, they were either traitors to their Church and Country, or liars in the sight of God. But we will talk of something more pleasant—yourself. Tell me what you have to say about yourself."

I related all that had taken place; how my aunt had proposed as it were to adopt me, and how my parents had consented, though not without a struggle with their own feelings; and how delighted I was at the prospect of being no longer treated as a child, and forbidden all expectation of being introduced into society till either Mildred or Aileen was married.

"Waiting for an elder sister's marriage is like waiting for dead men's shoes."

Miss Anstey Costello was silent for a time, then she took both my hands: "Yes, Kathleen, I do congratulate you. I can go back to the time when I was your age and had all the happy expectations you now are having. May your road not be the thorny one which I have travelled along since then."

Tears trickled down her poor, pale, thin cheeks; they did not fall on account of the past only, for she went on: "What shall I do without you? Mildred and Aileen seldom come to see me, and, when they do, they do not cheer me; they have no hearts to sympathise with me."

I ventured to whisper, " Have you forgiven General Lake?"

" No, Kathleen. I have prayed to be able to forgive, and I have imposed on myself harder penances than my Confessor has either enjoined or known of; but the grace has not yet been granted me."

" So long since! And have you never considered that he only did a soldier's stern duty?"

" Long since indeed; but the deed is always present to me. No fresh love ever did, or could, take the place of that which was crushed out of me."

" What! leave the world in an unforgiving spirit! Do you not fear——," and I hesitated.

" I know what you would say. You would remind me that in such a case, according to the doctrine of my church, a fiery expiation awaits me. I have thought of that. I may be surprised before I have attained the grace of forgiveness, and I have made provision accordingly. You know that my brother and I are the last of a family who once held the whole of the Kilkreen estate. The very small portion which we still call ours was all that was spared to our ancestors when *they* were expelled and *yours* were intruded by Cromwell. My brother and I have agreed that, on the death of either, the survivor shall sell our house and three hundred acres, giving your father the option of purchasing them, as he has often wished, for the purpose of making his estate complete. The produce is to be invested, and the survivor will be maintained on the interest yielded by the investment. On the survivor's death the principal will be devoted to religious uses, principally to masses for the repose of our souls."

" But why should the survivor leave the home of a life-time ? "

" Because your law of mortmain prevents the devise of any portion of God's *earth* to His service."

As she was entering on a subject in which I could not follow her, I put my arm round her waist caressingly, and said, " Dear Miss Anstey Costello, till that day in the hay-field, I used to wonder why you always turned away in disgust from strawberries."

" Apples of Sodom—grapes of Gomorrah ! "

CHAPTER THE FOURTH.

AUNT EVIE.

THE decision once made, no time was lost in carrying it into effect. By the same day's post a letter was despatched, accepting the offer made by my Uncle and Aunt Haughton.

I was to have an allowance of £30 a year for my dress, which my aunt was to expend for me. Besides, I was to start with a suitable supply of dresses and other articles of toilette, my mother being anxious that my first appearance should create a favourable impression. She had no notion of any daughter of her's needing to be apologised for.

To young ladies of the present day £30 a year may appear a paltry sum—barely sufficient for boots and gloves. But when I was started in life there were not the numerous entertainments, in-doors and out-doors, requiring, as now, toilettes so many and so varied. There were no garden parties, afternoon teas, croquet and archery meetings; there were no bazaars nor fancy fairs for charitable purposes, where ladies preside at stalls or itinerate about the room. It was not usual then for owners of good houses to throw them open for artistes to exhibit in before paying audiences, or for the holding of raffles for objects philanthropic or personal. Neither was the quantity of material amply sufficient for *two* dresses massed into *one*, in defiance of classical grace and the proper development of the natural form. My allowance, therefore, judiciously expended, was quite enough to answer all reasonable demands.

There was no great cordiality between my mother and Aunt Evie—"Miss Rochford senior," as she always introduced her to strangers. The designation was obnoxious to my aunt, as some people afterwards addressed her as "Miss Senior," and some even took the liberty of asking her whether she had taken the name of Senior upon coming into a large property.

There was no other cause of my mother's want of cordiality for Aunt Evie than this,—the Kilkreen estate was burdened to the amount of £12,000 settled on my aunt, of which she had the disposal by will, and on which, during her life, six per cent. interest was to be paid by my father. "As if it were not enough for the old gentleman to have gambled away the family jewels, without charging the estate with such an unconscionable sum as £12,000 for the benefit of a single woman!"

Whatever grievance this might be to my mother, she took good care to keep it to herself, and show no trace of it to her sister-in-law. As it would be the height of impolicy to give any offence to so important a person as one who had the sole power of disposition of £12,000, we were all brought up to pay great respect and attention to aunt Evie.

Since Eveleen's marriage and settling in the north of Ireland, my aunt had transferred to me the substantial proofs of affection which she had been in the habit of bestowing on her.

On the day fixed for taking leave of her before going to Waterford, my father drove me into Landford, and deposited me at her door, engaging to call for me in an hour. I found my aunt sitting bolt upright in front of the fire. The day was raw and chilly, and she had enveloped herself in a handsome Indian shawl—its soft texture causing it to fall in those graceful folds which no other than an Indian Cashmere can assume. To my aunt it was particularly becoming, concealing as it did the angularities of her spare figure, and enlivening her sombre surroundings. The furniture of her sitting-room was that which had been turned out of our house at Kilkreen by my mother, when she was installed as its mistress. By its associations it was sacred to aunt Evie, and she had taken it at a valuation. It was not "old trumpery" to *her* and *her mother*, whatever it might be to her brother's wife; and it was removed to the house which she had chosen for her residence at Landford.

I wondered why aunt Evie, who was so scrupulous in applying every article to its legitimate use, kept making her pocket handkerchief do duty for a handscreen. In time I detected the little manœuvre—it was that she might wipe away the tears that would involuntarily gather in her eyes.

It was one of Aunt Evie's maxims, which she persistently carried out, that dwellers alone—especially single ladies—ought to control their emotions, and should never yield to what are popularly called low spirits, which are generally the reaction of violent excitement. The old-fashioned cupboard in her sitting-room was no secret receptacle for decanters of Port or Sherry. Where no weeping was indulged in, no access to wine was needed. Giving way to the one is too often followed by having recourse to the other, and it requires no Seer to foretell what the end must be.

"Ah, Kathleen, coming to say good-bye?" and she described a semicircle with her handkerchief, brushing as it were accidentally her eyes in its course.

Medical practitioners tell us that in some disorders there exists so much acidity in the system, that, until *that* is expelled, there is no use applying direct measures for the cure of the disorder itself. It was morally so with my Aunt. Before she could bring herself into a state for kindly conversation, she must get rid of the acid sensations which had been generated by my Aunt Haughton's letter. She had been keen enough to detect at once that her Niece's advantage was not the sole nor the principal motive for the invitation—she had not the least doubt that there would be as much expected from as would be conferred on me; and, since no one else would, she would herself disillusionise me.

"Well, Kathleen, I hope you will give satisfaction to your Employers, and that you will, on trial, prove such a convenient drag on the wheels of time as to cause them to run their course smoothly and imperceptibly. Your cousin Geraldine's interests, at all events, will not suffer by her Father having to pay your milliner's bills; and no doubt your Aunt will soon find that the young monkeys to whom she alludes in her letter will pay their respects to her at other than feeding times."

I confess I was considerably taken down by the picture thus unexpectedly drawn of the position I was to hold in my new home. I had not reckoned upon being hired to play the part of a decoy-duck. Happily with this outbreak my Aunt's acidity was exhausted, and she soon launched out upon the pleasant part of the prospect which awaited me.

"You will have a happy life in Waterford. Naturally your Uncle and Aunt will make much of you, as you will render the house more lively, as well as attractive to the younger generation. You will have your harmless little flirtations, and the innocent amusements which fall to the lot of a popular young girl. You will meet in Society many friends of my youth, whom I have lost sight of for years and years; and you will not fail, when you write to me, to mention those who, reminded of me by your name, make inquiries after me."

"Mamma had a letter from Aunt Haughton this morning, in which she says that the young Marquis of Waterford is going to give a ball, and she has asked the Agent to send an invitation to me."

"What! the wild Marquis? It is a capital opportunity for your making your *début*."

"The great heiress, Miss Carmichael, is to make her's, so I shall be quite eclipsed, Aunt Evie."

"There will be partners enough and room enough for you both to dance in the same set, so you need not trouble yourself about that. There is no doubt of Miss Carmichael being a genuine heiress; most probably she is the only heiress the country possesses, as there is only one Duke it can boast of. She is singular in there being no mortgage nor incumbrance of any kind on her estate, which has had the benefit of her long Minority."

"Perhaps the young Marquis may fall in love with her——or her property."

"Not at all likely, my dear. He would not choose her for her beauty, and he is too rich himself to care for her wealth. He can afford to marry where he likes; and, as the fashion of marrying Actresses has gone out with the decline of the Drama, the chances are that he will marry one of his own rank."

I here recognised the step of my Father's hunter which he had lately put into harness, and I knew that the high-spirited animal would not bear waiting. I started up. My Aunt's arms were flung around me. Poor aunt Evie, determined to the last to repress all outward emotion if she could, upon releasing me busied herself in extracting from her purse a fresh crisp ten pound Bank of England note, which she hurriedly placed in my hand, kissed me, and prayed God to bless me.

The tears I wiped away were not all *my own*; some of *her's* were mingled with them, drawn forth at that last kiss—it was her *last*, we never met again.

CHAPTER THE FIFTH.

MY MOTHER.

"O who can sound the deep
And living sources of a mother's love!"

THE distance between Kilkreen and Waterford was about fifty miles, and was to be accomplished in one day. My Father was to take me as far as Kheveen, a small town with an Inn, where my Uncle's carriage was to meet us.

"There are two things I especially detest," said my Father, "combined movements, and being sent for. Some hitch invariably occurs in the best formed arrangements; if the coachman is punctual, the harness is found at the last moment to be out of gear, or a linch-pin has come out and can't be found, or one of the horses has gone lame—nobody knows how or why. Nevertheless, Kathleen, you have your Father to escort his young Princess as far as the boundary line which separates his county from that of her Uncle's."

Mildred and Aileen accused me of having no heart, because I was not for everlasting bursting into tears on the least provocation during the last week of my being at home. My Mother's large-hearted experience made all due allowance for my apparent indifference. How could it be expected that I should be sad and sorrowful on the threshold of a career in which I was to take my place as an only daughter, instead of remaining in the humble rank of the youngest of three.

My Mother's counsel to her daughter on entering life was pithy and practical,—to omit on no account my private prayers morning or evening,—to read a chapter in the Bible every day,—to take care of my health,—to be tolerant of the eccentricities and peculiarities of my Uncle and Aunt,—never to repeat to one person what another had said in dispraise,—and to be very cautious with whom I flirted, as a silly flirtation often ended in a foolish marriage; "there is much to be borne," she added, "and much to be suffered in this world, but the worst thing that can befal our sex is an unhappy marriage."

The last day which I passed at Kilkreen fled quickly away, in making my final preparations, and in taking leave of my village favourites and domestic pets. I patted the horses, caressed the dogs, and nursed the cats; and when night came, and Mildred and Aileen had given me their parting embraces, I went to bed exhausted in body and mind.

As we were to start early the next day, my Mother

arranged that I should go to her room when I was equipped and ready for the journey, that we might spend the last few minutes together alone.

On entering her room I found my mother dressed, but lying down on her bed, with her face turned toward the door that she might catch the very first glimpse of me. "Lie down beside me, Kathleen," she said; and my head was in a moment on her bosom, and both her arms were fondly clasped round me.

"My words of counsel and advice have already been spoken; my latest words must be words of love only, they may be the last words you will hear from my lips," and her voice faltered. "Kathleen, you will not forget me?"

"O never, never," I sobbed.

"Kathleen, I wish you to feel that parting with you is a great sacrifice to me. All the precious remembrances of endearing childhood seem to be clustered round you, my youngest born. In resigning you to others, I have had only your interests in view. The claims of Mildred and Aileen upon my time and care compelled me to leave you too much to yourself. Often and often, when visiting with them, my heart has leaped back to you. The clashing interests of her daughters are no small trial to a fond Mother. The time will come when you will understand this."

She was silent; but as I nestled still closer to her I felt the throbbings of her heart.

There was a sound of wheels without.

The time for parting had come.

One passionate embrace,—one long, long, loving kiss, and I was gone.

Kilkreen, as a home, knew me no more.

CHAPTER THE SIXTH.

TO WATERFORD.

> " Tosto
> Il fonte delle lagrime si secca,
> Ma il fiume della gioja abbonda sempre."
> *Guarini, Pastor fido.*

WE had not gone above three or four miles when I was brought to realise the sacrifice which my Father had made in accompanying me half way to Waterford. A sudden turn in the road brought us into the very midst of the Innisfellah Hunt. In a moment our carriage was surrounded.

"By the powers," cried a jovial squire, better known for his kindness of heart than choiceness of expression, "Rochford on a soft cushion instead of a saddle—on such a hunting morning as this!"

"Flying from the country," suggested another.

"Not so bad as that *yet*," said my Father significantly, who knew how irretrievably encumbered his interrogator was.

"At any rate," said Lord Drumsandle, "they will

leave *us* the green acres, though they rob the parsons of their tithes."

"Don't be so sure of that," said my Father, "once set the stone rolling down hill, and where will it stop?"

Innisfellah was a famous hunting county. A good run was expected this morning, and the whole country for miles round had turned out. There were Noblemen, and Squires, and Squireens,—there were Town gentry and Farmers,—there were shoeless gossoons, and ragged beggars. Pink was the prevailing colour, running through every possible shade, from the brilliancy of a first appearance to a nondescript tint of which it would be difficult to detect the origin. The steeds varied as much as their riders—from the faultless thoroughbred down to the most wretched of hacks. Before the end of the day, many horses changed masters; for these Meetings served a double purpose —Hunt first, Horse-fair afterwards. The day-labourers mustered strong; the National love of sport was as strong in *them* as in their betters; and they readily sacrificed their day's wages of Sixpence for a run with the hounds. Lithe, active fellows they were; knowing every inch of the ground as well as the running habits of the fox, and acquainted with all the short-cuts and bye-paths through wood and copse— they would outstrip many a well-mounted rider.

I had let down the window on my side, in order to have a better view of the picturesque scene. A young man, superbly mounted, wheeled round his horse, bringing his face almost on a level with mine. I hastily drew back.

"You see by my side," said my Father, "the cause of my not being with you this morning,—no other than my youngest daughter, whom I am escorting as far as Kheveen on her way to Waterford, where she is going to stay with the Haughtons. My dear," he added, turning to me—"Mr James Lysaght."

"Of course, I shall have the pleasure of meeting Miss Rochford at the Curraghmore Ball; may I hope for the honour of her hand for the first dance?"

I was too bashful to answer, but I suppose my looks did duty for words.

"Booked then," was all he had time to say. The horn sounded; the familiar cry was raised; forward dashed the dogs; and the horsemen, who but a minute before had been conversing in different groups, or quietly walking their horses up and down, were all at once engaged in a headlong promiscuous chace.

For the first part of the journey my Father dosed; waking up at intervals, he looked out and reported to me how many miles we had gone.

The scenery was unvaried and monotonous; stone walls for boundaries and enclosures, with gaps and decaying gates,—badly tilled fields,—pastures overgrown with rushes, from which lean stock were getting but scanty nourishment,—half-ruined slated houses,—thatched hovels with holes in the roof, admitting wind and rain,—such were the dreary and depressing landmarks, so that I was glad to shut my eyes, and revel in the thoughts of the coming Ball, and of the distinguished young man who was to be my partner for the first dance.

When we reached Kheveen, we found my Father's theory respecting combined-movements and being-sent-for happily falsified. My Uncle's carriage was awaiting our arrival. My Father hurried me into it; he evidently thought, as it was to be done, 'twere well if it were done quickly. He was just shutting the door, when I heard him say to himself, "Bless my soul, I had nearly forgotten it," and drawing from his coat pocket a morocco case, he placed it in my hand. When I opened it, I found it to contain a beautiful watch and chain.

From the time I could understand anything, I could recollect my Father's very strong and marked affection for me. I repaid it by a devoted attachment to him. I was never so happy as when I could do anything for him, nor so proud as when he called me his little secretary. It all rushed upon my mind in an instant after his shutting the carriage door, and I sobbed as if my heart would break. At that moment I would have gladly given up smart dresses, and society, and admiration, and balls, and all the Honourable Jameses in the world, only to be once again by his dear side, travelling back to Kilkreen, though it was to return to be a Nobody in the household, and to be elder-sistered over by Mildred and Aileen.

I cried myself to sleep like a child, for after all I was but a child, though for the last hour or two I had fancied that I had blossomed into young-lady-hood.

My Aunt had sent her Maid to be my companion by the way. With that quick insight into others' feelings, and ready sympathy with their distress, which is characteristic of the Irish, she had not interrupted me, but waited till the storm should expend itself; and now, when I awoke, she offered me sandwiches and wine, of which I was very glad in my exhaustion, and before long I regained my usual cheerfulness.

The carriage stopped. My Uncle and Aunt received me with open arms. Before the close of that first evening, I felt instinctively that I had created a favourable impression.

Book the Fifth.

CHAPTER THE FIRST.

AN EVENTFUL SUNDAY.

"I have not seen such a virago."
Twelfth Night, Act iii.
"She'll rail in the street else."
Othello, Act iv.

AMONG the members of the cathedral body at Waterford there was no *esprit de corps;* neither did they regard their ecclesiastical title of sufficient consequence as to "Mr Canon" each other. My Aunt was not of the same opinion; in her ears "Canon" sounded almost as grand as "Baron," and she supposed it must do the same in the ears of others; so when writing to her sister, between whom and herself there had been a long-standing dispute as to the social precedency of their respective husbands, she always designated her's as "the Canon."

The Reverend Canon Haughton was not a popular man. He saved money and invested it, which none of his acquaintances did, consequently he was, financially, a step in advance of his generation. There were few estates in the neighbourhood on which he did not hold a mortgage, and it was a great anxiety during the last decade of his life that there might possibly be some prior mortgages which would take precedence of his own. In religious matters he held with the old High-and-Dry School. He was highly esteemed as a preacher, his sermons being fashioned after those of Dr Blair, then regarded as the model of pulpit eloquence. His superior talents not only entitled him to take the lead in questions relating to the Church, but made him influential with the Laity. House-to-house visitation was neither practised nor expected; it was only on supreme occasions that the ministration of the Clergy were sought for, and then it was always the Rev. Ponsonby Haughton who was the first to be appealed to.

When the wave of Evangelicalism reached Waterford, the religious aspect of the place became altered. The old High-and-Dry opinions and habits were swept away. Earnest men sprang up. Clergymen of fervent zeal and persuasive eloquence hastened to occupy whatever pulpits were opened to them, and in homely and powerful language—hitherto unheard in Waterford—they denounced the indifference, lukewarmness, and worldliness of all ranks, and enforced the obligation of personal piety, heart-worship, and a devoted life.

The Rev. Ponsonby Haughton was fitted neither by feeling and disposition, nor by the habits of his previous life and study, to ride on the wave and direct its course. Thus his ministerial popularity declined, his polished but cold pulpit harangues no longer attracted, his prestige and influence waned.

To one who was both vain and proud, the descent from the eminence which he had so long held in public estimation—deservedly held too—was galling indeed. He had a ready wit, which too often took the satirical turn and naturally made him enemies. His memory at the age of sixty, when I first became an inmate of his house, was wonderfully accurate and retentive. He was never at a loss for a name, date, or locality. He was kind, but not generous to me. I liked and respected him in a half-and-half way, but I never could love him.

My Aunt had been a beauty, and was in a wonderful state of preservation. Her personal charms are best described by negatives. Her figure stopped short of *embonpoint*. Her complexion was neither fair nor dark. Her hair was without a silver thread, and of that peculiar shade of a filbert before it has attained its full ripeness. No feature prominently stood out, courting attention. When I looked at her *tout ensemble*, I could hardly conceive how she could have a married daughter, and how any day's Post might announce to her that she was a grandmother. She took to me at once, and very soon I came to love her, though, spite of her affection for me, she sometimes gave way to caprices of temper which sorely tried me; a capricious temper is indeed a trial even to the most equable.

My arrival in Waterford being on a Saturday, my first public appearance was at the next Morning's Cathedral Service. My Uncle had a pew in the Gallery appropriated to the members of his family, from which an uninterrupted view of the whole Church could be obtained. On this particular Sunday curiosity had drawn an unusually large congregation. A new Sect, fanatical in principle and rigid in conduct, had sprung up from within the Quaker Body, bearing the name of White Quakers. Their leader had given out that he, with a select party of his followers, intended to be present at the Morning Service, and to bear public testimony against the abomination of chanting and singing. The Dean, who was well versed in Ecclesiastical Law, arranged his measures for meeting the proposed intrusion.

When my Aunt and I entered the Cathedral Square, we found it filled with excited groups. The Building occupied by the White Quakers was in a narrow street debouching into the Square, though the main entrance to it was in the Square itself. A double line of spectators had been formed from this entrance all the way to the Cathedral to see the issuing forth of the procession.

We had not been long seated in our pew before a low hum and a shuffling of feet announced the entrance of the White Quakers. There were about a dozen of them, male and female, walking two and two. The men wore white cloth coats with capes and wide sleeves, their arms folded across their chests; and they had low-crowned, broad-brimmed, white felt hats on their heads. The women were in long white cloaks, white stockings and shoes. The verger showed them into a large pew in the middle aisle, where they sate, with downcast eyes, perfectly motionless. Directly after, the Cathedral Clergy and Choir, with the Dean bringing up the rear, entered and took their accustomed places. The Dean made a sign to the verger, and in a voice low but so clear as to be heard throughout the church said, " Order those men to take off their hats."

The verger walked leisurely to the pew,—" Gentlemen, the Dean orders you to take off your hats." In a moment every hat was removed. The Service began, and continued without any interruption until the chanting of the Jubilate, when the whole body of the White Quakers, who had till then remained sitting, rose simultaneously, and their leader in a loud voice protested against the profanation of God's worship by singing-men.

The Dean's voice was again heard: "Turn out those men who are brawling in Church."

The array of vergers and lay-clerks, determined on carrying the Dean's order into execution, was too formidable for any effectual resistance being made. The White Quakers were compelled to retreat, the vergers in their rear, while the Charity boys, whose place was in the aisle, found amusement in quiet kicks at their ankles, or attempts at tripping them up. They finished, or rather attempted to finish, their testimony in the Square, amid the hootings and derisive cheers of a motley mob.

My Uncle and Aunt took me to the Deanery after the Service. We were scarcely seated when a lady and a little girl were hurriedly ushered in. They were Mrs George Wyse and her daughter Winifred a beautiful interesting child of about twelve years old. Mrs Wyse was hardly able to speak from agitation, while the child clung to her mother, sobbing. As soon as she regained her self-possession, Mrs Wyse explained the cause which had compelled her to seek the shelter of the Deanery. She and Winifred were on their way home from visiting a sick friend, when Madame Bonaparte Wyse, who was driving past, ordered her coachman to stop.

"She overwhelmed me," said Mrs Wyse, "with violent invectives; she accused me of being the cause of the unhappiness between her and her husband, and of doing all in my power to bring about a separation between them. She threatened to expose me publicly, as she had already done privately. As I hurried on in order to escape from her, she made her coachman keep pace with me, while she went on showering on me the most scandalous accusations. Your door was my only hope of escape. Now, you know why I am here; and I cannot tell how long I must remain here—if you will keep me—as she threatened to wait till you turned me out, as she had not finished with me."

Mrs George Wyse was a general favourite, and she had the sympathy of the whole party. The Dean and his wife assured her that she was welcome to remain as long as she pleased.

"She will try and force her way into the house when she finds I will not come out," cried Mrs Wyse hysterically.

"That is easily prevented," said the Dean; and he rang the bell, and gave strict orders that Madame Bonaparte Wyse should not be admitted on any account.

I, aged seventeen, and Winifred Wyse, aged twelve, were presumed to be unfit hearers of a discussion on the manners and moralities of an Italian Princess; so we were sent off into the morning room. The windows of the room looked into the Cathedral Square, and there, before the Deanery entrance, we saw Madame Bonaparte Wyse standing up in the carriage holding the reins, while both coachman and footman were going up the steps to the hall door.

Her profile was turned to us : it was the very perfection of classical outline ; and, when she suddenly turned her full face, I was perfectly startled by its beauty. Her turbulent nature looked out of her large full eyes, while the rich colouring of her Southern blood alternately rushed into and receded from her cheeks. Her crimson velvet bonnet was worn far back on her head, and the dark masses of her hair were disposed in a style which none other than an Italian woman dare venture on.

Her intention evidently was to rush into the house as soon as the door was opened, and to further insult Mrs George Wyse in the presence of the Dean's family.

The butler had stationed himself at the open window of the Dean's Library, which was on a level with the hall door.

Rat-tat-tat—tat-a-tat—rat-a-tat—tat-a-tat.

" What are ye afther, boys ?—are these your forrin manners ? " cried the butler.

" Open de door," screamed Madame.

"I'm awaiting for orders, your Royal Highness," said the butler, with comic civility.

"Won't I smash your ugly face for you, you grinning rascal, when I have the chance," said the footman, again rapping at the door.

"Get the chance first, and then see whether you can do it: at any rate, it's a purtier face than your own."

Again a thundering rapping at the door.

"Your Princess will be a-larning to cool her hot blood, if she keeps there much longer, I'm a-thinking," was the butler's answer to the rapping.

Either the cold, or the evident hopelessness of forcing an entrance, caused Madame to toss her head in the direction of the driving-box; she impetuously flung the reins into the coachman's hands, and throwing herself back in the carriage, was driven off, and was soon out of sight.

"Do pray tell me who is Madame Bonaparte Wyse, and what her history is?" I asked my Uncle and Aunt as we were sitting over the fire in the evening.

"She is the daughter of Lucien, Prince of Canino, brother of the late Emperor Napoleon," answered my Uncle. "Mr Wyse, when travelling in Italy, visited her Father. He was struck by her beauty, he might have been ambitious, too, of an alliance with the Bonaparte family, he made her an offer of marriage, and was accepted."

"And a more unsuitable match there could hardly be," said my Aunt.

"The husband," proceeded my Uncle, "is reserved in manner, quiet in habits, and devoted to study. He has high political aims, and since he has become Member of Parliament for this City, a career is opened for him of which he will not fail to take advantage. His great acquirements, his classical and artistic tastes, and his perfect mastery of modern languages, mark him out for some high diplomatic post, for which he is eminently fitted."

"And meanwhile," interrupted my Aunt, "Madame complains that she is neglected; that her husband is shut up all the day long in his study; that she has no society such as she has been used to, and that she is devoured with ennui. The fact is, she can only exist in some Continental Capital, or some fashionable foreign resort."

"Now you see, Kathleen," said my Uncle, pointing the moral, "what comes of an ill-sorted marriage."

"Has she any children?" I asked.

"Two boys," said my Aunt; "but I fear that her love for them does not reconcile her to an uncongenial life. There is another cause of provocation; she complains of the devotion of Mr Wyse to his own family, who are fond and proud of him, and naturally take his side against her."

"Sad stories are told of her ungovernable violence," said my Uncle, "of which we have had an example to-day; I can see nothing for it but separation."

"And what will follow?" asked my Aunt. "Her life will be wrecked. Deprived of a husband's protection, her beauty will expose her to temptations very difficult to resist. Such is woman's hard lot. A man who swears never to forsake his wife till death parted them, will not make the least sacrifice for the woman he marries, though a singularly handsome woman, an Italian, and a Bonaparte!"

"Tom Wyse, M.P., is not the man to sacrifice his ambition and the prospects of a political career for any woman on earth—whether Bonaparte or Bourbon."

"You are right," said my Aunt, "it is not in his nature. At the same time, though we cannot respect this poor creature his wife, we must pity her for being doomed to such an unfortunate lot."

How any one so handsome, so beautifully dressed, and a princess too, could, under any circumstances, be an object of pity, was a perfect enigma to me.

CHAPTER THE SECOND.

THE EVANGELICAL WAVE.

" Lo ! God has now a house of prayer
Where Satan had a theatre."
De Foe.

FRONTING the Mall was the Town-hall, a large stone building where the City business was transacted. There was a handsome suite of rooms in which public dinners and balls were held, and where, during the Assizes, the Judges entertained the members of the Bar and the Grand Jury.

Attached to one end was a good-sized theatre. In Waterford's palmy days this theatre was well supported. When the great Tragedians, who trod the London stage, crossed the Channel and starred the Irish provinces, Waterford—as the third city in Ireland — was always visited. But when the Union drained Ireland of her wealthy inhabitants, and they who could not afford London migrated to Bath or Cheltenham, the theatre gradually declined for want of support, and was compelled at last to close its doors.

It was regarded as a crowning victory of Religion over Ungodliness, when the Rev. Randall Coote, the leading Evangelical Clergyman, purchased "the Devil's palace" as the party called it, and converted it into a Chapel. The Boxes and Galleries were removed, the Pit was filled up, and the stage was converted into a platform, on which the Rev. Randall, and other Clergymen, prayed, preached, and expounded to crowded audiences. But the most conspicuous use to which the late Theatre was turned, its special pride and glory, was the Sunday School, which numbered above six hundred children of all ranks and of both sexes. Great pains were taken with the Teachers, who met twice a week to receive directions and instruction from their Clerical Chief. Most of them were thoroughly devoted to their work for the work's sake. There were a few in whom a little vanity and love of display would peep out, when —in conducting their class—they were surrounded by an outer circle composed of their fashionable friends, who, though making no "Profession," were not unwilling to hear the Rev. Randall Coote's utterances as filtered through the lips of a pretty girl who had been "converted."

Strangers, on visiting Waterford, were always taken to the Town-Hall Sunday School, as one of the great institutions of the city.

To be a Teacher was a mark of distinction. Calvin was not more stern in his denunciation of worldly amusements, nor more resolute in enforcing on Geneva his strict code of laws, than was the Rev. Randall Coote in carrying out the rules and regulations which he drew up for the guidance of the Sunday School teachers. Balls, dances, and public entertainments of every kind, were utterly forbidden. If any Teacher were guilty of a violation of this prohibitory law, there would be no lack of tale-bearers to report the offence. The punishment followed swiftly. The next Sunday, on proceeding to take her accustomed seat, the offender would find it occupied by another. No notice of dismissal would be sent beforehand, a public degradation being considered the right method of applying the Apostolic order—" them that sin rebuke before all, that others also may fear." There was no respect of persons : even the daughters of the Bishop of the Diocese though religious and ready to join in every good work were excluded from being Teachers on account of their refusal to withdraw from the society of " the world."

It was not an unmixed good which was produced by the introduction of " the New Light," or, as it was contended, " the Old Light snuffed." In proportion as congregations became accustomed to extempore prayers and preachings in other than consecrated buildings, which—being contrary to Ecclesiastical Law —had to be announced as "Gospel Lectures or Expositions," Church Principles declined, Church Order was neglected, and reverence for sacred edifices (which never had any strong vitality in Ireland) was in danger of dying out altogether.

For a time the authority of the Rev. Randall Coote was paramount. By degrees, however, his severe code became too galling to be borne. Defections began to take place. The earlier fallers-away were branded as "apostates from the faith," but others followed in such respectable numbers that this hard term lost all its terror. In some instances continued attendance on the ministrations and the continued use of the phraseology of the Party remained, while there was a return—with keener relish—to worldly conformity. The mild dissipation of tea-drinkings—and the tame excitement of Missionary meetings—which had their attractions under the first impulse of a newly-awakened zeal—became tasteless and insipid; and Mothers began to find that they were not only not conducive to the best matrimonial interests of their daughters, but were actually likely to lead to unsuitable alliances. It was no great sacrifice for Mothers to renounce "worldly" society, as long as their daughters were in the school-room; but, on their emerging from it, it was impossible for

P

them to be confined within the narrow limits—and the low standard, both in birth and education, of the " Religious" circle : they returned, therefore, to the Society and amusements of their friends and equals.

That there were good, and earnest, and pious men engaged in this religious revolution,—that they succeeded in impressing many with a serious sense of personal responsibility who had never given a thought to their spiritual state,—cannot be denied ; but it was at the expense of creating much spiritual pride and censorious judgment, and of causing much discord and disunion in families.

Not the least part of the evil was the destruction of much of the wholesome quiet influence of Clergymen of far superior learning, and of equal but less active and obtrusive piety. Whether it was from timidity or dislike of noisy demonstration, or whether it was from a settled conviction that the hard soil was not to be broken up by the thunderbolt—but by patient unobserved tillage, these men did not—and it was a matter of lamentation that they did not—unite in taking their post in the van of the religious movement, and thus have *led* instead of being borne down by it.

The remissness of those who stand on the defence is proverbial; but perhaps it is shown nowhere so much as in Ireland. There is an impossibility almost of organising a steady and resolute opposition to any active aggression, theological or political. It was so on the Educational question. Had the Protestant Clergy and Laity heartily united together and determined either to maintain their own Schools without Government aid and to make up by their subscriptions the deficit caused by the withdrawal of the Government Grant from the Kildare Society, or else to throw themselves heartily into the Government plan of the National Board of Education, the Roman Catholics would not have been left—as they were— to monopolise almost the whole annual Parliamentary Grant, and, with it, the education of the masses.

The only party who have ever fought boldly and persistently—and therefore successfully, though against tremendous odds—have been the hardy Orangemen of the North of Ireland. They have been menaced, imprisoned, and fined; Acts have been passed for the suppression of their Lodges, Meetings, and Processions; yet they have triumphed. On the morning of the eighteenth of December, of glorious memory, the gates of Derry are closed, the bells ring out, the Orange flag waves from the Cathedral tower, the " 'Prentice Boys" throng the sacred building to hear a stirring discourse on the valour and patriotism of their forefathers: the celebration of the great historical event of the day is carried out with unabated enthusiasm and unmaimed rites.

CHAPTER THE THIRD.

THE WIDOW MOLLOY.

"God forgive me, I am not inclined, I must say,
To go and sit still to be preached at to-day."

IT was a dreary morning which ushered in the day on the evening of which the ball at Curraghmore was to take place.

The Cathedral chimes, followed by the Clock striking Eight, awoke me. It was still twilight, but through the dawn I could see the snow careering along in eddying whirls. A sudden fancy drove me out of bed, which I proceeded at once to carry out with great courage in spite of the fireless grate, the carpetless floor (such were the hardy habits of those times), and the thick coating of ice in the water jug. My fancy was to rehearse my part in the evening performance. The candles were soon lighted, the large looking-glass removed from the dressing-table to the floor, and in a semi-attire of silk stockings and white silk 'slip,' and, supported by an imagined arm, I was valsing round and round the limited space of my room. In the midst of my great achievement upon which I was complacently priding myself, — the curtsey in the Lancers, I was startled by Mrs Molloy's voice, who had entered unobserved with the hot water, "I was wondthring, Miss Kathleen, however you were to get up from your sate on the floor. It's the fairies that must have helped ye. But, bless me, only look at those mould-fours guttering down there! What will the Misthress say if they are burnt out afore ye are dressed for the ball?"

I felt flattered by Mrs Molloy's unconscious testimony to my successful execution of the ascending movement.

"O, the candles! never mind them; I shall not want them above half an hour this evening."

"Half an hour! why, barring the dressing of ye, ye'll be fighting for an hour and more with the hairs of yer head, in taking them down, and rolling them out, and twisting them round, and putting them up again, as sure as my name is Mrs Molloy and was Betsy Carroll."

"An hour or more! I should be ashamed of myself!"

But Mrs Molloy was ready with her proofs. "There was Miss Geraldine; no one could plaise her in the dressing of her hair. I wonder she had any hairs left at all, she tortured them so. An' a divil of a temper she was in all the time because I would not have the pincers hot enough; for, as I used to say to her, 'Miss Geraldine, I said to her, your hair will be quite grey afore the bloom has gone out of yer cheeks or the crows' feet be scratching about yer eyes.' 'That's my husband's look-out,' says she to me. But O, Miss Kathleen, what an aise 'tis to my mind that your hair curls naturally, and don't want no pincers!"

"Mrs Molloy," as she insisted on being called, was a good specimen of an Irish housemaid. Free of speech and full of humour and thoroughly good-natured she was, and obliging, too, provided you trusted her and took her into your confidence. She would take a deep interest in all your concerns, and troubles, and pleasures, and schemes. If you had a flirtation on hand, she would be on the trail of the young man, and soon find out whether he was true to the young lady, or whether he was only given to philandering, or on the look-out for a fortune. A hint would be sufficient to set her on the scent, and she would follow it up until she secured the desired information. Of an evening she exhaled largely the odour of peppermint, and when taxed with using it for the purpose of deceit, she would call all the Saints to witness that she never touched a drop of liquor, that she had a weakness in her inside, and carried a few peppermint lozenges just to warm her up. She never considered that she owed any regular duties to the bed-room over and above making the bed. She was no red-tapist; routine work she persistently resisted; the water jugs were as often empty as filled; you might write a memorandum on the dusty film upon the tables; under the bedstead there was always an accumulation of fluff. When I called her attention to her flagrant disregard of her duties as housemaid, she would break out with an irritable remark, " What's the use, Miss Kathleen, of spying about here and there, and poking your nose everywhere, just like those Englishers who come over and are always finding fault with everything?"

" Though I am no Englisher, any more than you, Mrs Molloy, yet I quite agree with them in thinking cleanliness absolutely necessary for our comfort."

" Then I beg lave to differ with you intirely, Miss Kathleen, and I give you my raisons to boot. What do they do in all the good Catholic Countries? and what's good for them must be good for us. Don't they keep their 'refuge' in their houses as long as they can? And as for what you call claneliness, why, in the holy city of Rome they tell me that all the godly monks and friars have as many fleas on their bodies as hairs on their heads."

"I have heard that Rome was an Augean stable, requiring the efforts of another Hercules to cleanse it."

"Well, I never heard of St Hercules, but I know all about the Stable; why, haven't they the very identical cradle in which the Holy Child laid in the Stable? An' isn't it in the grand Churches that the wives are telling their beads, and buying and sticking up candles in honour of the blessed Mother of God, and thus making their own souls for ever, as well as their husbands' and children's, instead of wasting their precious time in cleaning their houses, which will only get dirty again."

Cleanliness and heresy, dirt and orthodoxy, was the Creed of Mrs Molloy.

Arguing the question with her was quite out of the question, so I made this compact with her;—in consideration of her dusting daily every article of furniture, of filling the jugs and water-bottle, and of ceasing to make the vacant space under the bedstead the grand depository of the sweepings of the floor, she should receive all my left-off wearing apparel; otherwise, it should be divided between my Aunt's maid and the hangers-on of the family.

Mrs Molloy agreed to the terms, which were faithfully carried out on both sides.

Mrs Molloy's husband was a Corporal in a Regiment serving in India. She was perfectly sure he would rise from Corporal to Captain, and she looked forward to the time when she would be "Mrs Captain Molloy." She had no misgivings about becoming qualified for her grand position, for "hadn't she the iligant example of her Misthress—such a beautiful dresser, and such gracious manners? and if she did spake bad of her friends behind their backs, yet wasn't she mighty civil and the raal lady when she spake before their faces?"

Unfortunately, Mrs Molloy's anticipations of coming greatness were suddenly crushed. In the list of the killed at the battle of Sobraon was the name of Corporal John Molloy. The widow's greatest solace under this terrible blow was the wearing the three medals which he had received for his good services. I bought some black ribbon to hang them on, and she insisted on my arranging them so as to depend, in Chatelain fashion, on her left side,—his large silver watch she wore on the right side,—so that, as she explained, whichever way she turned her head, she could be reminded of her John.

On the arrival of the intelligence of her husband's death, Mrs Molloy was allowed to go and stay with her sister, the wife of a small farmer, within walking distance of us. My Uncle used often to take me there, and after the usual salutation "Well, Mrs Molloy, how are you to-day?" he would leave me with her for half an hour. During his absence I used to try my powers to rouse her from the stupor of her grief; and though the means I employed might be condemned by some as irrelevant and even trifling, they were so far successful as to make her desist from rocking herself to and fro like a Delphian Priestess on her tripod, and from that groaning and crooning which is the usual mode in which violent grief manifests itself among the lower class of Irish. One day she had become almost her former self, and was listening with even a lively interest to what I was telling her, when the wife of the Landlord of the farm entered. In a moment Mrs Molloy's apron was over her head, as it used to be in the first days of her grief, and she returned to her old rocking, and groaning, and crooning.

Mrs Torrens—a no welcome visitor, it was plain— could not have weighed less than eighteen stone. She was fair fat and flabby, and a long walk on a broiling day in July was enough to make her throw herself down on the first seat which came to hand, panting, breathless, and exhausted.

After some minutes spent in fanning and mopping herself, she began—" Mrs Molloy, I hope I find you in a better frame of mind than on my last visit."

The only response was a more vigorous rocking of the stool.

" I am perfectly shocked at you, Widow Molloy.

I do declare you look more like a Heathen than a Christian woman."

Mrs Molloy crossed herself, but did not speak.

Mrs Torrens turned to me—" If such superstitious practices satisfy her, she is not likely to be benefited by what I can say to her."

Mrs Torrens' diagnosis was faulty. How, then, could she touch the root of the disorder, or administer relief under the circumstances when the rich seek an inner chamber to weep and the poor cover their heads! Still she was not disheartened. Like a sanguine Protestant she produced a Bible out of her pocket, and said—" Well, Mrs Molloy, I am going to read you some comforting texts."

I knew this would not mend matters, for the Widow was a rigid adherent of her Church, and had been instructed that if the Protestant Bible was not altogether the Devil's book, it had been so tampered with and corrupted as to inculcate rank and damnable heresy. She used to boast to me that her faith was the old original faith—as old as the Virgin and her Son—as old as the Apostles, and Martyrs, and Popes, and Monks, and Nuns, and Churches, and Monasteries, and Convents; while the Protestant belief was only three hundred years old—the spawn of a renegade and apostate Monk.

" Now, Mrs Molloy, listen attentively to me while

I read you the 90th Psalm;" and she began at the beginning, and went on without any interruption to —" In the morning they are like grass which groweth up; in the morning it flourisheth and groweth up, in the evening it is cut down and withereth."

Here Mrs Molloy drew down the apron from her head, and fixed her eyes intently on Mrs Torrens.

Mrs Torrens was encouraged—at last she had touched the right cord in the Widow's heart.

"I am glad you feel what the Psalmist says, Mrs Molloy; tell me what is the thought that particularly strikes you now."

"Why, my lady, I'm thinking"———

"Well, what are you thinking?"

"Why, my lady, I'm thinking"—and she shook her head very solemnly—"I'm thinking, my lady, that when *ye* are cut down and withered, what a moighty foine haystack ye'll make."

CHAPTER THE FOURTH.

TITHE MASSACRE.

WHEN I entered the breakfast-room I found that some intelligence had painfully excited my Uncle and Aunt.

"What can the English Government be about?" said my Aunt.

"Waiting," said my Uncle, "till this crusade against the Tithes have reached a point imperilling the English hold on the country."

"Another murder?" I asked.

"Another murder!" said my Uncle—"a single murder is a trifle now-a-days." And he read aloud from the *Waterford Mail* the harrowing account of a wholesale massacre of a large body of police, who were guarding some process-servers. They were returning towards Knoctopher, in the adjoining county of Kilkenny, through a narrow pass; suddenly the hills on each side swarmed with men who hurled down great stones on them. Taken at a disadvantage, and having no power of resisting, they rushed forward to gain the open country; but they were confronted at the entrance by another mob armed with guns and bludgeons. It was but a minute's conflict; overpowered by numbers, the whole of that little party were either shot down or beaten to death.

"I do declare," said my Aunt indignantly, "that the Ministry are but puppets in the hand of O'Connell. How the great Agitator must chuckle at the successful progress his 'Agitation' scheme is making for coercing the English Government."

"Surely, Uncle, the English Government would never be so cruel as to sacrifice the rights of our Clergy?"—my thoughts flying back to poor Mr Ingram and his starving family.

"Whatever course they may adopt there can be no question that the Clergy will be plundered to a greater or less extent; it is the old story over again, of the weaker party being allowed to go to the wall."

"I cannot see that the Union has done much for the Established Church," said my Aunt; better to have been killed right out at once than to die by inches, as it is now doing. But do you think there is any chance of the arrears of Tithe being paid?"—she was in daily dread of her husband having to lay down the carriage and horses, and she put the question in some anxiety.

"As for that," replied my uncle, "we shall have to look to the English *people* rather than the English *Government*. Though they are fond of saying that there must be something indigenous to the Clergy of the Irish Established Church which compels their being mutilated, mangled, and murdered, still I don't doubt they will take compassion on our misfortunes. Public Meetings will be held, presided over by Noblemen and Church Dignitaries; Subscription Lists will be opened, headed by wealthy bankers and brewers; and considerable sums will be doled out to the sufferers, from whom everlasting gratitude will be expected. Gratitude indeed! If these charitable folks across the Channel would but shew their charity, by insisting on their Rulers fulfilling the first duty of a good Government, namely, the protection of life and property, and respect for solemnly guaranteed rights, then they would earn and receive our very warmest gratitude."

"Uncle, why do not the landlords insist on their tenants paying the Tithes?" I asked.

"You should have asked that question of your Landlord-papa, Kathleen. If you had done so, I suspect you would have heard some very plausible reasons for the Landlord's non-interference."

"I do now remember hearing Papa say that the odds would be too much against them unless they were supported by the Government, and that if they were to make the attempt they would be exposed to the same fate as the Clergy."

"Your Papa is quite right, my dear. Mark my

words, it will not be many years before the Landlords' turn will come, and there will be a similar crusade against the payment of Rents."

"It strikes me," said my Aunt, "that the Union of the two *Countries* has much the same result as that between an *individual* Englishman and an Irish heiress; her money is abstracted from *her own* country to increase the husband's grandeur and importance in *his*; and when they who are deserted, and therefore impoverished, cry for assistance in their distress, they are answered by a grudgingly-granted Rate-in-aid (to be repaid afterwards by instalments), instead of by a cheerful recognition of their justly-founded complaints. In short, England has got the Principal and grumbles at paying the Interest."

"At all events," said my Uncle, "this resistance to the payment of Tithes will compel me to part with the carriage and horses."

"I don't see the compulsion at all. You speak as if you were dependent on your tithes."

"And, pray, when I apply for my proportion of the fund raised for the relief of the Irish clergy who have been robbed of their property, do you suppose I am going to run the risk of its being thrown in my teeth —that I keep my carriage?"

I knew my Uncle was fond of money and careful in his expenditure; nevertheless, I was amazed to hear him speak of sending in a claim for his proportion of the Fund in question. And, yet, strictly he would have been justified; for, as he argued, since his losses were caused by the truckling policy of the English Government, and their cowardice in not enforcing the pledge given at the Union which secured to the Church of Ireland all her rights and privileges, they were bound in honour as well as in honesty to indemnify him to the utmost.

The threat of laying down the carriage was a bitter pill to my Aunt. Was she—a Canon's wife—to be reduced to the ignominy of a hired yellow Postchaise!

"Why, Kathleen," she said, turning to me, "we shall be as much laughed at as that Mrs Lawrence, who, you remember, was calling here yesterday."

"What for, Aunt?"

"Why, when she hires the yellow Postchaise—the same which your Uncle threatens to condemn me to—she has to cover the inside with a sheet to protect her white satin dress from the greasy lining and the protruding horse-hair."

"Mrs Lawrence in white Satin!" exclaimed my Uncle, lifting up his hands protestingly.

"And why not?" returned my Aunt rather sharply as I thought, but it glanced across me directly that she suspected that an indirect hit was intended against her own style of dress.

"Why not? Why should *Mutton* be dressed after *Lamb* fashion?"

"You surprise me, Ponsonby. It is ungallant for a gentleman to reflect on ladies' ages, and, as a Clergyman, you should remember that, it being so delicate a subject, *only one* woman's age is mentioned in the Bible."

A conjugal storm was blowing up. Happily it was diverted by the butler's entrance,—"A letter, sir, from Lady Brian Croker, — waiting for an answer."

Lady Brian Croker was the wife of one of Ireland's oldest Baronets, from whom she was separated on account of his dissipated habits. She was a devoted follower of the Rev. Randall Coote, an active member of the School Committee, an oracle at the Dorcas and the Maternity Societies' Meetings. Her only daughter, Helen—who had just entered her eighteenth year—had none of her Mother's tastes. She mercilessly criticised the expoundings to which she was taken, she ridiculed the sickly anecdotes told so unctuously at the missionary monthly gatherings, and she denounced all charity Bazaars as impositions, positively refusing to exert her talents in the formation of such useful and artistic wares as bookmarkers, pincushions, dolls' dresses, and clergymen's bands.

Upon Helen's declaring her intention that *she* at least would accept the invitation to the Curraghmore ball, and that she could easily get a Chaperone if her Mother refused to take her, she was overwhelmed with passages of Scripture, which proved most incontestibly that, if she persisted in such a wicked course, her case was that of a backslider verging towards very apostasy, and in imminent peril of everlasting condemnation.

Distressed by these terrible denunciations, which, though she believed them to be perfectly undeserved, she was unable to reply to, she flew for advice to my Uncle, who was by no means disinclined to take up the gauntlet which he considered had really been thrown down by the Rev. Randall Coote. With all possible delicacy, as was demanded by her sex and age, he pointed out to her that neither in language nor in spirit were those passages in the first Chapter of the Epistle to the Romans, and the seventh of the first Epistle to the Corinthians, so applicable to her case as her spiritual denouncers maintained they were; and he severely condemned, as either ignorance or dishonesty, the habit so common among those of a certain Religious School of wresting texts of Scripture from their original purpose and meaning, and applying them to persons and things for which they were never intended.

Lady Brian Croker's Letter.

" Dear Sir,

"I regard it as a sacred duty to protest against the false interpretations you have given to my daughter of those passages of Scripture which clearly declare such worldly amusements as balls, and such ungodly practices as dancing, to be sins, the commission of which must bring exclusion from the Kingdom of Heaven. By your instructions, or rather misinstructions, you are perilling my daughter's salvation, and encouraging her in her rebellion both against her Mother's wishes and the godly counsels of her *evangelical* Pastor, the Rev. Randall Coote. She insists on going to the Curraghmore Ball, and I am unable to prevent her. But while washing my hands of any complicity in the act, it is nevertheless incumbent on me to see that such precedence be accorded to her as befits her birth and rank. Of course you are aware of the great antiquity of our Family, and that Miss Brian Croker is a lineal descendant of the renowned King and Chieftain Brian Boirholme. I understand that the Agent selects the partners with whom the Marquis of Waterford is to dance; and I consider 'I have a right to call upon *You*—as being instrumental in her attending the Ball — to impress on the Agent the claim of my daughter to open the Ball with the Marquis in virtue of her Royal extraction.

"I am, dear Sir, Yours (I wish I could add—in the bonds of the Gospel), Selina Brian Croker."

"*P.S.*—Miss Brian Croker will be chaperoned by Mrs Lawrence, who will give orders to her coachman to keep close behind your carriage, so that they arrive at the same time with you, and accompany your party into the Reception room."

"A *mauvaise alliance* of spiritual intolerance and worldly pride"—was my Uncle's verdict.

"A gross impertinence," said my Aunt. "I am not going to be made a tool of by you, my Lady Brian Croker. If there is anything I especially dislike, it is the entering a ballroom with a tail of unattached petticoats. And in what terms are you going to refuse her request, Ponsonby?"

"Why, ignore it altogether."

"Then her Ladyship will take it for granted that your silence means consent."

"So she may. But Hennessy is not the man to be nursed for ten miles by a yellow Postchaise."

"Only fancy our driving up in company with such a conveyance, and having to listen to the titterings of the Flunkey Plushes on seeing Mrs Lawrence and Helen emerge from their ghastly receptacle,—it will be another version of Miss Pratt alighting from the hearse in the 'Inheritance.'"

CANON HAUGHTON'S ANSWER.

"Dear Lady Brian Croker,

"Your daughter came to me in much perplexity and distress of mind. I forbear recapitulating those passages of Scripture, which—as she told me—had been freely applied to her as a Heathen and Apostate, when she expressed her determination of accepting the invitation to the Ball at Curraghmore. Miss Croker implored me to tell her plainly, whether she would be in danger—if she persisted in going—of bringing upon herself Divine judgments in this world and everlasting perdition in the next. My answer, after explaining to her the condition and practices of the Heathen world at the time the Apostle wrote, and the perfect inapplicability of his language to society as at present constituted, was to this effect—that I could not conceive that the bitterest enemy of the Lord Primate, whom I am to have the honour of meeting this evening at the Ball, would accuse him of acting as High Priest of Baal, nor imagine that the guests at the Supper table could be classed with those who assisted at an idolatrous feast, nor that the female dancers could be tempted by their mothers to follow the example of the daughter of Herodias. I heartily wish my young friend Miss Helen a most pleasant evening ; but I must decline the office of being her Trumpeter, as I expect the Agent would that of being the Herald of her style, title, and dignities. I have the honour to remain, Your unworthy Servant,

PONSONBY HAUGHTON."

CHAPTER THE FIFTH.

THE YELLOW POSTCHAISE.

" Of the past the old man's thoughts are,
And the maiden's of the future."
Hiawatha.

My Aunt was right. Lady Brian Croker had taken my Uncle's silence, in regard to the postscript of her letter, as a sign of consent. When our carriage stopped at our door, there was the yellow Postchaise close behind. While my Aunt was settling herself down into a position, which engrossed two-thirds of the back and half the front seat, I had plenty of time, standing on the door steps, to take in the scene before me. There was a brilliant moon, which made the dry crisp snow along the street and on the house-roofs look as if it had been powdered with diamond fragments.

I was perfectly startled at the first glance I had of the yellow Postchaise with its occupants. Its interior had been lined with a sheet, and there, upright and motionless, sate Mrs Lawrence and Helen Brian Croker, the one in white satin and the other in white silk. In the moonlight they looked like corpses in bridal apparel enclosed in a huge glazed case. I could overhear exclamations far from complimentary from the windows of the houses on each side of us, out of which many a head was thrust out in order to see our turn-out for the Ball. I wonder whether the thought occurred to any of them that we were escorting a pair of Mummies to an Egyptian feast.

The body of the yellow Postchaise might have originally been built for a roomy double Sedan-chair, but—on its proving too heavy for hand transport—it had on a sudden inspiration been put on wheels by the constructor.

The horses, once upon a time, had been dappled greys, the pride of their owner, but age and hard work and neglect had changed their coats into a hue composed of slate, lime, and whitewash.

The harness had once been pliant polished and glittering; it was now hard, cracked, and rotten. It was dangerous to tighten the girths, and it would have been a hazardous attempt to drag the tongue of the rusty buckle into any other hole of the strap than that it was used to.

The Driver wore a dirty stained greatcoat—the possible purchase of some gentleman's roguish coachman, or which had been taken in payment for a score run up for whisky. His lower limbs were encased in a horse-cloth carefully tucked up under them. A grimy greasy woollen wrapper was round his throat and chin and ears, tilting up his smashed hat so far forward that little else could be seen of his ill-favoured countenance than a pair of shaggy eyebrows, cunning deep-set ferretty eyes, and a swollen red nose.

While waiting to take my seat in the carriage, I could hear this wretched Driver apostrophising his whip in no classical terms ; its upper part no longer formed a graceful curve—the nape of its neck being broken, and any attempt at a cheery crack would have separated the two component parts of the whole whip—leaving only the stock in the Driver's hand with which to " prod " the wretched animals whenever they slackened speed.

My Aunt seemed quite unconscious of our elegant appendage, but a low growl of dissatisfaction escaped from my Uncle.

I insinuated myself into the narrow space which had been left for me ; the door was shut with the usual consequential bang ; and off we started—with (as I was conscious) our yellow Tender and its spectral cargo following in our wake.

There was a long silence, which I broke by asking,

"Uncle, is there any connection between Politics and Post-chaises?"

"Very good, Kathleen; your Father will not have to be ashamed of his pupil. There *is* a connection; if England had not *absorbed* the Irish upper classes, we should have had a resident aristocracy with their becoming equipages, and a body of wealthy gentry taking a proper pride in keeping up carriages adapted to their position—very different to that which is hanging on *us*."

"A mark for the jeers of coachmen and postilions all along our route," said my Aunt sourly.

She had, however, taken sufficient precautions against our being involved in these jeers, as she had sent her Maid with a message in the morning to Hennessy the coachman, that he was to break loose directly from any yellow Postchaise which might attempt to tack itself on him.

"Tell the Misthress," was his answer, "she may make herself quite aisy; I know better what is due to the raal quality, than to take in tow any divil of a Po-shay with its sorry Screws and tatterdemalion Driver."

"It is just nine years," soliloquised my Uncle. "since our last visit to Curraghmore. Poor old Marquis—what a sad sufferer he was from the gout! how often he said to me that he envied the men who were waiting on him, as they never failed of getting a good night's rest, and he never had one."

My Aunt had her soliloquy—" there never was any Plate on the dinner table; of course they must have had plenty; why was it not produced?"

"Don't you remember," said my Uncle, "how the sailing vessel went down in mid-channel with their Plate-chest on board — valued at seven thousand pounds?"

"That's why Sugar had to do the duty of Silver, and we had—the first day—for the centre ornament on the dinner table a wonderful edifice representing a Chinese Summer palace in spun sugar. Greater economy was practised then than I expect there will be now; in the evening the Marchioness whispered to me that she was so mad at Waterford's pressing every one to taste the Caramel, when he must know that it was wanted for the Supper table afterwards at her Reception.

I remember, too, the next morning, before luncheon, while I was sitting with her in the garden, little Lord James running up and saying, " Mamma, Derrick says he wants more wine," and her drawing the key of the wine-cellar from her pocket, and telling him to bring it back to her when the butler had taken what was wanted."

"You cannot be too much on your guard against

these Irish butlers of ours," said my Uncle, "if you wish to give your guests good wine—or indeed have any at all for yourself. There was my friend Tom Reilly, who thought himself safe, because he trusted no one with the key of his cellar, and it had a lock which was unpickable. Yet his wine went, and he could not find out how. 'Look to your cellar, Sir,' whispered his cook to him one day. And he did look, to his cellar—only to find more wine gone; and he looked to the lock, and found that it had not been tampered with. 'Look to your cellar,' again said the cook; he could not question her, as he knew she would not only say nothing, but would never give him a hint again. He was sure no one could have got possession of the key,—he made a stricter scrutiny as to the condition of the hinges and lock of the door, and found them perfectly secure. Not long after, by the very merest accident—he discovered that bricks had been removed from a side wall sufficient for the butler to creep through, which had been carefully replaced after he had helped himself to a good supply."

"Of course," said my Aunt, "the rogue escaped punishment, as Irish servants will never swear away a fellow-servant's character, however base he may be. Perhaps, however, his Master took the law into his own hands?"

"I don't know whether he did on this occasion, but he did on another—as I witnessed. I happened to arrive at his house on a visit late on the very evening he was giving a grand Ball. I went into the Supper-room—which was all laid out—to help myself to some wine. The first decanter I tried was nauseous—so was the second, the third, the fourth. I withdrew my friend from the company, and asked him whether he really meant to give his friends such stuff. We pronounced it to be a weak solution of common beer. In a moment the butler was summoned. Taken by surprise, he had nothing to say for himself, and my friend kicked him first out of the room, and next down the kitchen stairs. For the next half-hour he and I were hard at work in superintending the washing of all the decanters, and the filling them with wine. It was working against time, as he was expected—exactly as the clock struck Twelve—to hand the *rankiest* lady in to supper."

And so my Uncle and Aunt went on relating and comparing their reminiscences, till first the one and then the other sank into a tranquil slumber, leaving me to speculate undisturbedly on the coming incidents of the Ball.

The carriage stopped—the ten miles' drive was over—my Uncle and Aunt awoke—the door was opened—the steps were dashingly let down—and we were ushered into the brilliantly-lighted entrance-hall of Curraghmore. For one moment I lingered to look back; there was a long line of carriages behind ours, but I could not detect among them the yellow Postchaise and the pale horses.

CHAPTER THE SIXTH.

THE CURRAGHMORE BALL.

"And all was beautiful, for all was new."

WE had advanced but a few paces in the Reception-room, when we encountered Lord John Beresford, Archbishop of Armagh, and Primate of all Ireland. His tall and commanding figure, his grand head with the organ of Veneration strongly developed, his courteous manner and address, and his melodious voice, made a powerful impression on me. Since then I have met with many of the greatest Prelates of the Anglican, Greek, and Roman Churches, but not one of them—in my opinion—could be compared with him. Last of the Prince-Bishops of the Irish Church, princely in descent, princely in munificence, he was fitted for an age of reverence and repose, when Rubrics were allowed to slumber, and Ritualisms were not. Who that had seen and known that calm, dignified, and stately Archbishop could imagine him wrangling with Ecclesiastical Commissioners, baited, bullied, and defied, steering the bark of the Irish Church over the troubled waters of angry controversy and acrimonious dissension? He was called to his rest before the evil days descended upon his Church and Order.

The Archbishop immediately recognised and addressed my Uncle and Aunt, and, observing me, he asked whether I was their daughter. Upon being told I was their niece, Kathleen Rochford. "Rochford, Rochford," he repeated to himself; "what, Rochford of Kilkreen?"

"The same, your Grace."

"I knew your father well, Miss Rochford, in former days," he said to me smiling; "we were school-fellows. I hope you will enjoy my Nephew's Ball."

My Uncle did not let the opportunity escape of having a fling at his clerical opponent. "My niece has not been frightened by the denunciations of the Reverend Randall Coote against balls and ball-goers."

"I see," said the Archbishop, "nothing sinful in such amusements if indulged in in moderation."

His words sounded in my ears almost like a benediction; and as we passed on I said to myself,—"As they can make him no higher than an Archbishop in this world, he will surely be an Archangel in the next."

Never could preconceptions be more contradicted than were mine upon my being taken up to be presented to the Ladies Anne and Catherine Beresford, who "received" for their nephew the Marquis of Waterford. Instead of the graceful and elegant, and even *grand* personages, who, as I pictured to myself, the sisters of the Archbishop *must* be, I was confronted with two ladies of not above the average height, with square thick-set figures, short fat necks, features unclassical, complexion sallow, expression austere ; and their dress, instead of being, as I had expected, of stately black velvet with point lace, was of bright brick coloured satin, and their Toques (then the fashionable head-dress) were of the same colour, embroidered with gold.

Standing behind them were the two Miss Beresfords, daughters of their brother Lord George Beresford, tall, slim girls, with a dejected look which I attributed to their being brought up by the severe spinsters in the Toques.

Being entire strangers to the names and persons of the invited guests, the Ladies Anne and Catherine Beresford were supported on each side by the Agent and his wife, who primed them against each presentation.

"Haughton, Cathedral dignitary ; wife, and *niece* not daughter," I overheard the prompter describing ourselves ; and a complacent nod of the Toques intimated that the lesson had been accurately learned.

"Very happy to see you, Mr and Mrs Morton Carysfort Digby," said Toque No. 1.

"And your grand-daughter also," said Toque No. 2.

On entering the ball-room I was struck by three distinguished-looking young men standing and talking together.

"Who are they, Uncle?" I asked.

"The Marquis of Waterford our host, the Earl of Powerscourt, and Lord Jocelyn the eldest son of Lord Roden."

The Marquis, as he impatiently shifted his position from one foot to the other, looked as if the acting the part of host in a ball-room was not the congenial sphere of his activities. He had a well-proportioned strongly-knit form and broad shoulders, betokening great muscular power. His features were prominent and manly, but not of an intellectual cast; later in the evening, when he became animated, they were fairly intelligent, but at this moment—though handsome, —they wore a heavy *bored* expression.

His two companions formed a striking contrast to himself. The Earl of Powerscourt was tall and slim, with finely-cut features, a complexion fair—with that unmistakeable tinge which tells of latent consumption, and light brown hair rippling back from his high forehead.

Lord Jocelyn, whose sister the Earl of Powerscourt

was on the point of marrying, was taller still, with piercing black eyes and black crisp curly hair—a man of fashion, with a decidedly military carriage.

The brothers-in-law (as they were soon to become) looked charged with spontaneous fun while watching the bright and graceful girls as they emerged from the Reception into the Ball room, and evidently impatient for the Band to strike up and release them from the irksome task of supporting their host.

While the Band were tuning their instruments, I strained my eyes in every direction in quest of Captain Lysaght, but in no nook or corner, doorway, arch, or window embrasure, could I discover the object of my search. Should I be thrown over by him at this my first Ball, what could I expect but to be superciliously overlooked by other eligible young men? and I made a resolution not to dance at all rather than be the partner of an Irish Lout or an English Tony Lumpkin.

Though I strove to put as good a face on the matter as if I were a well-seasoned young lady, I was conscious, by a gentle pressure of my Uncle's arm, that he was quite aware of the anxious suspense I was suffering.

It was not long; for almost immediately after, Captain Lysaght entered, with the Agent at his heels, both of them evidently hunting for some one.

My heart beat quickly. Would Captain Lysaght remember his promise? If he did, would he recognise ne? He had seen me but once, and then only for a minute or two, when I was muffled up in my travelling costume.

"Well, Kathleen," said my Uncle, "here's your hero of the hunting-field; he detects you at once. See, he is pressing his way through the crowd to us."

After shaking hands with my Uncle and Aunt, he offered his arm to me—"the set is formed; I have engaged our *vis-à-vis*."

"I was so afraid, Captain Lysaght, you would forget the engagement you made at our sudden encounter at the Meet."

"If you remembered your part of the engagement, why should I be suspected of forgetting mine? Besides, who ever forgets pleasant engagements?"

We had joined our set, and our *vis-à-vis* was Lord Jocelyn and Miss Beresford. She danced beautifully, her partner equally so. The Marquis of Waterford, who was in the same set, walked through the quadrille with a lovely girl, whose languid movements harmonized with her fragile figure.

The dance was finished, but my partner showed no intention of leading me back to my Aunt.

"Had we not better rest? Perhaps you would like me to point out to you some of the Notabilities of the company?"

"Oh, indeed, I should very much! And tell me

first, whom the Marquis of Waterford was dancing with."

"She is Miss L. He ought to have opened the Ball with the Hon. Lady Mulvelly. A precious row he made when he was told he must do so. He vowed that if in his own house he could not dance with whom he liked, he would not dance at all."

"Pray tell me next how it is that Lord Powerscourt and Lord Jocelyn are such excellent dancers."

"And why should they not?"

"Because the Earl's Mother prays, preaches, and expounds in public; and every one knows what Lord Jocelyn's Father's views are about worldly amusements."

"Then all the more reason why their sons should 'dance, and sing, and play,' to counterbalance the severe code of their Parents."

"You would not say that dancing was Lord Waterford's speciality?"

"At any rate you must give him the credit of appreciating Beauty."

"What a pity he came so late into the world! He ought to have lived in the days of the Knights of the Round Table. His acts might have come down to us enveloped in a halo of romance. In this prosaic age, mad pranks and pitiless practical jokes are regarded as neither chivalric nor romantic."

"Yes. We call it a prosaic age; but who can tell whether some centuries hence—should the world last so long—bards and troubadours will not be singing the exploits of that Chieftain of Erin—our noble Host."

"Who is that tall, elderly lady?" pointing with my bouquet.

"Why do you ask?"

"Because she seems so much courted by young men mostly. She must have great wit and talent to attract them in this way. See how Lords William and James Beresford are now talking and laughing with her."

Captain Lysaght made no answer, but hastily getting up, he proposed a turn round the rooms.

"The very thing I desire, and I shall be so obliged to you to point out to me the portrait of the lady to whom the ghost of her cousin Lord Tyrone appeared."

"It no longer hangs on the walls: it has been banished to the attic."

"Have you ever seen the picture?"

"Yes, I have often."

"Is it true that she has been taken with her wrist shrivelled and black?"

"No: when she found that her cousin's touch had shrivelled and discoloured her wrist—the proof that it was *himself* who had appeared to and touched her, and that it was no dream or fancy—she ever afterwards kept the part covered with a black band of ribbon, and so she is represented in the picture."

"She must have been a courageous woman to have chosen this ordeal, when the apparition proposed either writing in her pocket-book or tying the curtain in a particular knot."

"Surely, Miss Rochford, you would not approve of such a proceeding as unbelievers making a compact with each other that the one who died first should appear to the survivor in order to prove the reality of another world, and would not believe it if it were asserted that it had so happened?"

"But, what do you say to the wrist having been somehow injured, of which there seems to have been no doubt?"

"It is very possible that she walked in her sleep and wounded her wrist in a fall."

"Do you know, Captain Lysaght, that one of the rooms in my Uncle's house is haunted? it is the very room in which I sleep."

"Have you seen or heard anything Supernatural?"

"A little man in black—a former proprietor of the house—is said to appear in the room in which he died, on the night of the anniversary of his death."

"Have you been told when is the anniversary?"

"O yes,—it was on the very night of my arrival. My Aunt's Maid, while doing up my hair before going to bed, kept constantly twitching her head over her shoulder, as if she suspected some one was coming behind her, and, on my asking her the reason, she told me the tale."

"Of course your Uncle and Aunt thought it an idle superstition, or they would not have put you into that room. But did he pay you a visit?"

"Indeed he did. A short man dressed in black, with white hair and pale stern face, came from I don't know where—apparently through the wall—and walked up to my bed; he looked at me first with astonishment, then his countenance relaxed, and he smiled sweetly on me; then he raised his arms, as if blessing me, and, letting them fall, he gently stroked my hand, and disappeared through the wall as noiselessly as he entered. But see, Captain Lysaght," I said, taking off my glove, "his touch has left no ugly mark behind."

A strange conversation for a ball-room—a discussion about Ghosts! It was interrupted by Lord Jocelyn coming up and requesting my partner to introduce him to me: in another moment we were whirling round in the trois temps. Never since has it been my good fortune to have such a partner as I found in Lord Jocelyn.

I suppose he was equally satisfied with me, for it was long before he thought of pausing. It must be remembered that the dancing in those days was very different from the fast and furious style at present, which occasions—first, tattered trimmings, — next, sharp collisions,—and lastly, humiliating falls.

"Miss Rochford, you have all the graceful movement and light step which are said to be the national characteristic of Irish Ladies."

"From the last few minutes' experience I have had, *Irish Gentlemen* are no less indebted to their nationality for their superb dancing."

No response in word or look from the young Lord, but an unmistakably displeased expression on his face.

I saw at once that the double compliment I had intended to *him* and to *his country* was taken as quite the reverse of a compliment. I had made a blunder, that was certain, but *how* I could not for the life of me conceive.

Further acquaintance with Society revealed to me the fact that, with a certain class of Irishmen, any reference to their Nationality was distasteful, and that the suggestion of their being indebted by any possibility to their *Irish extraction* for any personal or intellectual gift would be contemptuously repudiated.

I did not add to the blunder—whatever it might be—by asking any question, but allowed my nose to take counsel of my bouquet for a brief space. Upon raising my eyes to my partner again, his gay good humour had returned. "We must not lose precious time, Miss Rochford; the valse will soon be over; we will have of it what we can,"—and again we were circling as merrily as before. When he led me to my Aunt and made his bow, the only displeasure he felt— as it seemed to me—was that of parting with me. How we girls do flatter and delude ourselves!

Seated beside my Aunt was Lady Mulvelly. She was fanning herself vigorously as if it were a midsummer's—instead of a midwinter's—night. Evidently she was not in a happy frame of mind; something must have gone wrong with her.

"The stupidest Ball I was ever at," were the first words I heard; "nothing to atone for its prevailing dullness. So few titled or distinguished guests!"

"My dear Lady Mulvelly," said my Aunt, "is it not too hard to charge our Host with not giving us the opportunity of mingling with Marchionesses and Countesses, when the Union has effected a clean sweep of the cream of the Irish Aristocracy?"

"But, at any rate, we might have expected something worthy of being called 'Reception Rooms.' I looked round in vain for the elegant furniture, cabinets, china, and crystal, which *should* adorn the Mansion belonging to the finest estate in the South of Ireland. And as to size, the whole building might be put into Mulvelly Castle and yet not half fill it."

I could not help smiling to myself at this mention of Mulvelly *Castle*, which was better known by the name of Mulvelly Craze. It had been built by the Grandfather of the present Baronet upon a scale so vastly out of all proportion to the value of the Estate, that a heavy mortgage had to be effected, and the family had had ever since to reside in one wing only of the building. Its final fate was—the property having been put up for sale under the Encumbered Estates Act, and no purchaser being found for the Castle—to be converted into a County Lunatic Asylum.

"Have you heard, Mrs Haughton, the Marquis' last practical joke?"

"No, what was it?"

"Early the other morning, when it was scarcely light, he drove up to the Rectory-house and roused the poor Rector out of his bed, by shouting to him to come down to him directly, without waiting to dress himself, as he had something of vital importance to tell him. Down hurried the poor man, with only a dressing-gown thrown hastily about him, and his naked feet in slippers. "Up," said the Marquis, "up as quick as you can, on to the box beside me, as none of those fellows behind must hear what I have to say to you." Up scrambled the Rector as well as he could, and was scarcely seated before off drove the Marquis at a furious rate, tearing up and down the street of the village—

and round and round—for at least half an hour, before setting down his unwilling Fare again at his own door. The victim of such a cruel joke has been in bed ever since. Were he any one but a Parson he would have had the Marquis up before the Magistrates and heavily fined for his vicious pranks."

My Uncle, who had come up while Lady Mulvelly was telling her tale, remarked—" If it be any satisfaction to you, Lady Mulvelly, to know it, the Marquis has been before now mulcted of large sums in the way of compensation for damages.

" In this case," sneered Lady Mulvelly, " he will compound by the promise of the first good Living in his gift—provided the sufferer's Apostolic constitution survives the exposure to *cold and nakedness.*"

" Come, Ponsonby," said my Aunt, rising and carefully adjusting the folds of her peach-coloured satin dress, " let us make the circuit of the rooms ;" and tapping me with her fan, we threaded our way through the throng.

The first incident which occurred to us was the transparent artifice of a triumphant Mother to draw our attention to the Marquis' devotion to her daughter—
" Have you seen my daughter Augusta, Mrs Haughton ?"

" No, indeed I have not, Lady L."

" Naughty child, where can she be ?" (though she

knew well enough). "I have not seen her since the Marquis carried her off for the first Quadrille."

The eldest daughter came up—bringing relief to the anxious mother,—"Mamma, I have found Augusta; she is sitting with the Marquis in the corridor."

"The future Mother-in-law—in anticipation—of the Marquis," laughed my Uncle, as we moved away.

Our next incident contained something of the ludicro-pathetic. We came suddenly upon Mrs Lawrence and Helen Croker. Mrs Lawrence was relating their adventures to a circle of listeners; she caught sight of us, and—from the look she bestowed on my Aunt—I was sure she suspected that it was owing to *her* that they had come to grief.

It was necessary to make a few civil inquiries; in reply to which we had this recital—"We got on smoothly enough for about half an hour, as long as we could keep your carriage in sight, Mrs Haughton. Suddenly we were alarmed by our coachman screeching at the top of his voice. On putting my head out of the window and asking what was the matter, he told me he was calling after your coachman to stop, as he was driving at such a pace that he could not keep up with him any longer. Without taking any further notice of me, he began to shower down curses and blows on the wretched animals, who did not seem provoked to more speed by the one any more than the other. Then—under pretext of getting some hay and water for them—he drove us into the yard of a Public-house, and left us there for half an hour or more, while he was drinking inside. He was in such a state—when at last he made his appearance—that he had to be lifted up on the driving-seat by a couple of as ill-looking fellows as I ever saw. It was a wonder that he kept his seat at all; but he did for some three or four miles, and then came to a dead halt. He said he had taken the wrong turn, and we were close to Portlaw,—and that the horses were so dead beat that they could not go a step further. There was no help for it, there we were—and there we must remain : our only hope—and a very scanty one it was—was that some friendly returning carriage might come our way and take us back to Waterford. Before long an 'Outside Car'—which had taken two officers from Portlaw to the Ball—was on its way back, and the Driver was very ready—for the pay we offered him—to convey us to Curraghmore. The military cloaks were lying on the seats, in which— necessity owning no law—we felt no scruple about wrapping ourselves ; and we arrived here without further mishap, astonishing the servants-in-waiting on their seeing two such smart ladies emerging from weather-stained roquelaires,—in fact, a pair of butter- flies from their chrysalid sheaths."

The most untoward accidents will generally be found to have their *compensations*—if we did but know *all* : the compensation in this case was,—that Lady Brian Croker was spared the bitter mortification of being told—as she must have been—that the Marquis of Waterford in opening the Ball preferred an untitled Miss L. to her daughter—the lineal descendant of King Brian Boirholme.

Early in the evening Captain Lysaght had engaged me for the " supper-dance ;" he was in attendance to lead me to the carriage, which—either intentionally or unintentionally—he was so slow in doing, that my Uncle was becoming impatient.

" I shall meet your Papa at the Meet on Thursday; am I to tell him that you enjoyed your first Ball."

" Tell him that I never enjoyed anything half so much before."

" And am I to tell him Who was your favourite partner ? "

" Canon Haughton's carriage stops the way "— which had been repeated over and over again while this short colloquy was going on—was now so impatiently shouted out, that in my alarm I hurried away—without making any answer, or accepting his profferred arm.

When we were well settled down in the carriage, " Well, Miss Helen," said my Uncle, for we were bringing Miss Brian Croker back with us, " have you found a ballroom to be such a scene of wickedness as it has been pictured to you?"

" I saw no wickedness; and dancing was so delightful that I had no time to be wicked myself."

" I need not ask *you*, Kathleen; you were in no haste to come away."

" Ponsonby," said my Aunt, " did you notice the high spirits in which that demure young English Earl of —— and Mrs · —— were at the supper-table?"

" Aunt," I said, " Captain Lysaght and I were close by them; and I was so surprised, that I could not help remarking to him that the Earl might have bestowed a little of his animation on his partners during the evening, and not reserved the whole of it for the supper-table."

" And what did he say?" asked my Aunt, with an impatient tone which seemed quite uncalled for.

" He said nothing, Aunt; but looking (as I thought angrily) at the pair, and muttering something between his teeth, he led me to the further end of the supper-table. But tell me, Aunt, what possible attractions could Mrs —— have for drawing out so shy a man as the Earl, who never spoke to nor looked at his partners, as far as I could see. I did feel so sorry for them."

" My dear Kathleen, when you are older by some

years you will find that young girls, however engaging, do not monopolise the attentions of *all* young men."

Time and experience became the interpreters of my Aunt's enigmatical reply. It was a painful discovery to make, that nobility of birth and nobility of mind did not always go together, and that outward graces and polished manners might co-exist with coarse tastes and a low morality. The scene at the supper-table at Curraghmore, that night has been recalled to my recollection, when I have seen women past their prime, no longer in the possession of youth or beauty, but still craving for the attentions which they used to receive and which had become almost a necessity of life, bidding for and courting the notice of men (no matter of what age) whom they could attract to them by an unscrupulous exercise of wit bordering on indelicacy, and by unblushing discussions of the esclandres of the day.

Of those three distinguished men, the observed of all observers on that night at the Curraghmore Ball, of whom I have even now after so many years the most distinct vision as they stood together, not one survives. In a few years all were prematurely snatched away by disaster or disease. The Earl of Powerscourt was carried off by consumption before attaining his thirty-first Birthday; Lord Jocelyn fell a victim to cholera, while on duty in the Tower of London, at the age of thirty-eight: and ten years later the Marquis of Waterford met his death in the hunting-field—he was killed on the spot by a fall from his horse.

"If in this life only we had hope!"

Book the Sixth.

CHAPTER THE FIRST.

MADAME BONAPARTE WYSE.

" Tranquillo varco
A piu tranquilla vita."
Guarini.

" For Men's and Women's hearts you cannot try
Beforehand, like the Cattle that you buy.
Nor human Wit nor Reason, when you treat
For such a purchase, can escape deceit ;
Fancy betrays us, and assists the cheat."
Theognis.

AGITATION had again been successful. O'Connell had driven the Government into further concession. The Irish Church must be plundered. The Clergy must be despoiled of one quarter of their incomes, which was to be bestowed on the Landlords in consideration of their paying the tithes directly, instead of indirectly through their tenants as heretofore.

This measure—as " Catholic Emancipation " before it—was hailed as a peace-offering ; but it failed, as signally, in securing peace.

It is remarkable, how in Ireland every conciliatory

act on the part of England, every remedial treatment, has produced the diametrically opposite results to those which had been designed and expected.

The passing of the *Spoliation* (in Parliamentary phrase "Impropriation") Act seemed but a new starting-point for renewed agitation, increased disloyalty, more daring Agrarian outrage.

This fresh outbreak of disaffection and violence had to be met by Special Commissions, Coercion Bills, Suspension of Habeas Corpus; the very Ministers who had now to wield the rod, were the same who, shortly before, had administered the (as they thought) healing draft; and they were in consequence held up by O'Connell to the hatred and execration of his Countrymen as the "base, brutal, and bloody Whigs."

It is the fatality of England in dealing with Ireland, never to become wiser by the experience of the Past. The latest concession which we have witnessed has been, not a partial, but an entire confiscation of the temporalities of the Irish Church. And what has been the result? Just the same as before, fresh violence, fresh agitation, and a clamorous demand for Home Rule. It could hardly be expected, that the Ministry, which *forcibly*, if not *unconstitutionally*, carried the measure, could escape being taunted with its utter failure in ushering in those halcyon days of peace and harmony which had been so grandiloquently described and promised; and the cool reply that was given was this, that we were too impatient by far, that no one but a fool would look for a harvest on the day in which the seed was sown, and that it was most unreasonable to expect that sores of centuries' continuance would yield to the best curative process in a less period than a century or two.

My Uncle had judged it prudent to lay down his carriage and horses. My Aunt was depressed and dyspeptic; she kept to the house, declaring in a humorous sort of way that it would take some time to learn how to tuck up her skirts, and put on her pattens, and gracefully trudge on foot to pay her afternoon visits.

"Why not engage the yellow Postchaise?" suggested my Uncle.

"What, after the experience we have had of the yellow Postchaise's performances!" said my Aunt.

"Then, why not take to an '*Inside Car,*' it is a very decent as well as comfortable vehicle?" asked my Uncle. An "*Inside*" was a carriage something like those now known as Waggonettes.

"An Inside indeed! Would you have me go to a Party in an '*Inside?*' Pray, who laughed so heartily as you did last week at Mrs Godolphin's Pic-nic, when the footman announced at the top of his voice — ' Mrs Levenge's Inside is coming up?'"

"My dear, other ladies besides Mrs Levenge must have been inconvenienced that day; for when I was going into a room to look for my overcoat, I was stopped by a footman—' plase, Sir, you must not go in there, Sir; its *there*, Sir, that the ladies sthrip.'"

Want of air and exercise produced their usual effects on my Aunt's constitution. She became nervous and hysterical; she had pains and aches here, there, and everywhere.

No one but Dr Jephson of Leamington could meet her case; and to Leamington she prevailed on her husband to send her. I, provided my parents consented, was to accompany her. What anticipations I had! what a grand thing it would be to visit England! to compare the two countries in their geographical and social contrasts! to judge for myself as to the intelligence and habits of their respective peoples! to determine whether Ireland was indeed a century behind England in civilization, whether England had really enriched herself at her Sister's expense, whether she was in truth that Great Country which alone could maintain peace in Europe, and had chained Napoleon to a rock in mid-ocean!

I had a half-consciousness, while speculating upon my opportunity or ability of solving these and other problems, of Mrs Molloy whisking about my room and dusting here and there with an unusual industry. I was in no humour to talk to her. After several abortive attempts to attract my notice, as if impatient of longer silence she broke out : " I wish the Boys," as she called the Peasantry, " had left off their thricks of frightening the Englishers afore they obleeged the Masther to send away the pretty carriage and horses. It's not for the likes of such an iligant lady as the Misthress to be footing it about the town. Any ways, I hope the Family won't come down to a She-Butler."

I was not going to discuss with Mrs Molloy the probabilities of what state of degradation the Family might or might not be reduced to, and pretended not to hear.

She was not to be thus shaken off. " Pray, tell me, Miss Kathleen, are ye, too, going across the Water ? "

" Yes, I hope so : I shall be miserable if I don't."

" 'Tis the more miserable the both of ye'll be, when ye come back. Nothing will then please ye, in the house or out of the house. Ye'll be turning up yer noses at every thing living or dead."

The Postman's familiar knock. I rushed down stairs. A letter directed to me in my Father's handwriting. It ran thus :—

"My very dear Daughter,

"Though I am overwhelmed with business, I will not delay sending an answer to your request. Your Mother and I are both agreed that a visit to England will be of so much advantange to you, that we can throw no hindrance in the way of your going. You have our willing consent, and I enclose a cheque for fifty Pounds for your personal expenses.

"There are hours when I sorely miss my little Secretary, more especially when this tithe settlement requires a great amount of calculation. The Government concession to the Party of brute force has not been followed, as it was promised it would be, by an instant and lasting peace. Far from it. In our unhappy Country, Agrarian crime is as rife as ever; and disaffection to the British Government increases. Sometimes I find myself crying out, O for an hour of Cromwell.

"Poor Miss Anstey Costello is dead. Yesterday I received a message urging me to lose no time in hastening to her. I rode off immediately. I found her with her head propped up on the pillow; she was breathing with difficulty; but there was an expression of restful calm on her face, and she smiled the old smile when I entered the room. I took the emaciated hand, which rested on the coverlid, in mine; it was cold and clammy. 'My dear, kind, true friend, the same throughout life, the same to the last.' She paused for breath and then went on : 'Every thing seems changed to me now. I see all that belongs to this world in such a different light to what I used to do. I used to think that it was no crime to get our Rights, or what we were taught to be our Rights, by violence and bloodshed; and I hardened my heart against all compunctions, when I heard of God's creatures being hurried out of this world by men of the same flesh and blood, and sometimes of the same kindred and creed. Now I dread that much innocent blood has been shed in the land, and that it is crying up from the ground to the Lord for vengeance, and He withholds peace. As I have lain here hour after hour in my solitary meditation, it has often come across my mind that the means used for redressing our wrongs were unrighteous and hateful in the sight of God, and that the leaders, who have been stirring up the wild passions of the people, will have a heavy account to render hereafter.'

"She gasped for breath. For a few moments there was a profound silence; a change came over her face; I bent down my head, as I saw she had something still to say—'Tell Kathleen,' she whispered, 'I die at peace with all the world. I have forgiven General Lake.' One sigh, and she was no more. At that moment the Romish Priest entered, to administer the last rites of his Church to the dying.

This must close my letter.

Your truly affectionate Father,

HENRY ROCHFORD."

My delight at being permitted to accompany my Aunt to England was dashed with sorrow by the intelligence of Miss Anstey Costello's death : and tears were running down my cheeks, which my Aunt naturally attributed to disappointment caused by a refusal, when I put the letter into her hands.

She, too, was much affected upon reading my Father's pathetic narrative of his farewell interview with his old friend and neighbour. She had barely time to make a remark on my Father's kindness and generosity, and her own pleasure in having me for her companion, when the door was hastily thrown open ; and, almost before she could be announced, Madame Bonaparte Wyse entered.

She was attired in a white morning dress profusely trimmed with Valenciennes lace, and a Leghorn hat with a plume of scarlet feathers ; her stockingless feet were thrust loosely into red morocco slippers. Superbly handsome, but with a pronounced expression of bitterness and defiance, such was the woman I looked at with a wondrous curiosity.

"Madame Haughton, I am come to take leave of you and your niece."

My Aunt expressed her regret, and at the same time her surprise at the announcement.

"I am sorry to part from *you*, but not from my husband and his family. He *do* sit in his library with his books when he ought to be driving about with me; and when we meet at table, he *do* talk to his *belle sœur* and his little niece, but never to me. O, I do so hate her. He takes me to no places; he says he has no money to take me to London, where I want to go. And this climate, *O mon Dieu, c'est affreux*. Nothing but rain and fog."

"But, Madame, you cannot complain of to-day—how bright and warm it is!"

"But how very few of them! and when you have any sun at all, there is not enough of it to make a *fête champêtre* tolerable."

"Where are you going, Madame?"

"To the palazzo of the Prince, my father. I shall not be a prisoner there, as I am here in your town of Waterford—a miserable prisoner in one little house, and no one I care to speak to. *There* I shall have the blue sky, and the fêtes, and the Opera."

"How long shall you be away from Waterford?"

"How long? Why for the whole of my life, to be sure."

"What can you mean, Madame? You cannot be serious?"

"Indeed, I am quite serious. There is to be what you call an *acte* of Separation, and my Husband will have to pay me a grand sum every year I live. My father took good care of that."

"And your two little boys, Madame?"

The mention of her children drew forth the only sign of softness she had shown during the conversation. I saw tears rush to her eyes. "Ah, Madame Haughton, I want to take them with me, but your laws say No. And if I were to remain, and go on enduring my present hateful life for their sake, I should see but little of them; they would soon be sent to a hideous school, after your barbarous custom. In Italy it would be very different; *there* I should always have them with me. An Abbé would educate them at home; and when they grew up they would become Officers in His Holiness' Guardia Nobile. There would be the *Villegiatura* at the Palazzo Canino in summer, and in winter either Rome or Paris."

"Surely not Paris, with the *décret* of banishment still in force against all the members of the Bonaparte Family!"

"O that will not be for long," and she laughed scornfully; "the French will soon be clamouring to have a Bonaparte again at their head."

My Aunt was far too prudent to be led into any political discussion with such a fiery spirit as Madame Bonaparte Wyse, whose private personal wrongs, which she always put in the strongest form, were ever driving her into paroxysms of excitement bordering on frenzy, without any reference to public and family misfortunes. Neither could my Aunt, however she might pity her for her anomalous position, express any hearty or partisan sympathy with her; in the first place she could not enter into the merits or demerits of private disputes between husband and wife, and in the next she much liked and was very intimate with the abused Wyse family who would still remain after Madame Bonaparte Wyse had disappeared from the scene.

My Aunt's coolness had the effect of exasperating Madame Bonaparte Wyse all the more; she worked herself up into a state of passionate screaming, which was followed by so much exhaustion that, after dosing her with a restorative, we had to support her down stairs and into her carriage.

Upon the scene being related to my Uncle, all the remark he made was, "Well! Tom Wyse has had to pay dear for his whistle."

The day's incidents were not over. Shortly after Madame Bonaparte Wyse's departure, the Agent of the Waterford Estate entered in great haste, and only stayed long enough to say that he was summoned to Curraghmore in consequence of the Marchioness having been pitched violently out of the high phæton in which the Marquis was driving her, and that there was only too much fear of serious concussion of the brain.

"I am more concerned than surprised," said my Uncle, "the wonder is, that it has not occurred sooner, considering the high-spirited horses he drives, and he though a good yet a most reckless driver."

"Dear, dear, how very sad," exclaimed my Aunt, "and she has been married only six months! Perhaps it may be some consolation to Lady L. when she hears it, that her daughter Augusta was not promoted to the Marchioness-ship and—the Coach-box."

CHAPTER THE SECOND.

ANECDOTES EPISCOPAL AND CLERICAL.

"Noble Lords had repeatedly asserted that the Measure (Catholic Emancipation) was dangerous to the Church of England. Was this danger to be apprehended from Legislation or Violence? . . . . . I beg further to observe on this point that *a fundamental Article of the Union of the two Countries* was the UNION OF THE TWO CHURCHES which then became THE UNITED CHURCH OF ENGLAND AND IRELAND; and *it was impossible that any mischief could happen to the Irish Branch of the United Church* WITHOUT DESTROYING THE UNION OF THE TWO COUNTRIES."—*Speech of the Duke of Wellington on the Catholic Emancipation Bill*, 1829.

THE Act which suppresses two Archbishoprics and four Bishoprics in Ireland was regarded by politicians who were not led away by party spirit as a piece of legislation both *unnecessary* and *mischievous*. It was unnecessary, because, as it was acknowledged, the Irish Clergy were then doing their work with a zeal tempered by judiciousness, and with an activity leavened by Christian charity, which had not been known for centuries; and it was attested, even by Roman Catholics of authority, that the services of the Protestant Clergy were invaluable, that they supplied in many instances the want of resident gentry, and that they showed kindnesses to the Roman Catholic portion of their Parishes (which the Roman Catholic Priest had it not in his power to show) without any attempt at proselytising. This was exemplified in a remarkable manner during the prevalence of the fearful Famine which ravaged Ireland in 1847.

And if it was *unnecessary*, it was also *mischievous*; because it had been proved to demonstration that every concession to the Church of Rome, instead of being received as a token of a spirit of conciliation, was made, as it were, a more advantageous fulcrum for the working of the Agitation lever, and that every act which weakened the Protestant, only strengthened the Roman Catholic Church and furnished fresh means for further aggressions.

Who could have supposed that this petty spoliation —petty by comparison—would be followed in the course of years, by a wholesale measure of Disestablishment and Disendowment? To neither the lesser nor the greater wrong could the Duke of Wellington have looked forward, when, in the words at the head of this Chapter, he was endeavouring to persuade the House of Lords to assent to the Bill for "Catholic Emancipation."

In the formation of public Companies and private

T

Firms, certain conditions are laid down as forming the base of agreement between parties interested, which are afterwards embodied in a Deed of Settlement, enrolled under Act of Parliament, and held to be strictly binding on those who have put their hands to it. If, after a time, any contracting Member violates or repudiates the terms of the Deed, there are but two courses—the enforcement of the penalties in that case made and provided, or a Dissolution of Partnership.

It is hard to see the distinction between a Mercantile partnership settled according to Law and confirmed by Act of Parliament, and a National partnership similarly settled and confirmed.

And it cannot be wondered at, that the cry for the Repeal of the Union, which was raised by the inveterate and irreconcilable enemies of England, has found an echo among those who have hitherto been (notwithstanding many discouragements) her most loyal and devoted adherents.

If England had but fulfiled her religious duty to Ireland, by appointing to Bishoprics none but men, not only of tried ability, but Irishmen well acquainted with the habits and language of their countrymen ; if the power of preaching and teaching in Irish had been made a *sine quâ non* for the holding of Livings ; if encouragement had been given to the translation of the Bible into the native tongue, and the circulation of small works explanatory of the doctrines of the Church of England, and the principles of the English Reformation, the power of the Roman Church would long ago have been broken, if not annihilated ; and there would have been none of that priestly agitation and those priestly denunciations which resulted in the Massacre of 1641, equalled only by that of St Bartholomew in France, in the Rebellion of 1798, and in those murderous outrages which have continued almost unceasingly ever since.

Instead of this, the Archiepiscopal and the Episcopal appointments were mostly political, as if the offices were made for the men and not the men for the offices. Interest was the rule, merit the rare exception : and but for such glorious names as Usher, Jeremy Taylor, Bedell, Berkeley, and a very few others, the Irish Bench would have presented nothing but incompetence, indolence, jobbery, and nepotism, ever since the Reformation.

" Beautiful indeed upon the mountains are the feet of them that bring good tidings of good, and publish Salvation ;" but no such feet were planted on the mountains of Ireland. The native population was left to a grossly ignorant and a fanatical Romish Priesthood.

In my earlier days the old race of Clergymen was

fast disappearing and giving place to more active, intelligent, and zealous men: but the spiritual neglect of ages could not be remedied in days, or weeks, or years, and the memory of past personal habits and manners was kept alive by many a characteristic anecdote.

A card-playing Bishop is now an impossibility: yet in those days the card-parties at the Palace at Waterford excited no scandal. Loo was the game. As soon the Cathedral clock struck Ten, a loud bell was heard in the hall—the meaning of which was well understood. Down went the cards upon their faces on the green-cloth, as if every hand which held them had received an electric shock; up sprang the guests to their feet and bustled down stairs into the dining-room, headed by the Bishop who said Prayers. Prayers over, the guests hurried upstairs—again led by their host: all, by an unerring instinct, settled into their own seats, and took up their own cards, and—apparently invigorated by their devotional exercise—resumed the game and continued it till midnight.

On one of these festive occasions the weather changed suddenly; it will do so in all pleasant lands, and Ireland can hardly expect to be an exception. The rain dashed against the windows, and some of the Company were repenting of their rash reliance on the fickle elements, when the butler entered, and in a very audible whisper said, " My Lord, the Kitchenmaid vows she won't go to the well for water, and there is not a drop in the house."

" Never mind," said his Lordship in the calmest tone, without ever taking his eyes from the cards, " then tell the coachman to put the horses to the carriage, and do you hand Peggy with her can into it, and go with her to the well; and mind she does not catch cold."

I am reminded here that the great mystery of the inequalities of our condition in this life was powerfully impressed on my mind at one of these wells. It was in the depth of winter, when every little pool in the streets was converted into a Nature's looking-glass, and long icicles were hanging from the eaves of houses like glassy lances reversed, that I stood, all warmly muffled up, watching a poor half-clad girl while her can was slowly filling. At last, poising it on her head, she was moving away, when her foot slipped and the can emptied itself over her shoulders and down her bare neck. " Ah, Musha, musha," was all the poor drenched creature said, eyeing me in my warm, dry dress, " Ah, Musha, musha, I wonder whether we shall be all alike in the next world."

Another Episcopal Subject of my early recollections is Bishop —— , a man of high family, polished manners, and the kindliest heart ; his hospitality was unlimited, his means very limited. He became inextricably embarrassed ; and only such a buoyant spirit as his could have borne up under the many annoyances and vexations which he had to endure, and the many humiliating shifts to which he was driven in order to stave off the inevitable result. Bailiffs were constantly prowling about the Palace, which, however, was strictly guarded by the faithful servants in the absence of their Master, who spent much of his time, for the sake of the society, in Dublin ; and the ingenious tricks employed for effecting an entrance, and the still more ingenious ways in which they were baffled, were duly reported to Dublin, and raised many a laugh at the dinner-tables there.

One day there appeared at the Palace gates a large dray with two great butts. What could they be ? Some fresh trick ? No. An order had arrived that morning from the Bishop, for two butts of beer to be sent to the Palace, there was the order to speak for itself. Suspicion was quite disarmed ; it was so like their generous Master to reward their fidelity in such a way. The gates were unbolted and thrown wide open, the dray rolled into the Court-yard, the draymen laboured hard (or pretended to do so) to lower the casks and wheel them into the house ; once in, some staves were removed and out from each cask crawled a couple of bailiffs. Thus the citadel was won at last. It was a homely and vulgar version of the wooden horse of the siege of Troy.

Thinking aloud is no peculiarity, as far as I am aware, of Irish Ecclesiastics; but I cannot help recording a singular instance of this infirmity in the Bishop of ———. He had a favourite sermon which he delivered in every part of his diocese, wherever he might have to preach. The subject was the little Israelitish maid who was carried away captive by Syrian marauders, and became a servant in Naaman's household. Some of the Clergy used to maintain that it was the only sermon which the Bishop had—that he was in fact *homo unius concionis*, but this I can positively contradict. At one of his Ordinations a nephew of his wife came for Priest's Orders. It was then the custom to appoint an incepting Priest to preach the Ordination Sermon : the appointment was regarded as a compliment to the appointee—being an acknowledgment of his having passed a superior examination when a Candidate the year before for Deacon's Orders. In this particular instance, the Preacher was indebted for the compliment to his connection with the Bishop, and not to his own merits. Either from utter inability to compose an appropriate sermon, or from diffidence as to his sermon (if he did compose one) being equal to the occasion, at any rate, when the time came, no sermon was ready. In his distress he had recourse to his Aunt, who, like an indulgent aunt but injudicious wife, relieved him from his difficulty by abstracting one of her husband's sermons. It happened to be the celebrated sermon on the Israelitish maid. Upon the text being given out, the Bishop was observed by his Examining Chaplain (who sate next him) to prick up his ears and to bend forward to listen with very unusual interest. At the end of the second or third sentence the Bishop exclaimed, in a voice loud enough to be heard by all within three yards of him, " Why, bless my soul, if the young blackguard has not gone and stolen my little maid ! "

The youthful Preacher, little thinking of the sensation he was creating in the Episcopal stall, proceeded with his sermon, bungling, and blundering, and miscalling the words, and running one sentence into another, when a second exclamation escaped from the Bishop, much louder than the first, " By ——, the brute is *murdering* my little maid."

I well remember Robert Daly taking up his residence at Waterford as Bishop of Cashel. He was *the last* Bishop of Cashel while it was an integral part of the " United Church of England and Ireland," and *the first* Bishop of *activity*.

The *Archbishopric* of Cashel had been suppressed,

as was also that of Tuam; and the Dioceses of Cashel, Emly, Waterford, and Lismore were merged into one Episcopate, of which the Episcopal Head was the Bishop of Cashel, and the Episcopal residence was Waterford as being the most central point.

Dr Daly, Bishop of Cashel, was not an ordinary man. His appearance was not prepossessing : he had a narrow head, angular features, long sharp nose, sallow complexion, and his gait was ungainly. He was a thorough-paced partisan, an eager controversialist *in* the pulpit (which he was fond of occupying) and *out of it;* and he was oftentimes not so choice in the language he employed as he should have been, when maintaining his own opinions or attacking those of others. And yet, occasionally, he exhibited traits of tenderness which could hardly be expected from him—as sometimes we see delicate flowers spring up from an apparently uncongenial soil ; he has been known to carry baskets of strawberries to sick people, tears would come into his eyes on hearing some tale of sad and real distress, and by his Will he bequeathed a legacy to every Curate in his Diocese, which he altered into an immediate gift.

The first time I saw him was at my Uncle's house, when a little *contretemps* occurred. On his being ushered into the drawing-room before dinner, the butler, who was a Roman Catholic, instead of the announcement which he had been instructed to make of "the Lord Bishop of Cashel," simply announced him as "Dr Daly." My Uncle showed his annoyance, and began to apologise to the Bishop, who was generous enough to say, that if the man could not conscientiously give him his spiritual title, he was right in not doing so.

During dinner, he talked *to the table*, and he told some stories which, I thought, he had better have kept to himself. He said that he had once occasion to consult the eminent physician Sir Philip Crampton, and went by appointment to his house in Merrion Square at nine o'clock. In the midst of the examination which the Doctor was making of him, he was called out of the room; the Bishop, seeing on the desk a pile of one pound Bank notes and shillings, had the curiosity to count them, in order to see how much business the Doctor had done at that early hour, and found that he had already had fourteen Patients. I question whether any of our sex, with all our proverbial curiosity, would have done such a thing, and I am quite sure that, if we had, we should never have confessed it.

He said that he always made a point of engaging in argument with Romish Priests whenever he had an opportunity; and he flattered himself that he was regarded as a formidable antagonist, from the fact of an order having been issued by the Cardinal Archbishop, that no Priest was to answer him on any religious question, but, however provoked, to maintain strict silence. " Once," went on the Bishop, " I had taken my place in the Mail Coach for Dublin, and found that my three fellow-passengers were Romish Priests. It was such a chance as I never had before, and was not to be neglected. I began at once to tackle them; but not a word could I extract from any one of the three, though I tried them over and over again. At last I said to them, 'Gentlemen, I see you have taken the vows of La Trappe, and I am sorry for it, as I am sure I should have been a great gainer by your conversation;' and then I took out my Bible, and read aloud all those passages which militated against Romish doctrines, as long as daylight lasted."

He was very severe on the Medical Profession, and in a graphic manner related this anecdote : " At the first visit which I paid to Sir Philip Crampton, among other questions he asked was one, what I drank at breakfast ? 'Tea, Sir Philip,' I answered. 'The worst thing in the world, my Lord,' he said, 'always take Coffee.' For nearly a year I followed his directions, without any perceptible benefit. I went to him again; he asked me just the same questions as before; after his prescription was placed in my hand, and my guinea in his, I was leaving the room when he hurried after me: 'My Lord, what do you drink at breakfast?' 'Coffee, Sir Philip,' I said. 'The worst thing in the world, my Lord,' said Sir Philip, 'always drink Tea.'"

One day we were startled by the announcement that the young wife of an elderly Clergyman, the Rector of a Parish at a short distance from Waterford, had eloped with the Village Doctor. My Uncle was much pained, as the deserted husband was highly respected by all his brethren; and he started off at once in order to consult with some of the Cathedral Clergy, whether anything could be done. It was the unanimous opinion, that if the husband could be prevailed on to receive back the erring wife, and the wife was willing to return in all penitence to her husband, the affair might, at this early stage, be hushed up, and much scandal as well as misery might be avoided. The management of these delicate negotiations was confided to my Uncle. After some persuasion he succeeded with the husband. He then posted after the fugitive wife, who had not gone very far. Twenty-four hours had been quite sufficient to reveal to her the terrible *blunder* she had made; and she was only too glad to accept at once my Uncle's proposals. On the journey back he talked long and earnestly to her of the injury she had done to Society —of the grievous wrong she had inflicted on an indulgent husband—and of the fearful sin she had committed in the sight of God. By the time they arrived at her forsaken home, he hoped that he had brought her to such a proper state of remorse and repentance, that he might confidently present her to her husband. He opened the door of the library where he was told he was; he expected the penitent wife to rush forward and cast herself at his feet in an agony of tears; instead of this, she skittishly tripped across the room, and, holding out her hand in a gracious way to her husband, said, " Henry, I forgive you."

" They *sometimes* pardon who commit the wrong."

Book the Seventh.

A REAL IRISH GRIEVANCE.

"Heaven take my soul, and England keep my bones."
K. John, Act IV.
"Father Abbot, I am come hither to lay my bones among you."
Card. Wolsey.

I HAD read and heard of the sufferings produced by sea-sickness, but like many other sufferings, whether mental or bodily, they must be really experienced before they can be realised.

The Steamers on the Waterford and Bristol Line conveyed merchandise and live stock as well as passengers. The lower deck was given up to the pigs, among which the Drovers had to be continually forcing their way, dragging their ears open and pouring water into them in order to preserve them from suffocation. It was necessary also to watch them closely and keep them upon their feet; as, once down, they would be trampled to death by their brethren. The effluvium arising from this Piggery, which the wind blew right in our faces as we sate on the upper deck, swelled the category of odours common to all Steamers. Horrible sounds proceeded from the hold into which the horses had been lowered; *they* suffer quite as much as human beings during a rough voyage.

Bad as it was on deck, it was much worse in the cabin, into which we were at last driven by darkness, rain, and wind. It was close and stifling, with an atmosphere impregnated with foul smells compounded of brandy, oil, paint, and tar.

Nature seeking relief in violent spasmodic action and then relapsing into nauseous prostration, by alternations, such was our painful and humiliating condition for the space of twenty-four hours.

The ladies' and the gentlemen's cabins were divided from each other by the very thinnest wooden partition. As I lay in my narrow berth, I wondered, whenever intervals in my paroxysms gave me liberty to think of anything at all, why, in the list of penances imposed by the Church of Rome, a sea-voyage, of longer or shorter duration proportioned to the amount of the sins confessed, was never included. We are familiar with the wearing of hair shirts, self-flagellations, crawling on all-fours round holy wells with an occasional sup of dust by the way, creeping up the Scala Santa on bare knees; but we have never yet heard of the imposition of a Marine penance. It is possible that the idea may have dawned upon the minds of those Pilgrims to Peray le Monial, who chose the longer voyage from Newhaven to Dieppe; they might have hoped, that a few hours of voluntary submission to a salt-watery Purgatory here, would win for them many years exemption from a fiery Purgatory hereafter.

Some Quaker ladies occupied berths adjoining my own. "How doth it fare with thee, Friend, this morning? Couldst thee sleep during the night for the grunting of those pigs?" said one. "Pigs," answered the one spoken to, "Pigs! why, sure it was Friend Joseph snoring as usual." "Doth Friend Joseph snore after that sort?" returned the first speaker, "then God help his poor wife."

How often during that night did I make the resolution, that once again at Waterford (should I ever return alive), nothing on earth should ever tempt me to run the risk of a repetition of such accumulated misery as I was then undergoing. And yet since then (how much easier it is to *make* than to *keep* resolutions), scarcely a year has come and gone without my breaking the resolution made on that miserable night; fortunately, however, the pains and penalties of later voyages have been greatly mitigated in consequence of their shorter duration. There was one exception, when I was tempted by the glassy smoothness of the sea, the unclouded brilliancy of the sky, and the absence of the very least breath of air, to take a voyage from Nice to Genoa—which the advertisement announced would occupy barely six hours. I had promised myself the greatest enjoyment in viewing from the deck of the Steamer the loveliness of the scenery of the Riviera. Scarcely had we emerged from the tiny harbour, when the peculiar motion of the vessel betrayed that under a smooth surface there was a treacherous ground-swell, which converted the six hours' voyage of anticipated delight into one of double the length of unexpected misery. This effectually cured me of trusting myself again to the faithless Mediterranean, and I performed the rest of my journey to Southern Italy by Vettura or Railway.

Our stay in England was to extend to three months. Clifton, Bath, Cheltenham, were to be visited *en route* to Leamington. My Aunt had never been in England since her marriage; previous to which she had passed two winters in Bath in its palmy days, and two seasons at Weymouth when George III. and Queen Charlotte had not ceased to visit that fashionable watering-place. Since then Cheltenham sprang up into notoriety on the strength of its saline springs, which were pronounced to be serviceable to livers, and conducive therefore to the prolongation of life.

These beautiful towns—though designed and built by English enterprise and skill, were not entirely supported by English gold, as we soon found that a large proportion of the occupiers of the best houses, and of the fashionable ladies who frequented the Assembly Rooms, thronged the Promenades, and shopped, and drove about in handsome equipages were *Irish Absentees*. My Aunt was severely eloquent about the injustice of Ireland being drained of her wealth and of the best blood of her people for the aggrandisement of England; she now saw with her own eyes how the stronger was preying upon the resources of the weaker, and she must admit that O'Connell had some reason on his side for the agitation he was so hotly carrying on for the Repeal of the Union.

At Cheltenham we spent a few days with the Macnamara family, relations of my Aunt, consisting of Father, Mother, and four grown-up Children. The eldest daughter, though past her first bloom, was still handsome. Upon her introduction, she had been singled out by the Duke of Gloucester, with whom she might be seen frequently walking in the Public gardens; she therefore became the fashion. Admiration by Royalty raised high hopes in the Family; if one Duke admired, why might not another propose? Titled flirtations ended with the season, untitled flirtations she haughtily repelled; and seasons, eight in number, left her Miss Macnamara still, unattached and unappropriated. This was a mortification, not confined to the young lady herself, but shared by both parents and brothers; it served to point a sarcasm whenever family jars arose. Barry, the eldest son, two years younger than his sister, was unable on his allowance to meet the expenses of a Cavalry Regiment, and disdaining — as heir to the family-estate—to enter the Line, was leading an idle life. He hoped to prop up the family credit, *and his own*, by marrying an English heiress; and he had succeeded in winning the affection of, and in being accepted by, Miss Adeline Kendrick. All went on smoothly till the question of settlement was brought on the carpet: then came enquiries, explanations, consultations, which were going on at this very time; and the uncertainty and suspense as to the result were making the young man irritable and even ill-tempered.

"Loo," he said in one of his fits of ill humour, "now that you have failed in landing a Duke, why don't you angle for a wealthy Commoner?"

Miss Loo was quite ready with her answer; "Yes, Barry, as it is absolutely necessary that money should be brought into the Family by one of us, I must try my luck as your venture does not promise to be successful."

"Nannie," turning to his younger sister, "what do

you think happened to me yesterday? Colonel Forrester is back from India, and has appeared at the Club. 'Why, Barry,' he said, 'I have not seen you since you were a boy; you must be twenty-four now.' 'Not a bit of it, Colonel, I am only twenty-two.' 'Come, Barry,' he said, 'that won't do; you are twenty-four if you are a day old; I remember standing for you as your Godfather.' Well, Colonel, you are right and you are wrong; according to the parish Register I am undoubtedly twenty-four; but then my sister, who is two years older than I am, sticks at twenty-four, and refuses to move on, and so I am kept at a stand-still.'"

The younger sister, who was the peace-maker of the Family, stopped further altercation by asking him, in one of her usual winning ways, to go and execute some commissions for her.

His absence was a relief; and we soon occupied ourselves in comparing notes as to our respective lives, pursuits, and amusements. I soon found how tame was life in Waterford, even with its Regiments, compared with life in Cheltenham without a Red-coat.

"We have Red-coats as good as your's, and better too," said Miss Macnamara the elder, "for we have the hunting men with their establishments down for the season, and they are always as ready for action in the ball-room as in the field."

"And," chimed in Miss Macnamara the younger, "there are Mr Close's attractive Exposition-receptions at home, and his stirring Lectures in the Church."

"Yes," said the elder sister, "a little Religion is not at all incompatible with a great deal of Fun."

"You astonish me," I remarked; "I thought people always belonged either to the Religious world or to the Worldly world."

"Not here in Cheltenham, at any rate," said the younger Sister; "there are certainly some who take their part either with the one or the other; but there are very many more who belong to both. If you go with me to Evening Service at St Mary's to-morrow, you will see pews crowded with ladies whose shawls conceal low dresses beneath; and as soon as the Service is over, they will hurry off to the Assembly Rooms and finish the evening with cards, conversation, or dancing."

The Irish possess a happy power of adaptation to the habits and customs of the people they sojourn among. In Ireland, the Macnamaras held the position of County magnates, living in a grand old Mansion with extensive demesne—hunting the County with their own pack—and exercising hospitality on such a lavish scale as to render Absenteeism an absolute necessity. Yet, upon their removal to Cheltenham, where they occupied a hired house in a Square, jobbed carriage and horses for the Season, and kept one hack for the Son, they took to their new life as complacently and readily as if they had never moved in any other sphere.

My Aunt was congratulating Mr and Mrs Macnamara upon exchanging the life at Ballyshan Castle, which was miserably dull and violently rollicking by turns, with the uniformly cheerful and sociable life at Cheltenham.

"You do not seem to take into account," smiled Mr Macnamara, "the loss of dignity which that change has brought us. We are no longer among the heads of a great County, but are mingled up among undistinguished gentry. Would you like to come down from your grandeur as the lady of Canon Haughton and become plain, simple Mrs Haughton?"

My Aunt, not perceiving that Mr Macnamara was speaking ironically, exclaimed energetically, "That I would; and I heartily wish I could prevail upon the Canon to follow your example in making England his home. There is one objection he could not get over —the English look down on the Irish, and seldom miss an opportunity of claiming superiority over them. At least I have been told that it is so; you have been here long enough to know whether it is true."

"Never in society," replied Mr Macnamara, "unless when provoked by some of our pretentious bragging countrymen. And even then it is done in a quiet, though effective way. As when, for instance, an Irishman boasts of his Country being the finest country in the world, possessing the most charming climate and the grandest scenery, the best hunting, fishing, and shooting; he is met with, 'O, indeed, you surprise me; but pray, tell me, if Ireland be such as you describe, how is it that there are so many Absentees?' When, however, it becomes a matter of *business* between an Englishman and an Irishman, then the national characteristic of the former comes out strong; caution in their dealing with us, and distrust of our professions. Old Kendrick, whose daughter is engaged to my son, brings his Solicitor to me, who first inspects my Title-deeds, and then wrings out of me all the charges upon the estate; and, upon my proposing that the girl's money should be handed over to me, and I would charge the Estate with a sum sufficient for the proper maintenance of the young couple until my death, he coolly informs me that the estate has already so many charges upon it that it resembles a target so riddled with bullets, that there was hardly space for another bullet mark."

What a highly cultivated country we traversed in our journey from Cheltenham to Leamington! fields bounded by green hedges and covered with luxuriant crops ripening for the harvest; rich pasture-land, where herds of cattle were feeding; avenues of fine old trees leading up to stately mansions, here crowning an eminence and displaying the whole length of the façade, there only peeping out from a surrounding of grand timber; Church spires or towers, with snug parsonage houses sheltering as it were beneath their shade; farm houses and homesteads, with stacks and ricks the produce of last year, standing like so many sentinels on guard. Beauty, wealth, industry, comfort, and security met my gaze as we sped along; however great might be the contrast between the Cities and Towns of England and Ireland, it was not greater than that between the rural and agricultural features and conditions of the two countries.

I was constantly calling my Aunt's attention to the picturesque beauty of the scenery—so different to what we had been accustomed to; no stone walls, no tumble-down farm buildings, no mud cabins, no wide dreary wastes separating Seat from Seat, as in Ireland, and making each seat to look like an Oasis in the Desert. She looked out on the succession of prospects with evident admiration, but with the jaundiced eye of an Irish woman who could not be brought to believe that England was not greatly indebted for its prosperity to Irish Capital and Labour.

"What magnificent crops!" I exclaimed.

"Very fine, indeed, Kathleen: but they would

have to stand till they dropped, if Irish labourers did not come over and reap them. And what do you think would become of those Hops, if Irish hands were not forthcoming to pick them ?"

After Cheltenham which struck me as being almost an Irish Colony, the visitors at Leamington looked wholly and thoroughly English as well as of a more aristocratic type.

Dr Jephson entered heartily into my Aunt's case, and promised a favourable issue in due course. Even from what I saw of his unfailing *bonhommie*, his adaptiveness to the various peculiarities of his patients, his intuitive discernment of their ailments, and the unlimited obedience which he had the art of enforcing to all his commands as to diet and exercise, I could quite understand how his successes were achieved and his great fame established.

The pleasant country round Leamington, and the many objects of interest within easy reach—such as the grand feudal Warwick Castle with its Picture treasures, Guy's Cliff which recals the Earl of Warwick of Edward the Second's time and the execution of the Favourite Gavestone, the ruins of that Castle of Kenilworth into which Queen Elizabeth was received in order to be fêted and from which poor Amy Robsart was forcibly carried away in order to be murdered, and especially Stratford-on-Avon with the house in which Shakespeare was born and the Church in which he was buried, rendered our stay one continued enjoyment.

We made more distant excursions; that to Coventry is strongly impressed on my mind. Standing on the platform of the station waiting for the train which was to take us back to Leamington, we were joined by an ecclesiastical dignitary of foreign caste of features, olive complexion, and portly figure, accompanied by a younger man in clerical costume. We all entered the same carriage, and as soon as we were seated I exclaimed abruptly, and I fear rudely:

"You are a Roman Catholic bishop."

"And pray, my dear young lady, how did you find out that?"

"By the ring you wear on your finger. Bishop Abraham—the Roman Catholic Bishop of Waterford—was dining with my uncle, and he wore a ring like yours. I asked him why he wore it, and he told me it was his wedding-ring; and then, remarking that I was looking at him in blank astonishment, he explained that the ring was the symbol and pledge of his being married to the Church."

"Allow me to introduce you to the Bishop of Melipotamos," said the younger man, who was his chaplain.

He was Nicholas Wiseman, afterwards Cardinal

Archbishop of Westminster. We found him a delightful companion. In the course of conversation Madame Bonaparte Wyse's name was mentioned, and my Aunt lamented that the steps that were then being taken for the separation between her and her husband could not be stopped. He lamented it equally, but did not see how any other course could be adopted, intimating that all the circumstances had been laid before him for his advice to be given.

"Among Protestants," remarked my Aunt, "the case would have been laid before lawyers, and prepared by them for the Divorce Court."

"You forget, madam, the Catholic Church does not allow of divorce."

"There must be exceptions, for the uncle of the very lady in question obtained a divorce in order to enable him to marry the Austrian Marie Louise."

"The law of the Church cannot be abrogated, though it may be defied."

As years passed on I used to hear of Papal aggressions in England, and of Bishop Wiseman's several appointments, his death, his public funeral; and at each successive notice of him I recurred in memory with great interest to my first and only meeting with him.

I was spending the winter of 1868 in Rome. One day in passing the Church of S. Tommaso degli

Inglesi, I was induced to enter it from being told by the *custode* that that day being the anniversary of the death of my countryman Cardinal Wiseman who had once been head of the English College attached to the Church, a commemorative service was being held. There was an immense catafalque, of fourteen feet high at least, in the centre aisle, with tall lighted candles at the four corners; quantities of tapers were burning on all sides; the air was laden with the smell of incense; and the choir was chanting a solemn dirge. It was an impressive scene, but my mind soon wandered from it, and I was once again in that railway carriage on the way from Coventry to Leamington when I had been so charmed with the playful wit and the kindly wisdom of him in whose memory this Service was performed. I was so absorbed in my own thoughts and recollections as to be only half aware of a long lighted taper being placed in my unresisting hand; and it was not till, either through absence or awkwardness, I had set my veil on fire, that I discovered I had been unconsciously assisting at the posthumous funeral obsequies, and honouring—" inani munere "—the memory of the man who was deservedly as popular in London as in Rome, and among Protestants almost as much as among Roman Catholics.

At length the term of our proposed absence was expiring, and my Aunt began to make preparation for returning to Waterford—in restored health, indeed, but with a regret she did not conceal at leaving the country where she had spent three eminently pleasant and profitable months. England had, indeed, become the land of her affection. At an early stage, even while staying at Cheltenham, she had formed the design, which she now revealed to me, of endeavouring to persuade her husband to pass the rest of his days in England. If he could not conscientiously put in a deputy to fulfil the legal and obligatory duties of the Prebend, then he might resign his stall; and in regard to his landed property, he might easily make an annual visit to Ireland and personally inspect it— thus avoiding the charge she had been in the habit of bringing against other landlords of leaving everything to their agents.

"Kathleen," she once impressively added, "my heart's fond wish and hope is, that you may marry an Englishman."

"My dear Aunt, then I shall be the first of my family to do so."

My Aunt lived to see her wish fulfilled, and my Father and Mother to bless my union with an Englishman. And England has been my peaceful and happy home for thirty years.

TURNBULL AND SPEARS, PRINTERS.

MAY, 1874.

A CLASSIFIED CATALOGUE OF
HENRY S. KING & CO.'S PUBLICATIONS.

CONTENTS.

	PAGE		PAGE
History and Biography	1	Books for the Young, &c.	16
Voyages and Travel	4	Works of Mr. Tennyson	19
Science	6	Poetry	20
Essays, Lectures, and Collected Papers	10	Fiction	22
		Cornhill Library of Fiction	25
Military Works	11	Theological	26
India and the East	14	Miscellaneous	31

HISTORY AND BIOGRAPHY.

AUTOBIOGRAPHY AND OTHER MEMORIALS OF MRS. GILBERT, FORMERLY ANN TAYLOR. By **Josiah Gilbert**, Author of "The Titian and Cadore Country," &c. In 2 vols. Post 8vo. With Steel Portraits, and several Wood Engravings. [*Preparing.*

AUTOBIOGRAPHY OF DR. A. B. GRANVILLE, M.D., F.R.S., &c. Edited, with a brief account of his concluding years, by his youngest Daughter. 2 vols. Demy 8vo. With a Portrait. [*Preparing.*

SAMUEL LOVER, THE LIFE AND UNPUBLISHED WORKS OF. By **Bayle Bernard**. In 2 vols. Post 8vo. With a Steel Portrait. [*Preparing.*

A MEMOIR OF THE REV. DR. ROWLAND WILLIAMS, with selections from his Note-books and Correspondence. Edited by **Mrs. Rowland Williams**. With a Photographic Portrait. In 2 vols. Large post 8vo. [*Shortly.*

POLITICAL WOMEN. By **Sutherland Menzies**. 2 vols. Post 8vo. Price 24s.

"Has all the information of history, with all the interest that attaches to biography."—*Scotsman.*

"A graceful contribution to the lighter record of history."—*English Churchman.*

65, *Cornhill;* & 12, *Paternoster Row, London.*

VOYAGES AND TRAVEL.

SOME TIME IN IRELAND; A Recollection. 1 vol. Crown 8vo.
[*Preparing.*]

WAYSIDE NOTES IN SCANDINAVIA. Being Notes of Travel in the North of Europe. By **Mark Antony Lower, M.A.** 1 vol. Crown 8vo.
[*Preparing.*]

ON THE ROAD TO KHIVA. By **David Ker**, late Khivan Correspondent of the *Daily Telegraph*. Illustrated with Photographs of the Country and its Inhabitants, and a copy of the Official Map in use during the Campaign, from the Survey of CAPTAIN LEUSILIN. 1 vol. Post 8vo. 12s.

VIZCAYA; or, Life in the land of the Carlists at the outbreak of the Insurrection, with some account of the Iron Mines and other characteristics of the country. With a Map and 8 Illustrations. Crown 8vo. [*Just ready.*]

ROUGH NOTES OF A VISIT TO BELGIUM, SEDAN, AND PARIS, in September, 1870-71. By **John Ashton.** Crown 8vo, bevelled boards. Price 3s. 6d.

"The author does not attempt to deal with military subjects, but writes sensibly of what he saw in 1870-71."—*John Bull.*
"Possesses a certain freshness from the straightforward simplicity with which it is written."—*Graphic.*
"An interesting work by a highly intelligent observer."—*Standard.*

THE ALPS OF ARABIA; or, Travels through Egypt, Sinai, Arabia, and the Holy Land. By **William Charles Maughan.** 1 vol. Demy 8vo, with Map. Price 12s.

"Deeply interesting and valuable."—*Edinburgh Review.*
"He writes freshly and with competent knowledge."—*Standard.*
"Very readable and instructive.... A work far above the average of such publications."—*John Bull.*

THE MISHMEE HILLS: an Account of a Journey made in an Attempt to Penetrate Thibet from Assam, to open New Routes for Commerce. By **T. T. Cooper,** Author of "The Travels of a Pioneer of Commerce." Demy 8vo. With Four Illustrations and Map. Price 10s. 6d.

"The volume, which will be of great use in India and among Indian merchants here, contains a good deal of matter that will interest ordinary readers. It is especially rich in sporting incidents."—*Standard.*

GOODMAN'S CUBA, THE PEARL OF THE ANTILLES. By **Walter Goodman.** Crown 8vo. Price 7s. 6d.

"A series of vivid and miscellaneous sketches. We can recommend this whole volume as very amusing reading."—*Pall Mall Gazette.*
"The whole book deserves the heartiest commendation... Sparkling and amusing from beginning to end."—*Spectator.*

FIELD AND FOREST RAMBLES OF A NATURALIST IN NEW BRUNSWICK. With Notes and Observations on the Natural History of Eastern Canada. By **A. Leith Adams, M.A.** In 8vo, cloth. Illustrated. Price 14s.

"Both sportsmen and naturalists will find this work replete with anecdote and carefully-recorded observation, which will entertain them."—*Nature.*
"Will be found interesting by those who take a pleasure either in sport or natural history."—*Athenæum.*
"To the naturalist the book will be most valuable... To the general reader most interesting."—*Evening Standard.*

ROUND THE WORLD IN 1870. A Volume of Travels, with Maps. By **A. D. Carlisle, B.A.**, Trin. Coll., Camb. Demy 8vo. Price 16s.

"We can only commend, which we do very heartily, an eminently sensible and readable book."—*British Quarterly Review.*

65, *Cornhill;* & 12, *Paternoster Row, London.*

Works Published by Henry S. King & Co., 5

VOYAGES AND TRAVEL—*continued.*

TENT LIFE WITH ENGLISH GIPSIES IN NORWAY. By **Hubert Smith.** In 8vo, cloth. Five full-page Engravings, and 31 smaller Illustrations, with Map of the Country showing Routes. Second Edition. Revised and Corrected. Price 21s.

"Written in a very lively style, and has throughout a smack of dry humour and satiric reflection which shows the writer to be a keen observer of men and things. We hope that many will read it and find in it the same amusement as ourselves."—*Times.*

FAYOUM ; OR, ARTISTS IN EGYPT. A Tour with M. Gérôme and others. By **J. Lenoir.** Crown 8vo, cloth. Illustrated. Price 7s. 6d.

"A pleasantly written and very readable book."—*Examiner.*
"The book is very amusing. . . . Who-ever may take it up will find he has with him a bright and pleasant companion."—*Spectator.*

SPITZBERGEN THE GATEWAY TO THE POLYNIA; OR, A VOYAGE TO SPITZBERGEN. By **Captain John C. Wells, R.N.** In 8vo, cloth. Profusely Illustrated. Price 21s.

"A charming book, remarkably well written and well illustrated."—*Standard.*
"Straightforward and clear in style, securing our confidence by its unaffected simplicity and good sense."—*Saturday Review.*

AN AUTUMN TOUR IN THE UNITED STATES AND CANADA. By **Lieut.-Col. J. G. Medley.** Crown 8vo. Price 5s.

"Colonel Medley's little volume is a pleasantly written account of a two-months' visit to America."—*Hour.*
"May be recommended as manly, sensible, and pleasantly written."—*Globe.*

THE NILE WITHOUT A DRAGOMAN. By **Frederic Eden.** Second Edition. In 1 vol. Crown 8vo, cloth. Price 7s. 6d.

"Should any of our readers care to imitate Mr. Eden's example, and wish to see things with their own eyes, and shift for themselves, next winter in Upper Egypt, they will find this book a very agreeable guide."—*Times.*
"It is a book to read during an autumn holiday."—*Spectator.*

IRELAND IN 1872. A Tour of Observation, with Remarks on Irish Public Questions. By **Dr. James Macaulay.** Crown 8vo. Price 7s. 6d.

"A careful and instructive book. Full of facts, full of information, and full of interest."—*Literary Churchman.*
"We have rarely met a book on Ireland which for impartiality of criticism and general accuracy of information could be so well recommended to the fair-minded Irish reader."—*Evening Standard.*

OVER THE DOVREFJELDS. By **J. S. Shepard,** Author of "A Ramble through Norway," &c. Crown 8vo. Illustrated. Price 4s. 6d.

"We have read many books of Norwegian travel, but . . . we have seen none so pleasantly narrative in its style, and so varied in its subject."—*Spectator.*
"As interesting a little volume as could be written on the subject. So interesting and shortly written that it will commend itself to all intending tourists."—*Examiner.*

A WINTER IN MOROCCO. By **Amelia Perrier.** Large crown 8vo. Illustrated. Price 10s. 6d.

"Well worth reading, and contains several excellent illustrations."—*Hour.*
"Miss Perrier is a very amusing writer. She has a good deal of humour, sees the oddity and quaintness of Oriental life with a quick observant eye, and evidently turned her opportunities of sarcastic examination to account."—*Daily News.*

65, Cornhill; & 12, Paternoster Row, London.

SCIENCE.

THE QUESTIONS OF AURAL SURGERY. By **James Hinton**, Aural Surgeon to Guy's Hospital. Post 8vo. Price 12s. 6d.

AN ATLAS OF DISEASES OF THE MEMBRANA TYMPANI. With Descriptive Text. By **James Hinton**, Aural Surgeon to Guy's Hospital. Post 8vo. Price £6 6s.

PHYSIOLOGY FOR PRACTICAL USE. By various Writers. Edited by **James Hinton**. 2 vols. Crown 8vo. With 50 Illustrations. 12s. 6d.

THE PRINCIPLES OF MENTAL PHYSIOLOGY. With their Applications to the Training and Discipline of the Mind, and the Study of its Morbid Conditions. By **W. B. Carpenter, LL.D., M.D., F.R.S.**, &c. 8vo. Illustrated. Price 12s.

SENSATION AND INTUITION. By **James Sully**. 1 vol. Post 8vo.
[*Nearly ready.*

THE EXPANSE OF HEAVEN. A Series of Essays on the Wonders of the Firmament. By **R. A. Proctor, B.A.** Second Edition. With a Frontispiece. Small crown 8vo. Price 6s.

"A very charming work; cannot fail to lift the reader's mind up 'through nature's work to nature's God.'"—*Standard.*

"Full of thought, readable, and popular."—*Brighton Gazette.*

STUDIES OF BLAST FURNACE PHENOMENA. By **M. L. Gruner**. Translated by **L. D. B. Gordon, F.R.S.E., F.G.S.**, &c. Demy 8vo. Price 7s. 6d.

"The whole subject is dealt with very copiously and clearly in all its parts, and can scarcely fail of appreciation at the hands of practical men, for whose use it is designed."—*Post.*

A LEGAL HANDBOOK FOR ARCHITECTS. By **Edward Jenkins** and **John Raymond**, Esqrs., Barristers-at-Law. In 1 vol. Price 6s.

"Architects, builders, and especially the building public will find the volume very useful."—*Freeman.*

"We can confidently recommend this book to all engaged in the building trades."—*Edinburgh Daily Review.*

CONTEMPORARY ENGLISH PSYCHOLOGY. From the French of **Professor Th. Ribot**. Large post 8vo. Price 9s. An Analysis of the Views and Opinions of the following Metaphysicians, as expressed in their writings :—

JAMES MILL, A. BAIN, JOHN STUART MILL, GEORGE H. LEWES, HERBERT SPENCER, SAMUEL BAILEY.

THE HISTORY OF CREATION, a Popular Account of the Development of the Earth and its Inhabitants, according to the theories of Kant, Laplace, Lamarck, and Darwin. By **Professor Ernst Hæckel**, of the University of Jena. With Coloured Plates and Genealogical Trees of the various groups of both plants and animals. 2 vols. Post 8vo. [*Preparing.*

Works Published by Henry S. King & Co.,

SCIENCE—*continued.*

A New Edition.

CHANGE OF AIR AND SCENE. A Physician's Hints about Doctors, Patients, Hygiène, and Society; with Notes of Excursions for health in the Pyrenees, and amongst the Watering-places of France (Inland and Seaward), Switzerland, Corsica, and the Mediterranean. By **Dr. Alphonse Donné**. Large post 8vo. Price 9s.

"A very readable and serviceable book. ... The real value of it is to be found in the accurate and minute information given with regard to a large number of places which have gained a reputation on the continent for their mineral waters."—*Pall Mall Gazette.*

"A singularly pleasant and chatty as well as instructive book about health."—*Guardian.*

MISS YOUMANS' FIRST BOOK OF BOTANY. Designed to cultivate the observing powers of Children. From the Author's latest Stereotyped Edition. New and Enlarged Edition, with 300 Engravings. Crown 8vo. Price 5s.

"It is but rarely that a school-book appears which is at once so novel in plan, so successful in execution, and so suited to the general want, as to command universal and unqualified approbation, but such has been the case with Miss Youmans' First Book of Botany. ... It has been everywhere welcomed as a timely and invaluable contribution to the improvement of primary education."—*Pall Mall Gazette.*

AN ARABIC AND ENGLISH DICTIONARY OF THE KORAN. By **Major J. Penrice, B.A.** 4to. Price 21s.

MODERN GOTHIC ARCHITECTURE. By **T. G. Jackson**. Crown 8vo. Price 5s.

"This thoughtful little book is worthy of the perusal of all interested in art or architecture."—*Standard.*
"The reader will find some of the most important doctrines of eminent art teachers practically applied in this little book, which is well written and popular in style."—*Manchester Examiner.*

A TREATISE ON RELAPSING FEVER. By **R. T. Lyons**, Assistant-Surgeon, Bengal Army. Small post 8vo. Price 7s. 6d.

"A practical work, thoroughly supported in its views by a series of remarkable cases."—*Standard.*

FOUR WORKS BY DR. EDWARD SMITH.

I. HEALTH AND DISEASE, as influenced by the Daily, Seasonal, and other Cyclical Changes in the Human System. A New Edition. Price 7s. 6d.
II. FOODS. Second Edition. Profusely Illustrated. Price 5s.
III. PRACTICAL DIETARY FOR FAMILIES, SCHOOLS, AND THE LABOURING CLASSES. A New Edition. Price 3s. 6d.
IV. CONSUMPTION IN ITS EARLY AND REMEDIABLE STAGES. A New Edition. Price 7s. 6d.

CHOLERA: HOW TO AVOID AND TREAT IT. Popular and Practical Notes by **Henry Blanc, M.D.** Crown 8vo. Price 4s. 6d.

"A very practical manual, based on experience and careful observation, full of excellent hints on a most dangerous disease."—*Standard.*

65, *Cornhill; & 12, Paternoster Row, London.*

SCIENCE—*continued*.

THE INTERNATIONAL SCIENTIFIC SERIES.

Fourth Edition.

I. THE FORMS OF WATER IN RAIN AND RIVERS, ICE AND GLACIERS. By **J. Tyndall, LL.D., F.R.S.** With 26 Illustrations. Crown 8vo. Price 5s.

Second Edition.

II. PHYSICS AND POLITICS; OR, THOUGHTS ON THE APPLICATION OF THE PRINCIPLES OF "NATURAL SELECTION" AND "INHERITANCE" TO POLITICAL SOCIETY. By **Walter Bagehot.** Crown 8vo. Price 4s.

Third Edition.

III. FOODS. By **Dr. Edward Smith.** Profusely Illustrated. Price 5s.

Third Edition.

IV. MIND AND BODY: THE THEORIES OF THEIR RELATIONS. By **Alexander Bain, LL.D.,** Professor of Logic at the University of Aberdeen. Four Illustrations. Price 4s.

Third Edition.

V. THE STUDY OF SOCIOLOGY. By **Herbert Spencer.** Crown 8vo. Price 5s.

Second Edition.

VI. ON THE CONSERVATION OF ENERGY. By **Professor Balfour Stewart.** Fourteen Engravings. Price 5s.

Second Edition.

VII. ANIMAL LOCOMOTION; or, Walking, Swimming, and Flying. By **Dr. J. B. Pettigrew, M.D., F.R.S.** 119 Illustrations. Price 5s.

Second Edition.

VIII. RESPONSIBILITY IN MENTAL DISEASE. By **Dr. Henry Maudsley.** Price 5s.

Second Edition.

IX. THE NEW CHEMISTRY. By **Professor Josiah P. Cooke,** of the Harvard University. Illustrated. Price 5s.

X. THE SCIENCE OF LAW. By **Professor Sheldon Amos.**
[*Just ready*.

65, *Cornhill;* & 12, *Paternoster Row, London.*

THE INTERNATIONAL SCIENTIFIC SERIES—*continued.*

FORTHCOMING VOLUMES.

Prof. E. J. MAREY.
The Animal Frame. [*In the Press.*

Prof. OSCAR SCHMIDT (Strasburg Univ.).
The Theory of Descent and Darwinism.
[*In the Press.*

Prof. VOGEL (Polytechnic Acad. of Berlin).
The Chemical Effects of Light.
[*In the Press.*

Prof. LONMEL (University of Erlangen).
Optics. [*In the Press.*

Rev. M. J. BERKELEY, M.A., F.L.S.,
and M. COOKE, M.A., LL.D.
Fungi; their Nature, Influences, and Uses.

Prof. W. KINGDOM CLIFFORD, M.A.
The First Principles of the Exact Sciences explained to the non-mathematical.

Prof. T. H. HUXLEY, LL.D., F.R.S.
Bodily Motion and Consciousness.

Dr. W. B. CARPENTER, LL.D., F.R.S.
The Physical Geography of the Sea.

Prof. WILLIAM ODLING, F.R.S.
The Old Chemistry viewed from the new Standpoint.

W. LAUDER LINDSAY, M.D., F.R.S.E.
Mind in the Lower Animals.

Sir JOHN LUBBOCK, Bart., F.R.S.
The Antiquity of Man.

Prof. W. T. THISELTON DYER, B.A., B.SC.
Form and Habit in Flowering Plants.

Mr. J. N. LOCKYER, F.R.S.
Spectrum Analysis.

Prof. MICHAEL FOSTER, M.D.
Protoplasm and the Cell Theory.

Prof. W. STANLEY JEVONS.
Money: and the Mechanism of Exchange.

Dr. H. CHARLTON BASTIAN, M.D., F.R.S.
The Brain as an Organ of Mind.

Prof. A. C. RAMSAY, LL.D., F.R.S.
Earth Sculpture: Hills, Valleys, Mountains, Plains, Rivers, Lakes; how they were Produced, and how they have been Destroyed.

Prof. RUDOLPH VIRCHOW (Berlin Univ.)
Morbid Physiological Action.

Prof. CLAUDE BERNARD.
Physical and Metaphysical Phenomena of Life.

Prof. H. SAINTE-CLAIRE DEVILLE.
An Introduction to General Chemistry.

Prof. WURTZ.
Atoms and the Atomic Theory.

Prof. DE QUATREFAGES.
The Negro Races.

Prof. LACAZE-DUTHIERS.
Zoology since Cuvier.

Prof. BERTHELOT.
Chemical Synthesis.

Prof. J. ROSENTHAL.
General Physiology of Muscles and Nerves.

Prof. JAMES D. DANA, M.A., LL.D.
On Cephalization; or, Head-Characters in the Gradation and Progress of Life.

Prof. S. W. JOHNSON, M.A.
On the Nutrition of Plants.

Prof. AUSTIN FLINT, Jr. M.D.
The Nervous System and its Relation to the Bodily Functions.

Prof. W. D. WHITNEY.
Modern Linguistic Science.

Prof. BERNSTEIN (University of Halle).
Physiology of the Senses.

Prof. FERDINAND COHN (Breslau Univ.).
Thallophytes (Algæ, Lichens, Fungi).

Prof. HERMANN (University of Zurich).
Respiration.

Prof. LEUCKART (University of Leipsic).
Outlines of Animal Organization.

Prof. LIEBREICH (University of Berlin).
Outlines of Toxicology.

Prof. KUNDT (University of Strasburg).
On Sound.

Prof. REES (University of Erlangen).
On Parasitic Plants.

Prof. STEINTHAL (University of Berlin).
Outlines of the Science of Language.

ESSAYS, LECTURES, AND COLLECTED PAPERS.

IN STRANGE COMPANY; or, The Note Book of a Roving Correspondent. By **James Greenwood,** "The Amateur Casual." Second Edition. Crown 8vo. 6s.

"A bright, lively book."—*Standard.*
"Has all the interest of romance."—*Queen.*

"Some of the papers remind us of Charles Lamb on beggars and chimney sweeps."—*Echo.*

MASTER-SPIRITS. By **Robert Buchanan.** Post 8vo. 10s. 6d.

" Good Books are the precious life-blood of Master-Spirits."—*Milton.*

" Full of fresh and vigorous writing, such as can only be produced by a man of keen and independent intellect."—*Saturday Review.*
"A very pleasant and readable book."—*Examiner.*

" Written with a beauty of language and a spirit of vigorous enthusiasm rare even in our best living word-painters."—*Standard.*
" Mr. Buchanan is a writer whose books the critics may always open with satisfaction . . . both manly and artistic."—*Hour.*

THEOLOGY IN THE ENGLISH POETS; COWPER, COLERIDGE, WORDSWORTH, and BURNS. Being Lectures delivered by the **Rev. Stopford A. Brooke,** Chaplain in Ordinary to Her Majesty the Queen. Crown 8vo. 9s.

SHORT LECTURES ON THE LAND LAWS. Delivered before the Working Men's College. By **T. Lean Wilkinson.** Crown 8vo. limp cloth. 2s.

"A very handy and intelligible epitome of the general principles of existing land laws."—*Standard.*

AN ESSAY ON THE CULTURE OF THE OBSERVING POWERS OF CHILDREN, especially in connection with the Study of Botany. By **Eliza A. Youmans.** Edited, with Notes and a Supplement, by **Joseph Payne,** F.C.P., Author of "Lectures on the Science and Art of Education," &c. Crown 8vo. 2s. 6d.

"This study, according to her just notions on the subject, is to be fundamentally based on the exercise of the pupil's own powers of observation. He is to see and examine the properties of plants and flowers at first hand, not merely to be informed of what others have seen and examined."—*Pall Mall Gazette.*

THE GENIUS OF CHRISTIANITY UNVEILED. Being Essays by **William Godwin,** Author of "Political Justice," &c. Never before published. 1 vol. Crown 8vo. 7s. 6d.

"Few have thought more clearly and directly than William Godwin, or expressed their reflections with more simplicity and unreserve."—*Examiner.*

"The deliberate thoughts of Godwin deserve to be put before the world for reading and consideration."—*Athenæum.*

MILITARY WORKS.

RUSSIA'S ADVANCE EASTWARD; Translated from the German of Lieut. Stumm. By Lt. C. E. H. Vincent. 1 vol. Crown 8vo. With a Map.

THE VOLUNTEER, THE MILITIAMAN, AND THE REGULAR SOLDIER; a Conservative View of the Armies of England, Past, Present, and Future, as Seen in January, 1874. By A Public School Boy. 1 vol. Crown 8vo.

THE OPERATIONS OF THE FIRST ARMY, UNDER STEINMETZ. By Major von Schell. Translated by Captain E. O. Hollist. Demy 8vo. Uniform with the other volumes in the Series. Price 10s. 6d.

THE OPERATIONS OF THE FIRST ARMY UNDER GEN. VON GOEBEN. By Major von Schell. Translated by Col. C. H. von Wright. Four Maps. Demy 8vo. Price 9s.

THE OPERATIONS OF THE FIRST ARMY IN NORTHERN FRANCE AGAINST FAIDHERBE. By Colonel Count Hermann von Wartensleben, Chief of the Staff of the First Army. Translated by Colonel C. H. von Wright. In demy 8vo. Uniform with the above. Price 9s.

"Very clear, simple, yet eminently instructive, is this history. It is not overladen with useless details, is written in good taste, and possesses the inestimable value of being in great measure the record of operations actually witnessed by the author, supplemented by official documents."—*Athenæum.*

THE GERMAN ARTILLERY IN THE BATTLES NEAR METZ. Based on the official reports of the German Artillery. By Captain Hoffbauer, Instructor in the German Artillery and Engineer School. Translated by Capt. E. O. Hollist. [*Preparing.*

THE OPERATIONS OF THE BAVARIAN ARMY CORPS. By Captain Hugo Helvig. Translated by Captain G. S. Schwabe. With 5 large Maps. Demy 8vo. In 2 vols. Price 24s. Uniform with the other Books in the Series.

AUSTRIAN CAVALRY EXERCISE. From an Abridged Edition compiled by Captain Illia Woinovits, of the General Staff, on the Tactical Regulations of the Austrian Army, and prefaced by a General Sketch of the Organisation, &c., of the Country. Translated by Captain W. S. Cooke. Crown 8vo, cloth. Price 7s.

History of the Organisation, Equipment, and War Services of

THE REGIMENT OF BENGAL ARTILLERY. Compiled from Published Official and other Records, and various private sources, by Major Francis W. Stubbs, Royal (late Bengal) Artillery. Vol. I. will contain War Services. The Second Volume will be published separately, and will contain the History of the Organisation and Equipment of the Regiment. In 2 vols. 8vo. With Maps and Plans. [*Preparing.*

65, *Cornhill;* & 12, *Paternoster Row, London.*

MILITARY WORKS—*continued.*

VICTORIES AND DEFEATS. An Attempt to explain the Causes which have led to them. An Officer's Manual. By **Col. R. P. Anderson.** Demy 8vo. Price 14s.

"The present book proves that he is a diligent student of military history, his illustrations ranging over a wide field, and including ancient and modern Indian and European warfare."—*Standard.*

"The young officer should have it al-ways at hand to open anywhere and read a bit, and we warrant him that let that bit be ever so small it will give him material for an hour's thinking."—*United Service Gazette.*

THE FRONTAL ATTACK OF INFANTRY. By **Capt. Laymann**, Instructor of Tactics at the Military College, Neisse. Translated by **Colonel Edward Newdigate.** Crown 8vo, limp cloth. Price 2s. 6d.

"An exceedingly useful kind of book. A valuable acquisition to the military student's library. It recounts, in the first place, the opinions and tactical formations which regulated the German army during the early battles of the late war; explains how these were modified in the course of the campaign by the terrible and unanticipated effect of the fire; and how, accordingly, troops should be trained to attack in future wars."—*Naval and Military Gazette.*

ELEMENTARY MILITARY GEOGRAPHY, RECONNOITRING, AND SKETCHING. Compiled for Non-Commissioned Officers and Soldiers of all Arms. By **Lieut. C. E. H. Vincent,** Royal Welsh Fusiliers. Small crown 8vo. Price 2s. 6d.

"This manual takes into view the necessity of every soldier knowing how to read a military map, in order to know to what points in an enemy's country to direct his attention; and provides for this necessity by giving, in terse and sensible language, definitions of varieties of ground and the advantages they present in warfare, together with a number of useful hints in military sketching."—*Naval and Military Gazette.*

THREE WORKS BY LIEUT.-COL. THE HON. A. ANSON, V.C., M.P.

THE ABOLITION OF PURCHASE AND THE ARMY REGULATION BILL OF 1871. Crown 8vo. Price One Shilling.

ARMY RESERVES AND MILITIA REFORMS. Crown 8vo. Sewed. Price One Shilling.

THE STORY OF THE SUPERSESSIONS. Crown 8vo. Price Sixpence.

STUDIES IN THE NEW INFANTRY TACTICS. Parts I. & II. By **Major W. von Schereff.** Translated from the German by **Col. Lumley Graham.** Price 7s. 6d.

"The subject of the respective advantages of attack and defence, and of the methods in which each form of battle should be carried out under the fire of modern arms, is exhaustively and admirably treated; indeed, we cannot but consider it to be decidedly superior to any work which has hitherto appeared in English upon this all-important subject."—*Standard.*

Second Edition. Revised and Corrected.

TACTICAL DEDUCTIONS FROM THE WAR OF 1870—71. By **Captain A. von Boguslawski.** Translated by **Colonel Lumley Graham,** late 18th (Royal Irish) Regiment. Demy 8vo. Uniform with the above. Price 7s.

"We must, without delay, impress brain and forethought into the British Service; and we cannot commence the good work too soon, or better, than by placing the two books ('The Operations of the German Armies' and 'Tactical Deductions') we have here criticised, in every military library, and introducing them as class-books in every tactical school."—*United Service Gazette.*

THE OPERATIONS OF THE SOUTH ARMY IN JANUARY AND FEBRUARY, 1871. Compiled from the Official War Documents of the Head-quarters of the Southern Army. By **Count Hermann von Wartensleben,** Colonel in the Prussian General Staff. Translated by **Colonel C. H. von Wright.** Demy 8vo, with Maps. Uniform with the above. Price 6s.

55, *Cornhill;* & 12, *Paternoster Row, London.*

Works Published by Henry S. King & Co.,

MILITARY WORKS—*continued.*

THE ARMY OF THE NORTH-GERMAN CONFEDERATION.
A Brief Description of its Organisation, of the different Branches of the Service and their "Rôle" in War, of its Mode of Fighting, &c. By a **Prussian General.** Translated from the German by **Col. Edward Newdigate.** Demy 8vo. Price 5*s.*

"The work is quite essential to the full use of the other volumes of the 'German Military Series,' which Messrs. King are now producing in handsome uniform style."—*United Service Magazine.*
"Every page of the book deserves attentive study.... The information given on mobilisation, garrison troops, keeping up establishment during war, and on the employment of the different branches of the service, is of great value."—*Standard.*

THE OPERATIONS OF THE GERMAN ARMIES IN FRANCE, FROM SEDAN TO THE END OF THE WAR OF 1870-71. With Large Official Map. From the Journals of the Head-quarters Staff, by **Major Wm. Blume.** Translated by **E. M. Jones,** Major 20th Foot, late Professor of Military History, Sandhurst. Demy 8vo. Price 9*s.*

"The book is of absolute necessity to the military student.... The work is one of high merit."—*United Service Gazette.*
"The work of Major von Blume in its English dress forms the most valuable addition to our stock of works upon the war that our press has put forth. Our space forbids our doing more than commending it earnestly as the most authentic and instructive narrative of the second section of the war that has yet appeared."—*Saturday Review.*

HASTY INTRENCHMENTS. By **Colonel A. Brialmont.** Translated by **Lieutenant Charles A. Empson, R.A.** Demy 8vo. Nine Plates. Price 6*s.*

"A valuable contribution to military literature."—*Athenæum.*
"In seven short chapters it gives plain directions for forming shelter-trenches, with the best method of carrying the necessary tools, and it offers practical illustrations of the use of hasty intrenchments on the field of battle."—*United Service Magazine.*
"It supplies that which our own text-books give but imperfectly, viz., hints as to how a position can best be strengthened by means ... of such extemporised intrenchments and batteries as can be thrown up by infantry in the space of four or five hours ... deserves to become a standard military work."—*Standard.*

STUDIES IN LEADING TROOPS. By **Colonel von Verdy Du Vernois.** An authorised and accurate Translation by **Lieutenant H. J. T. Hildyard,** 71st Foot. Parts I. and II. Demy 8vo. Price 7*s.*

₊₊* General BEAUCHAMP WALKER says of this work:—"I recommend the first two numbers of Colonel von Verdy's 'Studies' to the attentive perusal of my brother officers. They supply a want which I have often felt during my service in this country, namely, a minuter tactical detail of the minor operations of war than any but the most observant and fortunately-placed staff-officer is in a position to give. I have read and re-read them very carefully, I hope with profit, certainly with great interest, and believe that practice, in the sense of these 'Studies,' would be a valuable preparation for manœuvres on a more extended scale."—*Berlin, June, 1872.*

CAVALRY FIELD DUTY. By **Major-General von Mirus.** Translated by **Captain Frank S. Russell,** 14th (King's) Hussars. Crown 8vo, limp cloth. Price 7*s.* 6*d.*

DISCIPLINE AND DRILL. Four Lectures delivered to the London Scottish Rifle Volunteers. By **Captain S. Flood Page.** A New and Cheaper Edition. Price 1*s.*

"An admirable collection of lectures."—*Times.*
"The very useful and interesting work."—*Volunteer Service Gazette.*

65, Cornhill; & 12, Paternoster Row, London.

INDIA AND THE EAST.

THE THREATENED FAMINE IN BENGAL; How it may be met, and the Recurrence of Famines in India prevented. Being No. 1 of "Occasional Notes on Indian Affairs." By **Sir H. Bartle E. Frere, G.C.B., G.C.S.I.,** &c. &c. Crown 8vo. With 3 Maps. Price 5s.

THE ORIENTAL SPORTING MAGAZINE. A Reprint of the first 5 Volumes, in 2 Volumes, demy 8vo. Price 28s.

"Lovers of sport will find ample amusement in the varied contents of these two volumes."—*Allen's Indian Mail.*

"Full of interest for the sportsman and naturalist. Full of thrilling adventures of sportsmen who have attacked the fiercest and most gigantic specimens of the animal world in their native jungle. It is seldom we get so many exciting incidents in a similar amount of space... Well suited to the libraries of country gentlemen and all those who are interested in sporting matters."—*Civil Service Gazette.*

THE EUROPEAN IN INDIA. A Hand-book of Practical Information for those proceeding to, or residing in, the East Indies, relating to Outfits, Routes, Time for Departure, Indian Climate, &c. By **Edmund C. P. Hull.** With a MEDICAL GUIDE FOR ANGLO-INDIANS. Being a Compendium of Advice to Europeans in India, relating to the Preservation and Regulation of Health. By **R. S. Mair, M.D., F.R.C.S.E.**, late Deputy Coroner of Madras. In 1 vol. Post 8vo. Price 6s.

"Full of all sorts of useful information to the English settler or traveller in India."—*Standard.*

"One of the most valuable books ever published in India—valuable for its sound information, its careful array of pertinent facts, and its sterling common sense. It supplies a want which few persons may have discovered, but which everybody will at once recognise when once the contents of the book have been mastered. The medical part of the work is invaluable."—*Calcutta Guardian.*

THE MEDICAL GUIDE FOR ANGLO-INDIANS. Being a Compendium of advice to Europeans in India, relating to the Preservation and Regulation of Health. By **R. S. Mair, F.R.C.S.E.**, late Deputy Coroner of Madras. Reprinted, with numerous additions and corrections, from "The European in India."

EASTERN EXPERIENCES. By **L. Bowring, C.S.I.**, Lord Canning's Private Secretary, and for many years the Chief Commissioner of Mysore and Coorg. In 1 vol. Demy 8vo. Price 16s. Illustrated with Maps and Diagrams.

"An admirable and exhaustive geographical, political, and industrial survey."—*Athenæum.*

"This compact and methodical summary of the most authentic information relating to countries whose welfare is intimately connected with our own."—*Daily News.*

"Interesting even to the general reader, but more especially so to those who may have a special concern in that portion of our Indian Empire."—*Post.*

Works Published by Henry S. King & Co.,

INDIA AND THE EAST—*continued.*

TAS-HĪL UL KALĀM; OR, HINDUSTANI MADE EASY. By **Captain W. R. M. Holroyd**, Bengal Staff Corps, Director of Public Instruction, Punjab. Crown 8vo. Price 5s.

"As clear and as instructive as possible." —*Standard.*
"Contains a great deal of most necessary information, that is not to be found in any other work on the subject that has crossed our path."—*Homeward Mail.*

Second Edition.

WESTERN INDIA BEFORE AND DURING THE MUTINIES. Pictures drawn from Life. By **Major-Gen. Sir George Le Grand Jacob, K.C.S.I., C.B.** In 1 vol. Crown 8vo. Price 7s. 6d.

"The most important contribution to the history of Western India during the Mutinies which has yet, in a popular form, been made public."—*Athenæum.*
"Few men more competent than himself to speak authoritatively concerning Indian affairs."—*Standard.*

EDUCATIONAL COURSE OF SECULAR SCHOOL BOOKS FOR INDIA. Edited by **J. S. Laurie**, of the Inner Temple, Barrister-at-Law; formerly H.M. Inspector of Schools, England; Assistant Royal Commissioner, Ireland; Special Commissioner, African Settlements; Director of Public Instruction, Ceylon.

"These valuable little works will prove of real service to many of our readers, especially to those who intend entering the Civil Service of India."—*Civil Service Gazette.*

The following Works are now ready:—

	s. d.
THE FIRST HINDUSTANI READER, stiff linen wrapper	0 6
Ditto ditto strongly bound in cloth	0 9
THE SECOND HINDUSTANI READER, stiff linen wrapper	0 6
Ditto ditto strongly bound in cloth	0 9

	s. d.
GEOGRAPHY OF INDIA, with Maps and Historical Appendix, tracing the growth of the British Empire in Hindustan. 128 pp. Cloth	1 6

In the Press.

ELEMENTARY GEOGRAPHY OF INDIA.

FACTS AND FEATURES OF INDIAN HISTORY, in a series of alternating Reading Lessons and Memory Exercises.

EXCHANGE TABLES OF STERLING AND INDIAN RUPEE CURRENCY, UPON A NEW AND EXTENDED SYSTEM, embracing Values from One Farthing to One Hundred Thousand Pounds, and at rates progressing, in Sixteenths of a Penny, from 1s. 9d. to 2s. 3d. per Rupee. By **Donald Fraser**, Accountant to the British Indian Steam Navigation Co. Limited. Royal 8vo. Price 10s. 6d.

"The calculations must have entailed great labour on the author, but the work is one which we fancy must become a standard one in all business houses which have dealings with any country where the rupee and the English pound are standard coins of currency."—*Inverness Courier.*

65, *Cornhill;* & 12, *Paternoster Row, London.*

BOOKS FOR THE YOUNG AND FOR LENDING LIBRARIES.

AUNT MARY'S BRAN PIE. By the Author of "St. Olave's," "When I was a Little Girl," &c. [*In the Press.*

BY STILL WATERS. A Story in One Volume. By **Edward Garrett**. [*Preparing.*

WAKING AND WORKING; OR, FROM GIRLHOOD TO WOMANHOOD. By **Mrs. G. S. Reaney**. 1 vol. Crown 8vo. Illustrated. [*Preparing.*

PRETTY LESSONS IN VERSE FOR GOOD CHILDREN, with some Lessons in Latin, in Easy Rhyme. By **Sara Coleridge**. A New Edition. [*Preparing.*

NEW WORKS BY HESBA STRETTON.

CASSY. A New Story, by **Hesba Stretton**. Square crown 8vo, Illustrated, uniform with "Lost Gip." Price 1s. 6d.

THE KING'S SERVANTS. By **Hesba Stretton**, Author of "Lost Gip." Square crown 8vo, uniform with "Lost Gip." 8 Illustrations. Price 1s. 6d.

Part I.—Faithful in Little. Part II.—Unfaithful. Part III.—Faithful in Much.

LOST GIP. By **Hesba Stretton**, Author of "Little Meg," "Alone in London." Square crown 8vo. Six Illustrations. Price 1s. 6d.

*** *A HANDSOMELY BOUND EDITION, WITH TWELVE ILLUSTRATIONS, PRICE HALF-A-CROWN.*

DADDY'S PET. By **Mrs. Ellen Ross** (Nelsie Brook). Square crown 8vo, uniform with "Lost Gip." 6 Illustrations. Price 1s.

"We have been more than pleased with this simple bit of writing."—*Christian World.*

"Full of deep feeling and true and noble sentiment."—*Brighton Gazette.*

SEEKING HIS FORTUNE, AND OTHER STORIES. Crown 8vo. Four Illustrations. Price 3s. 6d.

CONTENTS.—Seeking his Fortune.—Oluf and Stephanoff.—What's in a Name?—Contrast.—Onesta.

Three Works by MARTHA FARQUHARSON.

I. ELSIE DINSMORE. Crown 8vo. 3s. 6d.
II. ELSIE'S GIRLHOOD. Crown 8vo. 3s. 6d.
III. ELSIE'S HOLIDAYS AT ROSELANDS. Crown 8vo. 3s. 6d.

Each Story is independent and complete in itself. They are published in uniform size and price, and are elegantly bound and illustrated.

THE AFRICAN CRUISER. A Midshipman's Adventures on the West Coast. A Book for Boys. By S. **Whitchurch Sadler, R.N.**, Author of "Marshall Vavasour." Illustrations. Crown 8vo. 3s. 6d.

"A capital story of youthful adventure. ... Sea-loving boys will find few pleasanter gift books this season than 'The African Cruiser.'"—*Hour.*

"Sea yarns have always been in favour with boys, but this, written in a brisk style by a thorough sailor, is crammed full of adventures."—*Times.*

BOOKS FOR THE YOUNG, ETC.—*continued.*

THE LITTLE WONDER-HORN. Series of "*Stories told to a Child.*" 3*s.* 6*d.* By Jean Ingelow. A Second Fifteen Illustrations. Cloth, gilt.

"We like all the contents of the 'Little Wonder-Horn' very much."—*Athenæum.*
"We recommend it with confidence."—*Pall Mall Gazette.*

"Full of fresh and vigorous fancy: it is worthy of the author of some of the best of our modern verse."—*Standard.*

BRAVE MEN'S FOOTSTEPS. A Book of Example and Anecdote for Young People. Second Edition. By the Editor of "**Men who have Risen.**" With Four Illustrations, by **C. Doyle.** 3*s.* 6*d.*

"A readable and instructive volume."—*Examiner.*
"The little volume is precisely of the stamp to win the favour of those who, in

choosing a gift for a boy, would consult his moral development as well as his temporary pleasure."—*Daily Telegraph.*

PLUCKY FELLOWS. A Book for Boys. By **Stephen J. Mac Kenna.** With Six Illustrations. Second Edition. Crown 8vo. 3*s.* 6*d.*

"This is one of the very best 'Books for Boys' which have been issued this year."—*Morning Advertiser.*
"A thorough book for boys . . . written

throughout in a manly straightforward manner that is sure to win the hearts of the children."—*London Society.*

GUTTA-PERCHA WILLIE, THE WORKING GENIUS. By **George Macdonald.** With Illustrations by **Arthur Hughes.** Crown 8vo. Second Edition. 3*s.* 6*d.*

"The cleverest child we know assures us she has read this story through five times. Mr. Macdonald will, we are convinced,

accept that verdict upon his little work as final."—*Spectator.*

THE TRAVELLING MENAGERIE. By **Charles Camden,** Author of "Hoity Toity." Illustrated by **J. Mahoney.** Crown 8vo. 3*s.* 6*d.*

"A capital little book . . . . deserves a wide circulation among our boys and girls."—*Hour.*

"A very attractive story." — *Public Opinion.*

THE DESERT PASTOR, JEAN JAROUSSEAU. Translated from the French of **Eugene Pelletan.** By **Colonel E. P. De L'Hoste.** In fcap. 8vo, with an Engraved Frontispiece. New Edition. 3*s.* 6*d.*

"A touching record of the struggles in the cause of religious liberty of a real man."—*Graphic.*
"There is a poetical simplicity and picturesqueness; the noblest heroism; unpre-

tentious religion: pure love, and the spectacle of a household brought up in the fear of the Lord. . . . ."—*Illustrated London News.*

THE DESERTED SHIP. A Real Story of the Atlantic. By **Cupples Howe,** Master Mariner. Illustrated by **Townley Green.** Crown 8vo. 3*s.* 6*d.*

"Curious adventures with bears, seals, and other Arctic animals, and with scarcely more human Esquimaux, form the mass of

material with which the story deals, and will much interest boys who have a spice of romance in their composition."—*Courant.*

HOITY TOITY, THE GOOD LITTLE FELLOW. By **Charles Camden.** Illustrated. Crown 8vo. 3*s.* 6*d.*

"Relates very pleasantly the history of a charming little fellow who meddles always with a kindly disposition with other people's

affairs and helps them to do right. There are many shrewd lessons to be picked up in this clever little story."—*Public Opinion.*

65, Cornhill; & 12, Paternoster Row, London.

18   *Works Published by Henry S. King & Co.,*

BOOKS FOR THE YOUNG, ETC.—*continued.*

SLAVONIC FAIRY TALES. From Russian, Servian, Polish, and Bohemian Sources. Translated by **John T. Naaké.** Crown 8vo. Illustrated. Price 5s.

AT SCHOOL WITH AN OLD DRAGOON. By **Stephen J. Mac Kenna.** Crown 8vo. Six Illustrations. Price 5s.

"Consisting almost entirely of startling stories of military adventure... Boys will find them sufficiently exciting reading."—*Times.*

"These yarns give some very spirited and interesting descriptions of soldiering in various parts of the world."—*Spectator.*

"Mr. Mac Kenna's former work, 'Plucky Fellows,' is already a general favourite, and those who read the stories of the Old Dragoon will find that he has still plenty of materials at hand for pleasant tales, and has lost none of his power in telling them well."—*Standard.*

FANTASTIC STORIES. Translated from the German of **Richard Leander,** by **Paulina B. Granville.** Crown 8vo. Eight full-page Illustrations, by **M. E. Fraser-Tytler.** Price 5s.

"Short, quaint, and, as they are fitly called, fantastic, they deal with all manner of subjects."—*Guardian.*

"'Fantastic' is certainly the right epithet to apply to some of these strange tales."—*Examiner*

Third Edition.

STORIES IN PRECIOUS STONES. By **Helen Zimmern.** With Six Illustrations. Crown 8vo. Price 5s.

"A pretty little book which fanciful young persons will appreciate, and which will remind its readers of many a legend, and many an imaginary virtue attached to the gems they are so fond of wearing."—*Post.*

"A series of pretty tales which are half fantastic, half natural, and pleasantly quaint, as befits stories intended for the young."—*Daily Telegraph.*

THE GREAT DUTCH ADMIRALS. By **Jacob de Liefde.** Crown 8vo. Illustrated. Price 5s.

"May be recommended as a wholesome present for boys. They will find in it numerous tales of adventure."—*Athenæum.*

"A really good book."—*Standard.*
"A really excellent book."—*Spectator.*

PHANTASMION. A Fairy Romance. A new Edition. By **Sara Coleridge.** With an Introductory Preface by the **Right Hon. Lord Coleridge of Ottery S. Mary.** In 1 vol. Crown 8vo. Price 7s. 6d.

LAYS OF A KNIGHT ERRANT IN MANY LANDS. By **Major-General Sir Vincent Eyre, C.B., G.C.S.I., &c.** Square crown 8vo. Six Illustrations. Price 7s. 6d.

Pharaoh Land.
Home Land.
Wonder Land.
Rhine Land.

BEATRICE AYLMER AND OTHER TALES. By the Author of "Brompton Rectory." 1 vol. Crown 8vo.   [*Preparing.*

THE TASMANIAN LILY. By **James Bonwick.** Crown 8vo. Illustrated. Price 5s.

"An interesting and useful work."—*Hour.*
"The characters of the story are capitally conceived, and are full of those touches which give them a natural appearance."—*Public Opinion.*

MIKE HOWE, THE BUSHRANGER OF VAN DIEMEN'S LAND. By **James Bonwick,** Author of "The Tasmanian Lily," &c. Crown 8vo. With a Frontispiece.

"He illustrates the career of the bushranger half a century ago; and this he does in a highly creditable manner; his delineations of life in the bush are, to say the least, exquisite, and his representations of character are very marked."—*Edinburgh Courant.*

65, Cornhill; & 12, Paternoster Row, London.

WORKS BY ALFRED TENNYSON, D.C.L.,
POET LAUREATE.

THE CABINET EDITION.

Messrs. HENRY S. KING & Co. have the pleasure to announce that they will immediately issue an Edition of the Laureate's works, in *Ten Monthly Volumes*, foolscap 8vo, to be entitled "The Cabinet Edition," at *Half-a-Crown each*, which will contain the whole of Mr. Tennyson's works. The first volume will be illustrated by a beautiful Photographic Portrait, and subsequent Volumes will each contain a Frontispiece. They will be tastefully bound in Crimson Cloth, and will be issued in the following order :—

Vol.
1. EARLY POEMS.
2. ENGLISH IDYLLS & OTHER POEMS.
3. LOCKSLEY HALL & OTHER POEMS.
4. AYLMER'S FIELD & OTHER POEMS.
5. IDYLLS OF THE KING.

Vol.
6. IDYLLS OF THE KING.
7. IDYLL OF THE KING.
8. THE PRINCESS.
9. MAUD AND ENOCH ARDEN.
10. IN MEMORIAM.

Subscribers' names received by all Booksellers.

	PRICE.
	s. d.
POEMS. Small 8vo.	9 0
MAUD AND OTHER POEMS. Small 8vo.	5 0
THE PRINCESS. Small 8vo.	5 0
IDYLLS OF THE KING. Small 8vo.	7 0
,, ,, Collected. Small 8vo.	12 0
ENOCH ARDEN, &c. Small 8vo.	6 0
THE HOLY GRAIL, AND OTHER POEMS. Small 8vo.	7 0
GARETH AND LYNETTE. Small 8vo.	5 0
SELECTIONS FROM THE ABOVE WORKS. Square 8vo, cloth extra	5 0
SONGS FROM THE ABOVE WORKS. Square 8vo, cloth extra	5 0
IN MEMORIAM. Small 8vo.	6 0
LIBRARY EDITION OF MR. TENNYSON'S WORKS. 6 vols. Post 8vo, each	10 6
POCKET VOLUME EDITION OF MR. TENNYSON'S WORKS. 10 vols., in neat case	45 0
,, gilt edges	50 0
THE WINDOW; OR, THE SONGS OF THE WRENS. A Series of Songs. By ALFRED TENNYSON. With Music by ARTHUR SULLIVAN. 4to, cloth, gilt extra	21 0

65, *Cornhill;* & 12, *Paternoster Row, London.*

POETRY.

LYRICS OF LOVE, Selected and arranged from Shakspeare to Tennyson, by **W. Davenport Adams**. Fcap. 8vo. Price 3s. 6d.

"We cannot too highly commend this work, delightful in its contents and so pretty in its outward adornings."—*Standard*.

"Carefully selected and elegantly got up... It is particularly rich in poems from living writers."—*John Bull*.

WILLIAM CULLEN BRYANT'S POEMS. Red-line Edition. Handsomely bound. With Illustrations and Portrait of the Author. Price 7s. 6d. A Cheaper Edition is also published. Price 3s. 6d.

These are the only complete English Editions sanctioned by the Author.

ENGLISH SONNETS. Collected and Arranged by **John Dennis**. Small crown 8vo. Elegantly bound. Price 3s. 6d.

"An exquisite selection, a selection which every lover of poetry will consult again and again with delight. The notes are very useful.... The volume is one for which

English literature owes Mr. Dennis the heartiest thanks."—*Spectator*.
"Mr. Dennis has shown great judgment in this selection."—*Saturday Review*.

Second Edition.

HOME-SONGS FOR QUIET HOURS. By the **Rev. Canon R. H. Baynes**, Editor of "English Lyrics" and "Lyra Anglicana." Handsomely printed and bound. Price 3s. 6d.

POEMS. By **Annette F. C. Knight**. Fcap. 8vo. [*Preparing.*

POEMS. By the **Rev. J. W. A. Taylor**. Fcap. 8vo. [*In the Press.*

ALEXANDER THE GREAT. A Dramatic Poem. By **Aubrey de Vere**, Author of "The Legends of St. Patrick," &c. Crown 8vo.
[*Nearly ready.*

THE DISCIPLES. A New Poem. By **Harriet Eleanor Hamilton King**. Crown 8vo. Price 7s. 6d.

ASPROMONTE, AND OTHER POEMS. Second Edition. Cloth, 4s. 6d.

"The volume is anonymous, but there is no reason for the author to be ashamed of it. The 'Poems of Italy' are evidently inspired by genuine enthusiasm in the cause espoused; and one of them, 'The

Execution of Felice Orsini,' has much poetic merit, the event celebrated being told with dramatic force."—*Athenæum*.
"The verse is fluent and free."—*Spectator*.

SONGS FOR MUSIC. By **Four Friends**. Square crown 8vo. Price 5s.

CONTAINING SONGS BY
Reginald A. Gatty.   Stephen H. Gatty.
Greville J. Chester.   Juliana H. Ewing.

"A charming gift-book, which will be very popular with lovers of poetry."—*John Bull*.

ROBERT BUCHANAN, THE POETICAL AND PROSE WORKS OF. Collected Edition, in 5 Vols. Vol. I. contains,—" Ballads and Romances;" "Ballads and Poems of Life," and a Portrait of the Author.

Vol. II.—"Ballads and Poems of Life;" "Allegories and Sonnets."

Vol. III.—"Cruiskeen Sonnets;" "Book of Orm;" "Political Mystics."

The Contents of the remaining Volumes will be duly announced.

THOUGHTS IN VERSE. Small crown 8vo. Price 1s. 6d.

This is a Collection of Verses expressive of religious feeling, written from a Theistic stand-point.

Works Published by Henry S. King & Co.,

POETRY—*continued.*

COSMOS. A Poem. Small crown 8vo. Price 3s. 6d.
SUBJECT.—Nature in the Past and in the Present.—Man in the Past and in the Present.—The Future.

NARCISSUS AND OTHER POEMS. By E. Carpenter. Small crown 8vo. Price 5s.
"Displays considerable poetic force."—*Queen.*

A TALE OF THE SEA, SONNETS, AND OTHER POEMS. By James Howell. Crown 8vo. Cloth, 5s.
"Mr. Howell has a keen perception of the beauties of nature, and a just appreciation of the charities of life. . . . Mr. Howell's book deserves, and will probably receive, a warm reception."—*Pall Mall Gazette.*

IMITATIONS FROM THE GERMAN OF SPITTA AND TERSTEGEN. By Lady Durand. Crown 8vo. 4s.
"A charming little volume. . . . Will be a very valuable assistance to peaceful, meditative souls."—*Church Herald.*

Second Edition.
VIGNETTES IN RHYME. Collected Verses. By Austin Dobson. Crown 8vo. Price 5s.
"Clever, clear-cut, and careful."—*Athenæum.*
"As a writer of Vers de Société, Mr. Dobson is almost, if not quite, unrivalled."—*Examiner.*
"Lively, innocent, elegant in expression, and graceful in fancy."—*Morning Post.*

ON VIOL AND FLUTE. A New Volume of Poems, by Edmund W. Gosse. With a Frontispiece by W. B. Scott. Crown 8vo. 5s.
"A careful perusal of his verses will show that he is a poet. . . . His song has the grateful, murmuring sound which reminds one of the softness and deliciousness of summer time. . . . There is much that is good in the volume."—*Spectator.*

METRICAL TRANSLATIONS FROM THE GREEK AND LATIN POETS, AND OTHER POEMS. By R. B. Boswell, M.A. Oxon. Crown 8vo. 5s.

EASTERN LEGENDS AND STORIES IN ENGLISH VERSE. By Lieutenant Norton Powlett, Royal Artillery. Crown 8vo. 5s.
"There is a rollicking sense of fun about the stories, joined to marvellous power of rhyming, and plenty of swing, which irresistibly reminds us of our old favourite."—*Graphic.*

EDITH; OR, LOVE AND LIFE IN CHESHIRE. By T. Ashe, Author of the "Sorrows of Hypsipyle," etc. Sewed. Price 6d.
"A really fine poem, full of tender, subtle touches of feeling."—*Manchester News.*
"Pregnant from beginning to end with the results of careful observation and imaginative power."—*Chester Chronicle.*

THE GALLERY OF PIGEONS, AND OTHER POEMS. By Theo. Marzials. Crown 8vo. 4s. 6d.
"A conceit abounding in prettiness."—*Examiner.*
"The rush of fresh, sparkling fancies is too rapid, too sustained, too abundant, not to be spontaneous."—*Academy.*

THE INN OF STRANGE MEETINGS, AND OTHER POEMS. By Mortimer Collins. Crown 8vo. 5s.
"Abounding in quiet humour, in bright fancy, in sweetness and melody of expression, and, at times, in the tenderest touches of pathos."—*Graphic.*
"Mr. Collins has an undercurrent of chivalry and romance beneath the trifling vein of good-humoured banter which is the special characteristic of his verse."—*Athenæum.*

EROS AGONISTES. By E. B. D. Crown 8vo. 3s. 6d.
"It is not the least merit of these pages that they are everywhere illumined with moral and religious sentiment suggested, not paraded, of the brightest, purest character."—*Standard.*

CALDERON'S DRAMAS. Translated from the Spanish. By Denis Florence MacCarthy. 10s.
"The lambent verse flows with an ease, spirit, and music perfectly natural, liberal, and harmonious."—*Spectator.*
"It is impossible to speak too highly of this beautiful work."—*Month.*

SONGS FOR SAILORS. By Dr. W. C. Bennett. Dedicated by Special Request to H. R. H. the Duke of Edinburgh. Crown 8vo. 3s. 6d. With Steel Portrait and Illustrations.
An Edition in Illustrated paper Covers. Price 1s.

WALLED IN, AND OTHER POEMS. By the Rev. Henry J. Bulkeley. Crown 8vo. 5s.
"A remarkable book of genuine poetry."—*Evening Standard.*
"Genuine power displayed."—*Examiner.*
"Poetical feeling is manifest here, and the diction of the poem is unimpeachable."—*Pall Mall Gazette.*

65, *Cornhill;* & 12, *Paternoster Row, London.*

POETRY—*continued.*

SONGS OF LIFE AND DEATH. By John Payne, Author of "Intaglios," "Sonnets," "The Masque of Shadows," etc. Crown 8vo. 5s.

"The art of ballad-writing has long been lost in England, and Mr. Payne may claim to be its restorer. It is a perfect delight to meet with such a ballad as 'May Margaret' in the present volume."—*Westminster Review.*

A NEW VOLUME OF SONNETS. By the Rev. C. Tennyson Turner. Crown 8vo. 4s. 6d.

"Mr. Turner is a genuine poet; his song is sweet and pure, beautiful in expression, and often subtle in thought."—*Pall Mall Gazette.*

"The light of a devout, gentle, and kindly spirit, a delicate and graceful fancy, a keen intelligence irradiates these thoughts."—*Contemporary Review.*

THE DREAM AND THE DEED, AND OTHER POEMS. By Patrick Scott, Author of "Footpaths between Two Worlds," etc. Fcap. 8vo. Cloth, 5s.

"A bitter and able satire on the vice and follies of the day, literary, social, and political."—*Standard.*

"Shows real poetic power coupled with evidences of satirical energy."—*Edinburgh Daily Review.*

GOETHE'S FAUST. A New Translation in Rime. By the Rev. C. Kegan Paul. Crown 8vo. 6s.

"His translation is the most minutely accurate that has yet been produced..."—*Examiner.*

"Mr. Paul is a zealous and a faithful interpreter."—*Saturday Review.*

SONGS OF TWO WORLDS. First Series. By a New Writer. Fcap. 8vo, cloth, 5s. Second Edition.

"These poems will assuredly take high rank among the class to which they belong."—*British Quarterly Review, April 1st.*

"No extracts could do justice to the exquisite tones, the felicitous phrasing and delicately wrought harmonies of some of these poems."—*Nonconformist.*

"A purity and delicacy of feeling like morning air."—*Graphic.*

SONGS OF TWO WORLDS. Second Series. By the Author of "Songs of Two Worlds." Crown 8vo. [*In the Press.*

THE LEGENDS OF ST. PATRICK AND OTHER POEMS. By Aubrey de Vere. Crown 8vo. 5s.

"Mr. De Vere's versification in his earlier poems is characterised by great sweetness and simplicity. He is master of his instrument, and rarely offends the ear with false notes."—*Pall Mall Gazette.*

"We have but space to commend the varied structure of his verse, the carefulness of his grammar, and his excellent English."—*Saturday Review.*

FICTION.

AILEEN FERRERS. By Susan Morley. In 2 vols. Crown 8vo, cloth. [*Immediately.*

IDOLATRY. A Romance. By Julian Hawthorne, Author of "Bressant." 2 vols. Crown 8vo, cloth.

VANESSA. By the Author of "Thomasina," "Dorothy," etc. 2 vols. Crown 8vo.

CIVIL SERVICE. By J. P. Listado. Author of "Maurice Rhynhart." 2 vols. Crown 8vo.

JUDITH GWYNNE. By Lisle Carr. In 3 vols. Crown 8vo, cloth.

TOO LATE. By Mrs. Newman. 2 vols. Crown 8vo.

LADY MORETOUN'S DAUGHTER. By Mrs. Eiloart. In 3 vols. Crown 8vo, cloth.

MARGARET AND ELIZABETH. A Story of the Sea. By Katherine Saunders, Author of "Gideon's Rock," etc. In 1 vol. Cloth, crown 8vo.

"Simply yet powerfully told.... This opening picture is so exquisitely drawn as to be a fit introduction to a story of such simple pathos and power.... A very beautiful story closes as it began, in a tender and touching picture of homely happiness."—*Pall Mall Gazette.*

FICTION—*continued.*

MR. CARINGTON. A Tale of Love and Conspiracy. By **Robert Turner Cotton.** In 3 vols. Cloth, crown 8vo.

"A novel in so many ways good, as in a fresh and elastic diction, stout unconventionality, and happy boldness of conception and execution. His novels, though free spoken, will be some of the healthiest of our day."—*Examiner.*

TWO GIRLS. By **Frederick Wedmore,** Author of "A Snapt Gold Ring." In 2 vols. Cloth, crown 8vo. [*Just out.*

"A carefully-written novel of character, contrasting the two heroines of one love tale, an English lady and a French actress. Cicely is charming; the introductory description of her is a good specimen of the well-balanced sketches in which the author shines."—*Athenæum.*

HEATHERGATE. In 2 vols. Crown 8vo, cloth. A Story of Scottish Life and Character. By a new Author.

"Its merit lies in the marked antithesis of strongly developed characters, in different ranks of life, and resembling each other in nothing but their marked nationality."—*Athenæum.*

THE QUEEN'S SHILLING. By **Captain Arthur Griffiths,** Author of "Peccavi." 2 vols.

"Every scene, character, and incident of the book are so life-like that they seem drawn from life direct."—*Pall Mall Gazette.*

MIRANDA. A Midsummer Madness. By **Mortimer Collins.** 3 vols.

"Not a dull page in the whole three volumes."—*Standard.*
"The work of a man who is at once a thinker and a poet."—*Hour.*

SQUIRE SILCHESTER'S WHIM. By **Mortimer Collins,** Author of "Marquis and Merchant," "The Princess Clarice," etc. 3 vols. Crown 8vo.

"We think it the best (story) Mr. Collins has yet written. Full of incident and adventure."—*Pall Mall Gazette.*
"So clever, so irritating, and so charming a story."—*Standard.*

THE PRINCESS CLARICE. A Story of 1871. By **Mortimer Collins.** 2 vols. Crown 8vo.

"Mr. Collins has produced a readable book, amusingly characteristic."—*Athenæum.*
"A bright, fresh, and original book."—*Standard.*

REGINALD BRAMBLE. A Cynic of the 19th Century. An Autobiography. 1 vol.

"There is plenty of vivacity in Mr. Bramble's narrative."—*Athenæum.*
"Written in a lively and readable style."—*Hour.*

EFFIE'S GAME; How she Lost and how she Won. By **Cecil Clayton.** 2 vols.

"Well written. The characters move, and act, and, above all, talk like human beings, and we have liked reading about them."—*Spectator.*

CHESTERLEIGH. By **Ansley Conyers.** 3 vols. Crown 8vo.

"We have gained much enjoyment from the book."—*Spectator.*

BRESSANT. A Romance. By **Julian Hawthorne.** 2 vols. Crown 8vo.

"One of the most powerful with which we are acquainted."—*Times.*
"We shall once more have reason to rejoice whenever we hear that a new work is coming out written by one who bears the honoured name of Hawthorne."—*Saturday Review.*

HONOR BLAKE: The Story of a Plain Woman. By **Mrs. Keatinge,** Author of "English Homes in India," etc. 2 vols. Crown 8vo.

"One of the best novels we have met with for some time."—*Morning Post.*
"A story which must do good to all, young and old, who read it."—*Daily News.*

OFF THE SKELLIGS. By **Jean Ingelow.** (Her First Romance.) In 4 vols. Crown 8vo.

"Clever and sparkling."—*Standard.*
"We read each succeeding volume with increasing interest, going almost to the point of wishing there was a fifth."—*Athenæum.*

SEETA. By **Colonel Meadows Taylor,** Author of "Tara," "Ralph Darnell," etc. 3 vols. Crown 8vo.

"Well told, native life is admirably described, and the petty intrigues of native rulers, and their hatred of the English mingled with fear lest the latter should eventually prove the victors, are cleverly depicted."—*Athenæum.*
"Thoroughly interesting and enjoyable reading."—*Examiner.*

WHAT 'TIS TO LOVE. By the Author of "Flora Adair," "The Value of Fosterstown." 3 vols.

FICTION—*continued.*

HESTER MORLEY'S PROMISE. By Hesba Stretton. 3 vols.

"Much better than the average novels of the day; has much more claim to critical consideration as a piece of literary work.—very clever."—*Spectator.*
"All the characters stand out clearly and are well sustained, and the interest of the story never flags."—*Observer.*

THE DOCTOR'S DILEMMA. By Hesba Stretton, Author of "Little Meg," &c. &c. 3 vols. Crown 8vo.

"A fascinating story which scarcely flags in interest from the first page to the last."—*British Quarterly Review.*

THE ROMANTIC ANNALS OF A NAVAL FAMILY. By Mrs. Arthur Traherne. Crown 8vo. 10s. 6d.

"Some interesting letters are introduced; amongst others, several from the late King William IV."—*Spectator.*
"Well and pleasantly told."—*Evening Standard.*

THOMASINA. By the Author of "Dorothy," "De Cressy," &c. 2 vols. Crown 8vo.

"A finished and delicate cabinet picture; no line is without its purpose."—*Athenæum.*

JOHANNES OLAF. By E. de Wille. Translated by F. E. Bunnett. 3 vols. Crown 8vo.

"The art of description is fully exhibited; perception of character and capacity for delineating it are obvious; while there is great breadth and comprehensiveness in the plan of the story."—*Morning Post.*

THE STORY OF SIR EDWARD'S WIFE. By Hamilton Marshall, Author of "For Very Life." 1 vol. Crown 8vo.

"A quiet, graceful little story."—*Spectator.*
"Mr. Hamilton Marshall can tell a story closely and pleasantly."—*Pall Mall Gaz.*

HERMANN AGHA. An Eastern Narrative. By W. Gifford Palgrave. 2 vols. Crown 8vo, cloth, extra gilt. 18s.

"There is a positive fragrance as of newly-mown hay about it, as compared with the artificially perfumed passions which are detailed to us with such gusto by our ordinary novel-writers in their endless volumes."—*Observer.*

A GOOD MATCH. By Amelia Perrier, Author of "Mea Culpa." 2 vols.

"Racy and lively."—*Athenæum.*
"This clever and amusing novel."—*Pall Mall Gazette.*

LINKED AT LAST. By F. E. Bunnett. 1 vol. Crown 8vo.

"The reader who once takes it up will not be inclined to relinquish it without concluding the volume."—*Morning Post.*
"A very charming story."—*John Bull.*

THE SPINSTERS OF BLATCHINGTON. By Mar. Travers. 2 vols. Crown 8vo.

"A pretty story. Deserving of a favourable reception."—*Graphic.*
"A book of more than average merits."—*Examiner.*

PERPLEXITY. By Sydney Mostyn. 3 vols. Crown 8vo.

"Written with very considerable power, great cleverness, and sustained interest."—*Standard.*
"The literary workmanship is good, and the story forcibly and graphically told."—*Daily News.*

MEMOIRS OF MRS. LÆTITIA BOOTHBY. By William Clark Russell, Author of "The Book of Authors." Crown 8vo. 7s. 6d.
"Clever and ingenious."—*Saturday Review.*
"Very clever book."—*Guardian.*

CRUEL AS THE GRAVE. By the Countess Von Bothmer. 3 vols. Crown 8vo.

"*Jealousy is cruel as the Grave.*"
"Interesting, though somewhat tragic."—*Athenæum.*
"Agreeable, unaffected, and eminently readable."—*Daily News.*

HER TITLE OF HONOUR. By Holme Lee. Second Edition. 1 vol. Crown 8vo.

"With the interest of a pathetic story is united the value of a definite and high purpose."—*Spectator.*
"A most exquisitely written story."—*Literary Churchman.*

SEPTIMIUS. A Romance. By Nathaniel Hawthorne. Second Edition. 1 vol. Crown 8vo, cloth, extra gilt. 9s.
The *Athenæum* says that "the book is full of Hawthorne's most characteristic writing."

COL. MEADOWS TAYLOR'S INDIAN TALES.
THE CONFESSIONS OF A THUG

Is now ready, and is the Volume of A New and Cheaper Edition, in 1 vol. each, Illustrated, price 6s. It will be followed by "TARA" (now in the press) "RALPH DARNELL," and "TIPPOO SULTAN."

65, Cornhill; and 12, Paternoster Row, London.

THE CORNHILL LIBRARY OF FICTION.

3s. 6d. per Volume.

IT is intended in this Series to produce books of such merit that readers will care to preserve them on their shelves. They are well printed on good paper, handsomely bound, with a Frontispiece, and are sold at the moderate price of 3s. 6d. each.

THE HOUSE OF RABY. By Mrs. G. Hooper.

A FIGHT FOR LIFE. By Moy Thomas.

ROBIN GRAY. By Charles Gibbon.

"Pure in sentiment, well written, and cleverly constructed."—*British Quarterly Review.*
"A pretty tale, prettily told."—*Athenæum.*

"A novel of tender and pathetic interest."—*Globe.*
"An unassuming, characteristic, and entertaining novel."—*John Bull.*

KITTY. By Miss M. Betham-Edwards.

"Lively and clever... There is a certain dash in every description; the dialogue is bright and sparkling."—*Athenæum.*

"Very pleasant and amusing."—*Globe.*
"A charming novel."—*John Bull.*

HIRELL. By John Saunders.

"A powerful novel... a tale written by a poet."—*Spectator.*
"A novel of extraordinary merit."—*Morning Post.*

"We have nothing but words of praise to offer for its style and composition."—*Examiner.*

ONE OF TWO; or, The left-handed Bride. By J. H. Friswell.

"Told with spirit... the plot is skilfully made."—*Spectator.*

"Admirably narrated, and intensely interesting."—*Public Opinion.*

READY-MONEY MORTIBOY. A Matter-of-Fact Story.

"There is not a dull page in the whole story."—*Standard.*
"A very interesting and uncommon story."—*Vanity Fair.*

"One of the most remarkable novels which has appeared of late."—*Pall Mall Gazette.*

GOD'S PROVIDENCE HOUSE. By Mrs. G. L. Banks.

"Far above the run of common three-volume novels, evincing much literary power in not a few graphic descriptions of manners and local customs.... A genuine sketch."—*Spectator.*

"Possesses the merit of care, industry, and local knowledge."—*Athenæum.*
"Wonderfully readable. The style is very simple and natural."—*Morning Post.*

FOR LACK OF GOLD. By Charles Gibbon.

"A powerfully written nervous story."—*Athenæum.*
"A piece of very genuine workmanship."—*British Quarterly Review.*
"There are few recent novels more powerful and engrossing."—*Examiner.*

ABEL DRAKE'S WIFE. By John Saunders.

"A striking book, clever, interesting, and original. We have seldom met with a book so thoroughly true to life, so deeply interesting in its detail, and so touching in its simple pathos."—*Athenæum.*

OTHER STANDARD NOVELS TO FOLLOW.

65, *Cornhill*; & 12, *Paternoster Row, London.*

THEOLOGICAL.

WORDS OF TRUTH AND CHEER. A Mission of Instruction and Suggestion. By the **Rev. Archer P. Gurney.** 1 vol. Crown 8vo. Price 6s. [*In the Press.*

THE GOSPEL ITS OWN WITNESS. Being the Hulsean Lectures for 1873. By the **Rev. Stanley Leathes.** 1 vol. Crown 8vo.

THE CHURCH AND THE EMPIRES: Historical Periods. By **Henry W. Wilberforce.** Preceded by a Memoir of the Author, by J. H. Newman, D.D. 1 vol. Post 8vo. Price 10s. 6d.

THE HIGHER LIFE. A New Volume by the **Rev. J. Baldwin Brown,** Author of "The Soul's Exodus," etc. 1 vol. Crown 8vo. Price 7s. 6d.

HARTHAM CONFERENCES; OR, DISCUSSIONS UPON SOME OF THE RELIGIOUS TOPICS OF THE DAY. By the **Rev. F. W. Kingsford, M.A.,** Vicar of S. Thomas's, Stamford Hill; late Chaplain H. E. I. C. (Bengal Presidency). "Audi alteram partem." Crown 8vo. Price 3s. 6d.

STUDIES IN MODERN PROBLEMS. A Series of Essays by various Writers. Edited by the **Rev. Orby Shipley, M.A.** Vol. I. Cr. 8vo. Price 5s.

CONTENTS.

Sacramental Confession. A. H. WARD, B.A.
Abolition of the 39 Articles. NICHOLAS POCOCK, M.A.
The Sanctity of Marriage. JOHN WALTER LEA, B.A.
Creation and Modern Science. GEORGE GREENWOOD, M.A.
Retreats for Persons Living in the World. T. T. CARTER, M.A.
Catholic and Protestant. EDWARD L. BLENKINSOPP, M.A.
The Bishops on Confession. THE EDITOR.

A Second Series is being published, price 6d. each part.

UNTIL THE DAY DAWN. Four Advent Lectures delivered in the Episcopal Chapel, Milverton, Warwickshire, on the Sunday Evenings during Advent, 1870. By the **Rev. Marmaduke E. Browne.** Crown 8vo. Price 2s. 6d.

"Four really original and stirring sermons."—*John Bull.*

A SCOTCH COMMUNION SUNDAY. To which are added Discourses from a Certain University City. Second Edition. By **A. K. H. B.,** Author of "The Recreations of a Country Parson." Crown 8vo. Second Edition. Price 5s.

"Some discourses are added, which are couched in language of rare power."—*John Bull.*
"Exceedingly fresh and readable."—*Glasgow News.*
"We commend this volume as full of interest to all our readers. It is written with much ability and good feeling, with excellent taste and marvellous tact."—*Church Herald.*

EVERY DAY A PORTION: Adapted from the Bible and the Prayer Book, for the Private Devotions of those living in Widowhood. Collected and Edited by the **Lady Mary Vyner.** Square crown 8vo, printed on good paper, elegantly bound. Price 5s.

"Now she that is a widow indeed, and desolate, trusteth in God."

65, *Cornhill;* & 12, *Paternoster Row, London.*

THEOLOGICAL—*continued*.

CHURCH THOUGHT AND CHURCH WORK. Edited by the Rev. Chas. Anderson, M.A., Editor of "Words and Works in a London Parish." Demy 8vo. Pp. 250. 7s. 6d. Containing Articles by the Rev. J. LL. DAVIES, J. M. CAPES, HARRY JONES, BROOKE LAMBERT, A. J. ROSS, Professor CHEETHAM, the EDITOR, and others.

Second Edition.
WORDS AND WORKS IN A LONDON PARISH. Edited by the Rev. Charles Anderson, M.A. Demy 8vo. 6s.

"It has an interest of its own for not a few minds, to whom the question 'Is the National Church worth preserving as such, and if so, how best increase its vital power?' is of deep and grave importance."—*Spectator.*

ESSAYS ON RELIGION AND LITERATURE. By Various Writers. Edited by the Most Reverend Archbishop Manning. Demy 8vo. 10s. 6d.

CONTENTS:—The Philosophy of Christianity.—Mystical Elements of Religion.—Controversy with the Agnostics.—A Reasoning Thought.—Darwinism brought to Book.—Mr. Mill on Liberty of the Press.—Christianity in relation to Society.—The Religious Condition of Germany.—The Philosophy of Bacon.—Catholic Laymen and Scholastic Philosophy.

WHY AM I A CHRISTIAN? By Viscount Stratford de Redcliffe, P.C., K.G., G.C.B. Crown 8vo. 3s. Third Edition.

"Has a peculiar interest, as exhibiting the convictions of an earnest, intelligent, and practical man."—*Contemporary Review.*

THEOLOGY AND MORALITY. Being Essays by the Rev. J. Llewellyn Davies. 1 vol. 8vo. Price 7s. 6d.

"The position taken up by Mr. Llewellyn Davies is well worth a careful survey on the part of philosophical students, for it represents the closest approximation of any theological system yet formulated to the religion of philosophy. . . We have not space to do more with regard to the social essays of the work before us, than to testify to the kindliness of spirit, sobriety, and earnest thought by which they are uniformly characterised."—*Examiner.*

THE RECONCILIATION OF RELIGION AND SCIENCE. Being Essays by the Rev. T. W. Fowle, M.A. 1 vol. 8vo. 10s. 6d.

"A book which requires and deserves the respectful attention of all reflecting Churchmen. It is earnest, reverent, thoughtful, and courageous. . . . There is scarcely a page in the book which is not equally worthy of a thoughtful pause."—*Literary Churchman.*

HYMNS AND SACRED LYRICS. By the Rev. Godfrey Thring, B.A. 1 vol. Crown 8vo.

HYMNS AND VERSES, Original and Translated. By the Rev. Henry Downton. Small crown 8vo. 3s. 6d.

"Considerable force and beauty characterise some of these verses."—*Watchman.*
"Mr. Downton's 'Hymns and Verses' are worthy of all praise."—*English Churchman.*
"Will, we do not doubt, be welcome as a permanent possession to those for whom they have been composed or to whom they have been originally addressed."—*Church Herald.*

65, *Cornhill;* & 12, *Paternoster Row, London.*

THEOLOGICAL—*continued.*

MISSIONARY ENTERPRISE IN THE EAST. By the **Rev. Richard Collins.** Illustrated. Crown 8vo. 6s.

"A very graphic story told in lucid, simple, and modest style."—*English Churchman.*
"A readable and very interesting volume."—*Church Review.*
"We may judge from our own experience, no one who takes up this charming little volume will lay it down again till he has got to the last word."—*John Bull.*

MISSIONARY LIFE IN THE SOUTH SEAS. By **James Hutton.** 1 vol. Crown 8vo. [*In the Press.*

THE ETERNAL LIFE. Being Fourteen Sermons. By the **Rev. Jas. Noble Bennie, M.A.** Crown 8vo. 6s.

"The whole volume is replete with matter for thought and study."—*John Bull.*
"Mr. Bennie preaches earnestly and well."—*Literary Churchman.*
"We recommend these sermons as wholesome Sunday reading."—*English Churchman.*

THE REALM OF TRUTH. By **Miss E. T. Carne.** Crown 8vo. 5s. 6d.

"A singularly calm, thoughtful, and philosophical inquiry into what Truth is, and what its authority."—*Leeds Mercury.*
"It tells the world what it does not like to hear, but what it cannot be told too often,
that Truth is something stronger and more enduring than our little doings, and speakings, and actings."—*Literary Churchman.*

LIFE: Conferences delivered at Toulouse. By the **Rev. Père Lacordaire.** Crown 8vo. 6s.

"Let the serious reader cast his eye upon any single page in this volume, and he will find there words which will arrest his attention and give him a desire to know
more of the teachings of this worthy follower of the saintly St. Dominick."—*Morning Post.*

Second Edition.

CATHOLICISM AND THE VATICAN. With a Narrative of the Old Catholic Congress at Munich. By **J. Lowry Whittle, A.M.**, Trin. Coll., Dublin. Crown 8vo. 4s. 6d.

"We may cordially recommend his book to all who wish to follow the course of the
Old Catholic movement."—*Saturday Review.*

SIX PRIVY COUNCIL JUDGMENTS—1850-1872. Annotated by **W. G. Brooke, M.A.**, Barrister-at-Law. Crown 8vo. 9s.

"The volume is a valuable record of cases forming precedents for the future."—*Athenæum.*
"A very timely and important publication. It brings into one view the great
judgments of the last twenty years, which will constitute the unwritten law of the English Establishment."—*British Quarterly Review.*

THE MOST COMPLETE HYMN BOOK PUBLISHED.

HYMNS FOR THE CHURCH AND HOME. Selected and Edited by the **Rev. W. Fleming Stevenson,** Author of "Praying and Working."

The Hymn-book consists of Three Parts:—I. For Public Worship.—II. For Family and Private Worship.—III. For Children: and contains Biographical Notices of nearly 300 Hymn-writers, with Notes upon their Hymns.

⁂ Published in various forms and prices, the latter ranging from 8d. to 6s. Lists and full particulars will be furnished on application to the Publisher.

THEOLOGICAL—*continued*.

WORKS BY THE REV. H. R. HAWEIS, M.A.

Sixth Edition.
THOUGHTS FOR THE TIMES. By the Rev. H. R. Haweis, M.A., "Author of Music and Morals," etc. Crown 8vo. Price 7s. 6d.

"Bears marks of much originality of thought and individuality of expression."—*Pall Mall Gazette*.
"Mr. Haweis writes not only fearlessly,

but with remarkable freshness and vigour. In all that he says we perceive a transparent honesty and singleness of purpose."
—*Saturday Review*.

SPEECH IN SEASON. A New Volume of Sermons. By the Rev. H. R. Haweis. Crown 8vo. Price 9s.

UNSECTARIAN FAMILY PRAYERS, for Morning and Evening for a Week, with short selected passages from the Bible. By the Rev. H. R. Haweis, M.A. Square crown 8vo. Price 3s. 6d.

WORKS BY THE REV. C. J. VAUGHAN, D.D.

THE SOLIDITY OF TRUE RELIGION.
[*In the Press*.

FORGET THINE OWN PEOPLE. An Appeal for Missions. Small Crown 8vo. Price 3s. 6d.

WORDS OF HOPE FROM THE PULPIT OF THE TEMPLE CHURCH. Crown 8vo. Price 5s.

Fourth Edition.
THE YOUNG LIFE EQUIPPING ITSELF FOR GOD'S SERVICE. Being Four Sermons Preached before the University of Cambridge, in November, 1872. Crown 8vo. Price 3s. 6d.

"Has all the writer's characteristics of devotedness, purity, and high moral tone."—*London Quarterly Review*.
"As earnest, eloquent, and as liberal as everything else that he writes."—*Examiner*.

WORKS BY THE REV. G. S. DREW, M.A.,
VICAR OF TRINITY, LAMBETH.

Second Edition.
SCRIPTURE LANDS IN CONNECTION WITH THEIR HISTORY. Bevelled Boards, 8vo. Price 10s. 6d.

"Mr. Drew has invented a new method of illustrating Scripture history—from observation of the countries. Instead of narrating his travels, and referring from time to time to the facts of sacred history belonging to the different countries, he writes an outline history of the Hebrew nation from Abraham downwards, with special reference to the various points in which the geography illustrates the history. . . He is very successful in picturing to his readers the scenes before his own mind."—*Saturday Review*.

Second Edition.
NAZARETH: ITS LIFE AND LESSONS. Second Edition. In small 8vo, cloth. Price 5s.

"We have read the volume with great interest. It is at once succinct and suggestive, reverent and ingenious, observant of small details, and yet not forgetful of great principles."—*British Quarterly Review*.
"A very reverent attempt to elicit and develop Scripture intimations respecting our Lord's thirty years' sojourn at Nazareth. The author has wrought well at the unworked mine, and has produced a very valuable series of Scripture lessons, which will be found both profitable and singularly interesting."—*Guardian*.

THE DIVINE KINGDOM ON EARTH AS IT IS IN HEAVEN. In demy 8vo, bound in cloth. Price 10s. 6d.

"Entirely valuable and satisfactory. . . . . . There is no living divine to whom the authorship would not be a credit."
—*Literary Churchman*.

"Thoughtful and eloquent. . . . Full of original thinking admirably expressed."
—*British Quarterly Review*.

65, *Cornhill;* & 12, *Paternoster Row, London.*

THEOLOGICAL—*continued*.

WORKS OF THE LATE REV. F. W. ROBERTSON.

NEW AND CHEAPER EDITIONS.

SERMONS.
Vol. I. Small crown 8vo. Price 3s. 6d.
Vol. II. Small crown 8vo. Price 3s. 6d.
Vol. III. Small crown 8vo. Price 3s. 6d.
Vol. IV. Small crown 8vo. Price 3s. 6d.

EXPOSITORY LECTURES ON ST. PAUL'S EPISTLE TO THE CORINTHIANS. Small crown 8vo. 5s.

AN ANALYSIS OF MR. TENNYSON'S "IN MEMORIAM." (Dedicated by permission to the Poet-Laureate.) Fcap. 8vo. 2s.

THE EDUCATION OF THE HUMAN RACE. Translated from the German of Gotthold Ephraim Lessing. Fcap. 8vo. 2s. 6d.

LECTURES AND ADDRESSES, WITH OTHER LITERARY REMAINS. A New Edition. With Introduction by the Rev. Stopford A. Brooke, M.A. In One Vol. Uniform with the Sermons. 5s. [*Preparing.*

A LECTURE ON FRED. W. ROBERTSON, M.A. By the Rev. F. A. Noble. Delivered before the Young Men's Christian Association of Pittsburgh, U.S. 1s. 6d.

WORKS BY THE REV. STOPFORD A. BROOKE, M.A.

Chaplain in Ordinary to Her Majesty the Queen.

THE LATE REV. F. W. ROBERTSON, M.A., LIFE AND LETTERS OF. Edited by Stopford Brooke, M.A.
 I. In 2 vols., uniform with the Sermons. 7s. 6d.
 II. Library Edition, in demy 8vo, with Two Steel Portraits. 12s.
 III. A Popular Edition, in 1 vol. 6s.

THEOLOGY IN THE ENGLISH POETS. Being Lectures delivered by the Rev. Stopford A. Brooke. 9s.

Seventh Edition.
CHRIST IN MODERN LIFE. Sermons Preached in St. James's Chapel, York Street, London. Crown 8vo. 7s. 6d.

"Nobly fearless, and singularly strong. . . . carries our admiration throughout."—*British Quarterly Review.*

Second Edition.
FREEDOM IN THE CHURCH OF ENGLAND. Six Sermons suggested by the Voysey Judgment. In 1 vol. Crown 8vo, cloth. 3s. 6d.

"A very fair statement of the views in respect to freedom of thought held by the liberal party in the Church of England."—*Blackwood's Magazine.*

"Interesting and readable, and characterised by great clearness of thought, frankness of statement, and moderation of tone."—*Church Opinion.*

Seventh Edition.
SERMONS Preached in St. James's Chapel, York Street, London. Crown 8vo. 6s.

"No one who reads these sermons will wonder that Mr. Brooke is a great power in London, that his chapel is thronged, and his followers large and enthusiastic. They are fiery, energetic, impetuous sermons, rich with the treasures of a cultivated imagination."—*Guardian.*

THE LIFE AND WORK OF FREDERICK DENISON MAURICE: A Memorial Sermon. Crown 8vo, sewed. 1s.

A NEW VOLUME OF SERMONS IS IN THE PRESS.

65, *Cornhill; & 12, Paternoster Row, London.*

MISCELLANEOUS.

VILLAGE HEALTH. By **Horace Swete, M.D.** [*In the Press*.

THE POPULAR EDITION OF THE DAILY NEWS' NARRATIVE OF THE ASHANTEE WAR. 1 vol. Crown 8vo. [*In the Press*.

HAKAYET ABDULLA. A Tale of the early British Settlement in the Malaccas. By a **Native**. Translated by **John T. Thompson**. 1 vol. Post 8vo.

THE SHAKESPEARE ARGOSY: containing much of the wealth of Shakespeare's Wisdom and Wit, alphabetically arranged by **Captain A. Harcourt**. Crown 8vo. [*In the Press*.

SOCIALISM: its Nature, its Dangers, and its Remedies considered by the **Rev. M. Kaufman, B.A.** 1 vol. Crown 8vo. [*In the Press*.

CHARACTERISTICS FROM THE WRITINGS OF Dr. J. H. NEWMAN: being Selections Personal, Historical, Philosophical, and Religious; from his various Works. Arranged with the Author's personal approval. 1 vol. With a Portrait.

Second Edition.
CREMATION; THE TREATMENT OF THE BODY AFTER DEATH: with a Description of the Process and necessary Apparatus. Crown 8vo, sewed. 1s.

'ILAM EN NAS. Historical Tales and Anecdotes of the Times of the Early Khalifahs. Translated from the Arabic Originals. By **Mrs. Godfrey Clerk**, Author of "The Antipodes and Round the World." Crown 8vo. Price 7s.

"As full of valuable information as it is of amusing incident."—*Evening Standard*.
"Those who like stories full of the genuine colour and fragrance of the East should by all means read Mrs. Godfrey Clerk's volume."—*Spectator*.

THE PLACE OF THE PHYSICIAN. Being the Introductory Lecture at Guy's Hospital, 1873-74; to which is added
ESSAYS ON THE LAW OF HUMAN LIFE AND ON THE RELATION BETWEEN ORGANIC AND INORGANIC WORLDS.
By **James Hinton**, Author of "Man and His Dwelling-Place." Crown 8vo, cloth. Price 3s. 6d.

Third Edition.
LITTLE DINNERS; HOW TO SERVE THEM WITH ELEGANCE AND ECONOMY. By **Mary Hooper**, Author of "The Handbook of the Breakfast Table." 1 vol. Crown 8vo. Price 5s.

THE PORT OF REFUGE; OR, COUNSEL AND AID TO SHIPMASTERS IN DIFFICULTY, DOUBT, OR DISTRESS. By **Manley Hopkins**, Author of "A Handbook of Average," "A Manual of Insurance," &c. Cr. 8vo. Price 6s.

SUBJECTS:—The Shipmaster's Position and Duties.—Agents and Agency.—Average.—Bottomry, and other Means of Raising Money.—The Charter-Party, and Bill-of-Lading. Stoppage in Transitu; and the Shipowner's Lien.—Collision.

MISCELLANEOUS—*continued.*

LOMBARD STREET. A Description of the Money Market. By **Walter Bagehot.** Large crown 8vo. Fourth Edition. 7s. 6d.

"Mr. Bagehot touches incidentally a hundred points connected with his subject, and pours serene white light upon them all."—*Spectator.*

"Anybody who wishes to have a clear idea of the workings of what is called the Money Market should procure a little volume which Mr. Bagehot has just published, and he will there find the whole thing in a nut-shell."—*Saturday Review.*

"Full of the most interesting economic history."—*Athenæum.*

THE ENGLISH CONSTITUTION. By **Walter Bagehot.** A New Edition, revised and corrected, with an Introductory Dissertation on recent Changes and Events. Crown 8vo. 7s. 6d.

"A pleasing and clever study on the department of higher politics."—*Guardian.*

"No writer before him had set out so clearly what the efficient part of the English Constitution really is."—*Pall Mall Gazette.*

NEWMARKET AND ARABIA; AN EXAMINATION OF THE DESCENT OF RACERS AND COURSERS. By **Roger D. Upton,** Captain late 9th Royal Lancers. Post 8vo. With Pedigrees and Coloured Frontispiece. 9s.

"It contains a good deal of truth, and it abounds with valuable suggestions."—*Saturday Review.*

"A remarkable volume. The breeder can well ponder over its pages."—*Bell's Life.*

"A thoughtful and intelligent book... A contribution to the history of the horse of remarkable interest and importance."—*Baily's Magazine.*

MOUNTAIN, MEADOW, AND MERE: a Series of Outdoor Sketches of Sport, Scenery, Adventures, and Natural History. By **G. Christopher Davies.** With 16 Illustrations by W. HARCOURT. Crown 8vo. Price 6s.

"Mr. Davies writes pleasantly, graphically, with the pen of a lover of nature, a naturalist, and a sportsman."—*Field.*

"Pervaded throughout by the graceful melody of a natural idyl, and the details of sport are subordinated to a dominating sense of the beautiful and picturesque."—*Saturday Review.*

HOW TO AMUSE AND EMPLOY OUR INVALIDS. By **Harriet Power.** Fcap. 8vo. 2s. 6d.

"A very useful little brochure... Will become a universal favourite with the class for whom it is intended, while it will afford many a useful hint to those who live with them."—*John Bull.*

REPUBLICAN SUPERSTITIONS. Illustrated by the Political History of the United States. Including a Correspondence with M. Louis Blanc. By **Moncure D. Conway.** Crown 8vo. 5s.

"A very able exposure of the most plausible fallacies of Republicanism, by a writer of remarkable vigour and purity of style."—*Standard.*

"Mr. Conway writes with ardent sincerity. He gives us some good anecdotes, and he is occasionally almost eloquent."—*Guardian.*

STREAMS FROM HIDDEN SOURCES. By **B. Montgomerie Ranking.** Crown 8vo. 6s.

"We doubt not that Mr. Ranking's enthusiasm will communicate itself to many of his readers, and induce them in like manner to follow back these streamlets to their parent river."—*Graphic.*

"The effect of reading the seven tales he presents to us is to make us wish for some seven more of the same kind."—*Pall Mall Gazette.*

GLANCES AT INNER ENGLAND. A Lecture delivered in the United States and Canada. By **Edward Jenkins, M.P.,** Author of "Ginx's Baby," &c. Crown 8vo. 5s.

65, Cornhill; & 12, Paternoster Row, London.

MISCELLANEOUS—*continued*.

Thirty-Second Edition.
GINX'S BABY: HIS BIRTH AND OTHER MISFORTUNES. By **Edward Jenkins.** Crown 8vo. Price 2s.

Fourteenth Thousand.
LITTLE HODGE. A Christmas Country Carol. By **Edward Jenkins,** Author of "Ginx's Baby," &c. Illustrated. Crown 8vo. 5s.
A Cheap Edition in paper covers, price 1s.

Sixth Edition.
LORD BANTAM. By **Edward Jenkins,** Author of "Ginx's Baby." Crown 8vo. Price 2s. 6d.

LUCHMEE AND DILLOO. A Story of West Indian Life. By **Edward Jenkins,** Author of "Ginx's Baby," "Little Hodge," &c. 2 vols. Demy 8vo. Illustrated. [*Preparing.*

TALES OF THE ZENANA, OR A NUWAB'S LEISURE HOURS. In 2 Vols. Crown 8vo. [*Preparing.*

PANDURANG HARI; or, MEMOIRS OF A HINDOO. A Tale of Mahratta Life sixty years ago. With a Preface by **Sir H. Bartle E. Frere, G.C.S.I.,** &c. 2 vols. Crown 8vo. Price 21s.

"There is a quaintness and simplicity in the roguery of the hero that makes his life as attractive as that of Guzman d'Alfarache or Gil Blas, and so we advise our readers not to be dismayed at the length of Pandurang Hari, but to read it resolutely through. If they do this they cannot, we think, fail to be both amused and interested."—*Times.*

GIDEON'S ROCK, and other Stories. By **Katherine Saunders.** In 1 vol. Crown 8vo. Price 6s. [*Just out.*

CONTENTS.—Gideon's Rock.—Old Matthew's Puzzle.—Gentle Jack.—Uncle Ned.—The Retired Apothecary.

JOAN MERRYWEATHER, and other Stories. By **Katherine Saunders.** In 1 vol. Crown 8vo.

CONTENTS.—The Haunted Crust.—The Flower-Girl.—Joan Merryweather.—The Watchman's Story.—An Old Letter.

MODERN PARISH CHURCHES; THEIR PLAN, DESIGN, AND FURNITURE. By **J. T. Micklethwaite.** Crown 8vo. Price 7s. 6d.

LONGEVITY; THE MEANS OF PROLONGING LIFE AFTER MIDDLE AGE. By **Dr. John Gardner,** Author of "A Handbook of Domestic Medicine," &c. Small Crown 8vo.

STUDIES AND ROMANCES. By **H. Schutz Wilson.** 1 vol. Crown 8vo. Price 7s. 6d.

"Open the book, however, at what page the reader may, he will find something to amuse and instruct, and he must be very hard to please if he finds nothing to suit him, either grave or gay, stirring or romantic, in the capital stories collected in this well-got-up volume."—*John Bull.*

THE PELICAN PAPERS. Reminiscences and Remains of a Dweller in the Wilderness. By **James Ashcroft Noble.** Crown 8vo. 6s.

"Written somewhat after the fashion of Mr. Helps's 'Friends in Council.'"—*Examiner.*

"Will well repay perusal by all thoughtful and intelligent readers."—*Liverpool Leader.*

65, *Cornhill;* & 12, *Paternoster Row, London.*

MISCELLANEOUS—*continued*.

BRIEFS AND PAPERS. Being Sketches of the Bar and the Press. By **Two Idle Apprentices.** Crown 8vo. 7s. 6d.

"Written with spirit and knowledge, and give some curious glimpses into what the majority will regard as strange and unknown territories."—*Daily News*.

"This is one of the best books to while away an hour and cause a generous laugh that we have come across for a long time."—*John Bull*.

THE SECRET OF LONG LIFE. Dedicated by Special Permission to Lord St. Leonards. Third Edition. Large crown 8vo. 5s.

"A charming little volume."—*Times*.
"A very pleasant little book, cheerful, genial, scholarly."—*Spectator*.

"Entitled to the warmest admiration."—*Pall Mall Gazette*.

SOLDIERING AND SCRIBBLING. By **Archibald Forbes**, of the *Daily News*, Author of "My Experience of the War between France and Germany." Crown 8vo. 7s. 6d.

"All who open it will be inclined to read through for the varied entertainment which it affords."—*Daily News*.

"There is a good deal of instruction to outsiders touching military life, in this volume."—*Evening Standard*.

BRADBURY, AGNEW, & CO., PRINTERS, WHITEFRIARS.